HALIFAX
TRANSGRESSION

HALIFAX
TRANSGRESSION

ROGER SIMPSON

BLACK
STONE
PUBLISHING

Printed in the United States of America
Originally published in hardcover by Blackstone Publishing in 2023

First paperback edition: 2023
ISBN 979-8-212-37718-8
Fiction / Thrillers / Suspense

Version 1

Blackstone Publishing
31 Mistletoe Rd.
Ashland, OR 97520

www.BlackstonePublishing.com

For Sally

1

"Hello, Jane. It's Eric Ringer."

Jane stood with her mobile held to her ear.

"You probably don't remember me."

She remembered him very well.

"It's probably been twenty years."

It had been twenty-three.

"We worked together on the Point Cook shooting."

How could anyone fail to remember that?

"Hello, Eric," she said at last. "I must admit you were the last person I expected to phone. Especially at half past eight on a Friday night. Are you still in Canberra?"

"No, I came back to be closer to the family. I was happy with the Federal Police, but this Covid thing made travel too hard—and with the ex and the kids still in Melbourne . . . I'm back with Victoria Police again, as Head of Homicide."

"So, how can I help you, Eric?"

"Work, I'm afraid."

"Don't apologize for that."

"This one you probably won't thank me for."

Which seemed a strange thing for a policeman to say.

"I'm at the crime scene now if you're interested—and

available. It's one you should see for yourself. I don't usually say this, but I genuinely don't know where to start."

"Something I won't thank you for?" she said, her imagination already racing. She was at the same time attracted and repelled by the invitation.

"I won't even begin to describe it. If you can come, I'll send a car."

Jane hung up the phone and got herself ready: a tailored jacket and a plain white shirt; never over-dress for work. She had the lift to herself as she descended from her apartment on the seventh floor. A police car was already waiting outside. Apart from the usual greetings and talk about the weather, she barely spoke to the female constable for the twenty minutes it took to drive to Toorak, nor did she ask anything about the case. Ringer seemed to think it important that she assessed the crime scene, though photographs or first-person accounts usually sufficed. Did she really have to see this for herself?

The memories of the Point Cook shooting came flooding back, the mass killing that had more to do with counseling survivors than solving the crime, though they managed to do that too. It was the first time she and Ringer had met, he a newly minted detective who looked like Hugh Jackman, she only a few years older and comparatively new to forensic psychiatry. She remembered too the New Year's Eve they had spent together, an unexpected digression from the pressures of that particularly distressing case, a sweet moment in time when they both were young and single. Would he remember it as fondly as she? Opening the presents under the Christmas Tree, her "magic trick" with the champagne, her apartment high above the city, a less luxurious version of the one she had now.

The police car wound around the river and turned up

St. Georges Road, the houses becoming more opulent as the better-heeled burghers of Melbourne displayed the elegance and acreage their wealth allowed. Police vehicles outside the crime scene announced they had arrived at their destination. In any other suburb, crowds of onlookers would have assembled by now, but not in Toorak. It's not becoming for the rich to stand and stare.

Jane signed herself in at the gate. The mansion and its expansive gardens were illuminated by a battery of arc lights. She was handed gloves and plastic over-boots and told to stick to the laneway marked by police tape that snaked across the lawn as the driveway was still being checked by forensics. As she approached the house, Ringer was waiting to greet her.

"Hello, Jane."

"Hello, Eric." It was good to see him and see that he still looked like Hugh Jackman.

At fifty-three and fifty-seven they had both aged very well: he didn't have the spread of the usual policeman, nor she any signs she'd surrendered to middle-age. She supposed he could credit his exercise regime; she her mother's genes.

It was hard not to relive their original meeting all those years ago. Jane had prepared for the dead bodies the Point Cook killer had left in his wake—apart from the last one, the one she'd stumbled upon as she'd pushed through a side door in search of fresh air, heeding too late Ringer's warning to "look away."

You can attend pathology classes over years of university but you can't unsee what a high-powered rifle can do at close range to the brain, bone, and flesh of a living head.

"It's good to see you, Jane."

"You too." But she wasn't here to reminisce.

"You need to know that the victim is Nigel Woods and that this is his home."

"Nigel Woods, the billionaire?"

"The same. I don't know what you'll make of this, Jane. As I said on the phone, I've no idea. If you're ready, I'll take you through."

Jane nodded, though she wanted to turn and run.

"Walk on the plastic." Ringer indicated the runner on the floor and opened the door with his gloved hand.

Nigel Woods's house was as much a gallery for his extensive collection of Australian art as it was a home for his family. The vaulted foyer, more than two stories high, was dominated by a sculpture by Jaroslav Petranovic, *The House of the Stolen*. Jane knew it well. She had been to the launch in Jaroslav's studio, one of the last-remaining Collingwood factories that hadn't been converted into a dwelling. Petranovic had emigrated to Australia from Czechoslovakia in 1971 and had gone on to establish himself as one of its most celebrated sculptors. Embracing the life and culture of his adopted country, Petranovic had learned to believe again. He had not felt that way since he'd been a student during that time of hope they called the Prague Spring, but in Australia, his belief returned: the belief that things could change, the belief that life could be better. He knew what it was like to face the invader. He had suffered dispossession. He had stood arm in arm with his friends when the Russian tanks rolled in, and though he had chosen to flee, he had selected his path and he knew how it would go: outlaw, exile, refugee. Grateful citizen of a welcoming nation, a nation which at last was facing up to its own transgressions.

Moved by the struggles of Australia's Indigenous people and to show his support for their cause, Jaroslav Petranovic had made *The House of the Stolen*. His inspiration was *The House of the Suicide*, a tribute to Jan Palach, a student who had given his life to protest the Soviet occupation of

Czechoslovakia by setting himself on fire. The sculpture featured a large central spear to represent hope for the future surrounded by smaller spears of declining size to acknowledge the losses of the past.

Like its inspiration, *The House of the Stolen* was tall and majestic and fashioned from steel. It was designed for a public space and the sculptor contented himself with the knowledge it would stand one day in the National Gallery as part of the Nigel and Melissa Woods Bequest, ensuring Nigel—and hopefully Jaroslav Petranovic—would be remembered long after they were dead.

Both men would be remembered all right, but not for the reasons they hoped.

The first thing that caught Jane's eye was a pool of what looked like blood at the base of the sculpture. As she looked up, she saw what she hoped was some kind of macabre installation: the white, waxen figure of a man, the bottom half of his clothes removed, skewered on a spike that ran up through his rectum and out through his neck. But this was no artistic statement about the white invader, no nightmare monument to man's inhumanity. This was utterly and chillingly real. Jane was looking up at the recently deceased body of Nigel Woods, a man who, by the torment still etched on his face, had endured a slow and agonizing death. His knees were spread outward as if to push back against the pain, his hands open, fingers curled against the direction of his arms. His rigid body hung above her, suspended in time and space, lifeless but alive with his suffering. Though Jane could barely breathe, she could not look away from the horror.

Jesus, Mary, and Joseph.

Ringer took Jane through to one of the reception rooms to introduce his team, the distorted figures of Brett Whiteley paintings mute witnesses on the walls. The art was eclectic—Tuck, Shead, Quilty, Petyarre, and Mombassa—but there was no time to appreciate any of that. Senior Sergeant Nita Marino, compact and watchful and on the right side of forty, was Ringer's 2IC. She had been promoted to Homicide from the Sexual Victims Unit, where the worst side of human nature was constantly on display. As Marino would say herself, she had seen it all—though nothing at all like this. Sergeant Graeme Gawler, or "Showbag" to his mates, was fifty, a bulky old-school cop who liked to work on his own. As hard and tough as a cop could be, he was so affected by the body in the other room, he could barely grunt "Hello." Senior Detective Raymond Cheung went the other way, with an outpouring of speculation about the crime and the offender until Ringer quietened him down. At twenty-eight, he was the youngest member of the unit, but his IT and technical skills made up for his lack of experience in the field.

"Do we know how the body got there?" asked Jane.

"Well, we know he didn't jump from the landing," said Ringer as if to eliminate the obvious.

"We think the perpetrator used the mechanism that lowers and raises the chandelier for cleaning," Marino explained. "Some kind of harness was attached, we think, then removed to leave the weight of the body to do the rest."

"Was the victim conscious at the time?" asked Jane.

"That's yet to be established," answered Marino.

"And the time he took to die?"

"That too."

"Anything else? Any threats or demands?"

"Nothing as yet."

"Family situation?"

"Happily married," said Ringer. "The widow is on her way back from their holiday house at Portsea. Woods was supposed to join the family there later this evening. I've ordered the body to be removed before she gets here, so this is the last chance for everyone. After this, we're down to photographs and videos and written accounts. But what I need is first reactions—raw and unadorned. It's always the best shot we have."

The team was silent. They had already given Ringer their impressions and now the spotlight was firmly on Jane.

"It's probably an unfair question, Jane, but do you know what we're dealing with here?"

"I think there are two possibilities. Either someone cruel and deliberate who had something very personal in mind. Or a psychopath or thrill killer who did this for his own grat-ification. I tend toward the former, though at this stage it's speculation. In which case," she said, looking kindly at Cheung, "the detective's prognostications are probably as useful as mine.

"But if I'm right, the killer is organized, knew this loca-tion and came prepared. He's also meticulous, obsessive and extremely sadistic. I don't think the crime is ritualistic—but with an example of one, I can't rule that out. There is torture involved, which is extremely unusual: something quite medie-val, like the obscenities committed during the Crusades in the name of the Catholic Church. So, I would look for a hate crime or a religious motive or extreme prejudice of some kind. But most of all I would say this killer is clever, vengeful and quite probably narcissistic. And there is something else I would like to add. There's an arrogance to this crime and quite possibly a challenge, a challenge directed at you, the police. *See what I've done, try and stop me, for I am cleverer than any of you.* Let's pray that isn't the case."

Jane and Ringer headed outside. The fire brigade had arrived to remove the body, not something they wanted to watch. The air was sweet with night-scented jasmine so they stood as far away from the smokers' pungent bubble as they could. Ray Cheung remained inside to ensure the integrity of the crime scene, to the extent that that was possible.

"Did you really need to put me through that?"

"Nobody can read a crime scene like you can, Jane. That's something I remember like yesterday."

Yesterday. It seemed both far away and close. Was he remembering their sexual encounter on that New Year's Eve in 1998, Jane telling him the relationship had no future and his wry response, "I don't know; it could last all the way into next year"?

So much had happened to them both since then. With so many colleagues in common, they weren't totally unaware of what the other had done. He heading off to the Federal Police when his marriage fell apart. She retreating to academia to recharge her batteries, and beginning a relationship with Ben, which would last for seventeen years. But did Ringer know how Ben had died? Did he know of the tensions between Jane and her stepdaughter, Zoe, after Zoe's mother was found guilty of her father's murder? Jane knew nothing about Ringer's private life beyond the fact he had come back to Melbourne.

"Thanks for coming at such short notice," said Ringer, his eyes examining her face with the fondness of someone who had been a special friend.

"Wouldn't have missed it for quids," said Jane, hiding her feelings behind her irony, feelings she was yet to process.

Ringer grinned. Jane could tell he liked her ease and familiarity with the black humor world of a cop, a world few on the outside understood.

With the body removed and on its way to the morgue,

Marino announced that the car with Mrs. Woods was at the gate. Ringer gave instructions to avoid the foyer and escort her in through the kitchen—he would meet her in the lounge. He looked at Jane. He didn't ask, but she could see he needed support. She was curious, anyway, so when Marino suggested she might like to join them, Jane agreed.

With the aid of a personal trainer and a skilled cosmetic surgeon, Melissa Woods looked much younger than her fifty-three years and not at all like the mother of four children, two from her previous marriage now aged in their late twenties, the younger ones in their teens. Being the wife of a rich-lister had helped; wanting for nothing can do wonders for your worry lines. Her clothing came from Milan, her jewelry from New York, her poise from the knowledge that her position in society was secure. As head of the Nigel and Melissa Woods Foundation, she bestowed her husband's largesse on a number of cultural and philanthropic institutions and glowed in their reflection. But none of that was comfort now. She was, like anyone else whose husband had been the victim of a sudden and violent crime, in shock and despair.

"Mrs. Woods, I'm Inspector Eric Ringer. This is Doctor Jane Halifax and Senior Sergeant Nita Marino."

Melissa scrutinized Jane like she was someone she may have met.

"Please, call me Melissa." She introduced her companion, Maurice Engels, a lawyer and family friend, and invited everyone to sit.

"Do you have somewhere to stay tonight?" asked Ringer. "I'm sorry, but your home will be a crime scene until we've completed forensics."

"We'll go back to Portsea to be with the children. Maurice's wife is with them now."

"Inspector, could you tell us, please, what you know?" said the lawyer, showing impatience on his client's behalf.

"Not a lot more than I said on the phone."

"Is there a chance this was an accident?"

"No. We think he was lowered onto the sculpture."

"Lowered," whispered Melissa. "How?"

"We think the mechanism that controls the chandelier may have been used."

Melissa Woods closed her eyes to blot out the image.

"Do you know if your husband had received any threats?"

"What kind of a question is that?"

"A necessary one," said the lawyer gently. "I am sorry, Mel, but they have to ask."

"This whole thing is a nightmare. Can I see my husband's body?"

"Of course. We can take you to the morgue after this. Before we do the autopsy."

"I'm sure you're trying to protect me, but I need to know what happened."

Where to begin? She was barely holding herself together.

"Inspector, can I see the crime scene, please?" It was an unnecessary request from Engels, but Ringer wasn't going to be pedantic. And it would be easier to tell the lawyer what they knew without the widow present.

"You'll need to be kitted up, Mr. Engels. Marino will find you some gloves and over-boots." The detectives went off with the lawyer, leaving Melissa and Jane alone.

"Did you see him?"

Melissa's question caught Jane off guard.

"My husband's body?"

"Yes, I did." She couldn't lie.

"And?"

"I don't think he suffered too long. He would have lost consciousness."

"From the pain?"

"And loss of blood." Despite the bluntness of her answers, Jane knew Melissa needed to know.

"Why would anyone want to kill someone in such a horrible way?"

"We've no idea at this point, but I promise you, we will discover what happened."

"You've been through something similar, haven't you?"

So that's why Melissa had looked at Jane so intently when they were introduced. Ben's violent murder had filled the newspapers the year before, shot in the head as he sat beside Jane in her car. His murder and the investigation of the Melbourne Shooter had dominated the headlines for weeks. It was publicity that Jane didn't seek or want—but she got it anyway. And now Melissa Woods was about to find out what that was like.

"Is that why you're here?"

It wasn't of course, unless Ringer was smarter than Jane imagined. He had said it was Jane's work with the Point Cook survivors that made her involvement so valuable. Was she back now for more of the same?

"Stay close to your children, don't read the papers and seriously think about going interstate for a while."

"You begin to believe life is perfect. Apart from the usual issues with children. Do you have children, Jane?"

"I have a stepdaughter who lives in New York. A musician. She's twenty-four." But Melissa was only asking to be polite.

"Nigel was the center of everything. Such a busy life, such high expectations, the children never quite up to the mark. Everything done on the run. Business, functions, travel, holidays, obligations. The foundation was a full-time occupation.

Rewarding, of course, but exhausting. And now everything stops. Our world has lost its planet, Jane. We're moons around a black hole."

"Melissa, I'm a doctor. I can prescribe you something, if you like."

"No, you can't. Unless you've got something to go back in time. Do you have any concept of a billion dollars? Well, Nigel had fourteen of those and he wanted more. It becomes an addiction. A competition for where you sit on the list. A measure of how important you are. It defines you and it defines your friends, who can't be normal people. Normal people don't understand a billion dollars. No wonder your kids get lost. But it doesn't make any difference. You can't spend that much money. It multiplies so quickly, you can't even give it away."

Melissa Woods seemed suddenly small and in danger of being swallowed by the enormous couch on which she sat. Despite her wealth she looked vulnerable and without resources. Jane wanted to put her arms around this stranger, this woman all at sea in her own home, suffering the pain of unbearable loss.

"Melissa, I'm so sorry."

The two women sat together in silence, the sad eyes of Reg Mombassa watching from his self-portrait on the wall.

2

The Homicide Squad worked through the weekend and assembled for a briefing at 8:00 a.m. on Monday morning. Ringer circulated copies of the autopsy and asked Jane to talk them through the salient points. Her medical knowledge would help her explain the detail.

Time of death had been put at 6:45 p.m., about three hours after Nigel Woods had come home. Traces of the drug ketamine had been found in his body and it was clear he'd been tranquilized before being lowered onto Jaroslav Petranovic's sculpture. Jane explained that ketamine, which could be obtained illegally as a party drug, was effective for up to half an hour so had probably been injected to prevent Woods resisting while the murderer removed the clothing from the bottom half of his body and attached him to the chandelier mechanism with some kind of makeshift harness.

"Woods probably recovered consciousness with the main spear of the sculpture having already pierced his bladder and his large and small intestine," said Jane. "As the weight of his body caused him to slowly descend on the spike, the point of the spear was probably at his liver when he came around. That was the organ that had bled the most as gravity caused the spear to continue up through his lung and eventually out in front of the right clavicle. The murderer may or may not have pulled down on his legs to assist the process."

Jane concluded by observing that Nigel Woods had died from loss of blood, but not in a timely manner. "Fortunately—or unfortunately, depending on your point of view—the femoral artery, aorta, vena cava, and heart had not been penetrated. Had they been, death would have occurred much sooner. Instead, the victim survived, conscious and in extreme pain, for up to two hours and forty-five minutes."

The autopsy's findings didn't surprise Jane. She had seen the urine, blood, and fecal matter at the crime scene. She had lied to Melissa Woods about her husband quickly losing consciousness because it had seemed a kinder assessment.

Nita Marino followed with a summary of the forensic information.

"With no obvious sign of forced entry, the perpetrator either entered with Woods or was already waiting inside. Either way, the implication was that they were familiar with the house and possibly known to the victim. There was no sign of a scuffle either inside or outside the house and the security cameras outside the building revealed no one inside the grounds—which either meant the murderer was lucky or knew where the cameras were and how to avoid them."

Marino explained that the Woodses' normal routine was for Melissa and the family to head down to Portsea on Friday afternoons with Nigel joining them after work, having swung by the house to select wine for the weekend from his extensive cellar; this was not a task he would delegate to his wife. Wine was Nigel's great passion in life and what he presented would balance the status of his guests for the weekend with how much he wanted to impress them.

What the CCTV cameras had managed to pick up was a telephone technician working in the street along the road from the house from midday through to 4:30 p.m. He had been there with his bag of tools the Friday before and the Friday a week before that, yet Telstra was adamant it had not had a technician in the area for months. Had it been the murderer, tracking Woods's movements?

"Course it was," grunted Showbag. "What tradesman do you know works after 3:00 p.m.? They get up at bloody five in the morning." He was scrutinizing a blown-up image of the supposed technician taken from CCTV footage. It was grainy and shot at a distance, making any identification other than his gender impossible. "Looks totally sus to me: big hat and sunnies and a hi-vis vest with no logo." He passed the photo on to the others.

Ringer looked at Jane. "So, are we any the wiser as to what makes this torturer tick?" he asked.

It was a strange question under the circumstances. Why all this focus on the killer? Jane wondered. They had a victim, which was a much better place to start.

"It's still speculation—unless you can tell me how long he stayed?" she said.

Marino shook her head, so Jane continued, "Torturers are usually comfortable with their actions because they are driven by religious or ideological conviction. Or they do it through obedience or chain of command. But outside authoritarian regimes, torture is unusual, so I am going to refer to our perpetrator as a sadist. A genuine sadist would have hung around to watch."

Ray Cheung's eyes widened with fascination.

"Sadists are motivated by a desire to bring suffering to others or pleasure to themselves, often of a sexual nature. If we'd found semen at the crime scene, then it would probably be the latter, though a meticulous criminal like ours would probably use a condom to avoid leaving any trace."

"Do we know why he left when he did?" asked Ringer, turning to Marino. "Maybe he was interrupted?"

"No. He had left by the time the cleaners discovered the body."

"Now nighttime cleaners as well," said Showbag with his usual cynicism. "Isn't that suspicious?"

Marino looked at him over her spectacles. "Melissa Woods insisted the cleaners worked when she wasn't there."

"Instead of speculating on the killer, shouldn't we concentrate on Woods?" suggested Jane as diplomatically as she could. "If we fully understand the victim, then I can start by profiling him."

Ringer summarized what they knew. "Nigel Damien Woods was a former merchant banker who formed his own investment company in 2001, focusing on venture capital and new technologies. He went on to amass a fortune including an extensive portfolio in mining and property. He had one of the most valuable art collections in Australia outside a public gallery. He was a generous philanthropist, especially in the arts, and was prominent in the Catholic Church, having been made a Papal Knight in 2017.

"Woods married his current and only wife Melissa in 1997, adopting her two young children from a previous marriage before having two of their own. With influential friends including prominent businessmen, politicians, celebrities, and rich-listers, Woods managed to keep his family and his private life out of the headlines.

"Interviews with friends and employees are ongoing," said Ringer as he wrapped things up, "but at this stage we have no known threats, disputes or enemies. His life was ordered, without controversy. And extremely comfortable."

"Until he was hoist on his own Petranovic."

Nothing like a tortured metaphor from Showbag to reduce a briefing to laughter.

As the others welcomed the interruption, Jane's focus remained on Ringer. As much as she liked this cop, with his ready grin and easy charm, there was something about the way he was acting that made her uneasy, something about the case she sensed he was withholding.

Ringer caught her look and smiled fondly. It was impossible to ignore the intensity of their past encounter. He would probably mistake it for something else, but she would make things clear when the moment was right. Jane couldn't deny her attraction, but however she felt, workplace relationships were way out of bounds and as far as Eric Ringer was concerned, Jane Halifax was definitely not available.

3

Jane and Ringer attended Nigel Woods's funeral at St. Patrick's Cathedral. It was both a sign of respect and a routine part of any police investigation, a matter of looking and listening. Among the dignitaries in attendance were the Premier, the Leader of the Opposition, senior clergy, leading Melbourne businessmen and women, prominent arts administrators and representatives of the Melbourne Football Club.

The archbishop began by quoting the motto of the young architect and engineer William Wardell, who had designed the cathedral in 1897. "*Inventi Quod Quaesivi*: I have found that which I sought."

Jane imagined Nigel Woods's ascent into heaven may well have been his ultimate intention in life, though not at this time and certainly not in this manner.

After a succession of hagiographic eulogies from politicians and prominent businessmen, advertising executive and fellow Portsea identity Barry Boucher introduced some humor into proceedings.

"I attend this service today at great personal risk as possibly the only self-confessed atheist in this magnificent building. Should lightning strike, you have my permission to applaud.

Nigel and I were neighbors and rivals for fifteen years. He coveted my wife . . . sorry," he said as he corrected his speech, "that should be 'wine'—and I coveted his.

"Nigel was a very good tennis player but a very poor linesman. His close calls were always 'in' whereas my close calls were always 'out.' And as a tribute to his memory, bad calls on his magnificent court at Portsea shall from this day forth be called 'a dead Nigel.'

"Though we were very good friends he never understood my world and I never understood his. He had no need of advertising and I had no need of a billion dollars . . ." Barry scribbled on his printed speech. "My secretary's keyboard skills again. That should have been no need of *fourteen* billion dollars."

The humor loosened everyone up and even brought smiles from Woods's family.

After the casket had been removed through an honor guard formed by the Melbourne Football Club, Jane and Ringer mingled at the after-service function as inconspicuously as they could. Jane earned a grateful nod from Melissa Woods; Ringer, a guarded one from Maurice Engels.

A funeral is like tossing a pebble into a pond. At the center, where the wake is strongest, the family and close friends stand in unison and perpetuate the myth. But as the ripples spread through the lesser reaches, you get a more accurate sounding. Meeting at the urn of undrinkable coffee, Ringer asked Jane what she had gleaned.

"There's a gargoyle of Jeff Kennett above the restored eastern transept. There's no mistaking his long, lean face. When it rains, his enormous mouth gushes water and nothing else, which is a consolation to some, I suppose."

"I didn't know the former premier was a Catholic?"

"He's not. The architect designs the building but the

gargoyles are left to the stonemason. At least this one had a sense of humor. What about you?"

"Nigel Woods wasn't as universally admired as we've been led to believe. I heard someone say it was about time 'someone stuck it up him'. And someone else that it gave a whole new meaning to 'a probe into someone's affairs'. Everyone seems to know about how Woods died. I'd put my money on Engels being the leak."

Between them they'd discovered that Nigel Woods was feared and admired—called "the Jesuit" by some and "the Toe-cutter" by others—but he wasn't liked. In Nigel's world, people were expendable as he built his empire like a corporate Viking, shielded by the cloak of his Papal dispensation. Many despised his take-no-prisoners approach to making money and doing deals, though all agreed he'd been a man of his word.

Ringer returned to police headquarters to get his troops to compile a list of people in the business world who'd been "bruised or worse" by Woods. It loomed as a formidable task but at least they now had an angle. Jane had lingered with the funeral goers in the hope Melissa might invite her to the inner-sanctum function so she could continue to gather intelligence. But the esprit de corps of the Sisterhood of the Widows of Tragedy obviously didn't run that deep, not yet, so Jane ubered off to work on her profiling at home.

———

Jane's process was more esoteric than the detectives'. Profiling the victim was her first step in profiling the killer. It was a process of triangulation. Around an empty circle in the middle of a page she listed what she knew about Nigel Woods: rich-lister, art collection, Catholic, ruthless reputation, feared/admired, powerful/uncompromising, married, four children.

Highlighted to one side she wrote, *The House of the Stolen.* Beyond being the means of death, was the sculpture a significant clue in itself? Was it incidental or vital? Was it an object of convenience or did it in fact inspire the torture? There were some who would claim Petranovic's work as an act of cultural appropriation, that it was for the Indigenous people to make their own statements of loss, not for a Czech refugee who had adapted a sculpture from the nation of his birth about an entirely different time and place. But given the violence and sadism involved, Jane felt that bow was too long and excised "cultural appropriation" from her list.

Jane made herself a cup of tea and continued the process in the kitchen, leaving the circle blank for her conclusions while adding a list of what she knew, a list that would grow as the investigation proceeded, aided by her psychological overlay. It was a process she enjoyed, her sleuthing working in parallel with the police operation, their evidence physical and forensic, hers based on the maneuvers of the mind.

Jane was utterly lost in the process when Ringer phoned.

"Have you eaten?" he asked.

"No, have you?"

"Great. I'll pick you up in fifteen."

They headed for some late-night dining at the Magic Mountain Saloon in Little Collins Street. Finding a quiet booth, they ordered curried soft-shell crab, Peking duck salad, and a bottle of Mr. Hyde Montepulciano from the Clare Valley.

"Have you told me everything about this case?" Jane asked once their dishes had arrived.

Ringer seemed genuinely puzzled by the question. "Of course. What do you mean?"

"Just an impression I get—that you're holding back on something. Not telling me what you really think."

Ringer grinned at her perception. "How I don't like Nigel Woods on principle?"

"Aren't you supposed to be impartial?"

"I'm focused on catching the villain. I don't have to like the victim."

"So what's your problem?"

"I don't like billionaires. The rich in general. Their accumulation of wealth does nobody any good. Especially the planet."

"I never picked you as a greenie, Eric. Congratulations."

"More Pol Pot than Greta Thunberg. I wouldn't call me green. Like most cops, I hang to the right."

"Well, you can forget about us getting together. I am way, way left of center." Jane regretted the one-liner as soon as it left her lips. She had already sensed he wanted more than she did, yet there she was, tossing throwaways like throw-down crackers.

"That was a joke," she said as plainly as she could.

"I know." He grinned but she could tell he was filing the comment away for future reference.

"So, you envy the rich?"

"No."

"So you think that one bad billionaire ruins the barrel?"

"No. They're all rotten by definition."

"And tell me, Mr. Pol—or is it Mr. Pot?—what would you do if you could?"

"Impose a progressive tax rate that allows them to be what they want to be, but extracts an ever-increasing bounty for the rest of us."

"You are a very unusual policeman, Eric Ringer. Is this what happens when you work in Canberra?"

"I should have been born in Sweden. I like the welfare state but I hate the weather. I was there on exchange for a year and barely got through the six months of dark. Scandinoir isn't a crime genre, it's the reason the Swedish are so miserable. People murder to ward off the cold."

Now Jane was laughing out loud, and hoping her throw-away had fizzled and been forgotten.

They strolled along the path by the Yarra to walk off the wine, the river reflecting the city lights. The CBD glimmered around them, benign and reassuring and already half asleep. It was hard to believe there was a killer out there, waiting and biding his time.

A party boat pushed downstream, the revelers under the influence of Lady Gaga. Jane and Ringer paused to look back at the city.

"So give me a prediction," said Jane.

"I think our torturer will strike again." Ringer's use of the word seemed deliberate. "Sadist" wasn't something he understood. "Ritualistic or otherwise—I'll leave that stuff to you—he's telling us something we can't see yet."

"Are you hoping there'll be another one?"

"It could help us make more sense of it all. But no, I'm hoping this is an aberration. What about you?"

"The slow and deliberate infliction of cruelty in such a calculated manner lies at the heart of this. It probably reflects the murderer's pain, which he's attempting to transfer to someone else. I think the relationship between perpetrator and victim is close and intimate—but I could be wrong—an element of 'you did this to me, so I'm doing the same to you'. A very personal and extreme vengeance."

"Like someone he screwed in business?"

"Possibly."

"It's an interesting concept. That the murderer is suffering as much as his victim."

"Isn't that often the case?"

4

Franco Bernero didn't have the time to attend Nigel Woods's funeral. A man with a sprawling charity to run, a demanding wife, and two mistresses on the go, Bernero had too many balls in the air.

Since resigning in disgrace from Victoria's Upper House after accepting a number of questionable donations from a Chinese businesswoman, Bernero had transformed a little-known Catholic charity into a sprawling social service. With depots all across Melbourne, the Ferraro Bequest had become the Ferraro Foundation. Utilizing unoccupied buildings marked for rezoning or redevelopment, the foundation received donations of clothing and furniture which was lovingly restored by an army of volunteers. It paid no rent and little in the way of salaries—apart from generous stipends to Bernero and his two personal assistants. Very close personal assistants.

The foundation didn't only recycle clothing and furniture, which was then provided free to the poor. The landowners whose generosity provided the premises gained access to Bernero's extensive network of politicians and local counselors who would look kindly on the development plans of anyone who contributed so selflessly to their communities. Meetings would typically take place at a number of Lygon Street eateries and, to show his bona fides, Bernero would accept a stake in the development as well: "Everyone's a winner when Franco comes to dinner."

The charity was headquartered in a former engineering works in North Melbourne. Upstairs was Bernero's office and a small apartment where he could stay when the trip back to his wife and five children at Woodend was too daunting after a long day keeping his not-for-profit on course. People had no idea of the paperwork involved.

Mary McCluskey was Bernero's assistant during the first half of the week. Short and dumpy with bottomless appetites, it was a case of like attracting like. As she handed him a folder of planning department correspondence, Bernero slipped his hand under her skirt and plucked her G-string like a banjo. Mary melted. Such a sweet talker, he didn't need to open his mouth. She did that for him with her tongue as the paperwork ejaculated across the floor.

Bernero was so self-deluding he thought that no one knew about his office arrangements. But somebody did. They'd been watching the building for weeks.

The onlooker was a patient man and a perfectionist. He knew when Mary would leave to go home to her aging mother. She had left her with a microwave meal and a replacement Confidence Diaper and would lovingly bathe her in the morning. Her mother knew Mary always worked back on Wednesdays: it was an expectation of her employment.

On cue, Mary tottered out to her Cortina at half past ten and puttered off into the night. Bernero opened another bottle of Sangiovese and put on some music. It should have been "Air on the G String" but he didn't have the wit for that. With glass in hand, he moved around the building to turn off lights and check the locks. He didn't bother picking up the spilled correspondence. His other assistant, Preyah Mendoza, who pampered him during the second half of the week and who was as quick and efficient as Mary was sluggish and approximate, could do that in the morning. As Bernero would say himself, his assistants complemented each other perfectly.

At the top of the steel stairs that led to the mezzanine on the second level, Bernero paused. What was that sound? An open window, creaking in the wind? Or something closer, like a footstep? It was said a worker had died here decades ago after falling from the gantry. Was it the footfall of his ghost?

Bernero peered into the darkness and saw two mounds of heavy industrial chain by the goods lift. Strange, he hadn't noticed those before. He would talk to his people in the morning. Someone could do themselves an injury.

A length of pipe slammed into the back of Franco Bernero's head. It was designed to stun, not kill. His assailant wanted him to be present for his demise.

————

For once, Jane didn't mind that the traffic was heavy. Locked in the rush-hour madness Melbourne motorists accept every day, she had time to think, time to prepare.

When her mobile had rung at seven fifteen that morning, Jane knew it wouldn't be good news.

"He's struck again," Ringer had said. It was barely two weeks since the first murder.

Walking into a crime scene was harrowing at the best of times and Jane knew that this one would be anything but routine. Not that entering the scene of a murder is ever a neutral experience. The arena of someone's death is always charged with sadness and reflection.

But this killer wanted to shock, to punish his victim and those dear to him—and the investigators as well. Jane had to go into operative mode. As a scientist, she needed to be objective. She knew that empathy got in the way of analysis, that emotion was unhelpful and self-indulgent. So much for good intentions.

As she approached the building, she saw it first in the faces of the police who guarded the crime scene: something unspeakable had happened here.

Ringer met her at the entrance. As head of the investigation, his demeanor imparted authority and reassurance, but as his eyes met with Jane's, they flickered with apology. He didn't want to put her through this again, but she knew he needed her more than ever.

Franco Bernero's earthly remains hung in the void at the end of the cavernous building. Suspended ten meters above the ground, like a carcass in an abattoir, the victim appeared at first as a silhouette against the sun that pierced the grime of the eastern windows. Heavy chains were attached to his wrists and ankles and, as Jane moved closer, she could see that sections of an athlete's compression sleeve had been placed beneath the shackles to prevent the skin from tearing. Remarkably considerate, she thought, for a killer whose currency was pain.

But then the awful truth was revealed: Bernero had been incrementally stretched to ensure he had suffered a slow and excruciating death. His limbs had been wrenched from their sockets, dislocated to a point short of separation so his corpus remained intact. Desecrated like Nigel Woods.

The chains attached to Bernero's legs ran down to U-bolts that secured them to an iron railing, while those attached to his wrists disappeared up over the edge of the concrete mezza-nine on the second floor. From there the chains ran across to the goods lift where they'd been dropped down the shaft. The killer had attached the other end of the chains to the back of a forklift loaded with a container. The stacker had then been parked on a ramp leading down to the cart dock. With its brake released, the weight took up the strain and the rest was a matter of physics.

"The container on the forklift is full of clothes and blan-kets," explained Ringer. "A fire hose had been poked into the top of the container so water soaked the contents, progres-sively increasing the weight."

Jane looked up at Bernero's brutalized body. It seemed disrespectful to speak in his presence, but she knew Ringer needed answers.

"It's the same person who killed Nigel Woods. The same MO: medieval torture."

"I thought you didn't approve of the word?"

"Well, it's not a category in the *Clinician's Guide to Diag-nosis*."

"Anything else?"

"Where do I start? Religion. The Inquisition. Vengeance. Sadism. Suffering. Hate. Fury. Purification. A Cleansing."

"Cleansing?" Ringer's voice registered his disbelief.

"It's important to keep an open mind," said Jane. Though apparently not if you were Eric Ringer. "Were the victims known to each other? I mean, did Woods know . . . whoever this victim is?"

"Franco Bernero, former Labor politician and fixer. This building was part of a charity he ran—the Ferraro Founda-tion. It's associated with the Catholic Church . . ."

"So did they know each other?"

"Bernero would have known of Woods; maybe not the other way round. They moved in different circles."

"What about Catholic circles?" said Jane, stressing the connection.

"We don't know that yet. 'It's important to keep an open mind.'"

"What's that lesion on his side?" Jane indicated a wound on the right-hand side of Bernero's torso.

"The murderer didn't do that. Well, not directly."

"Then how did it get there?"

Ringer indicated a wire basket that had fallen to the floor with some frayed lengths of twine attached. "Rodents. We think he attached the basket to Bernero's stomach and filled it with rats. Starving rats. If you deprive them of food for long enough—well, your imagination can do the rest. They obviously had what they wanted, then gnawed through the ties and escaped."

Jane closed her eyes to eradicate the image. Instead, it seared into her brain.

5

Walking through the grounds of Melbourne University on a shimmering summer day, Jane wondered why she had left. She had enjoyed her years here as Professor of Forensic Psychiatry, inspiring students and jousting with colleagues. Ben had encouraged her to apply for the post in the first place and had resisted when she'd returned to active police work to help Tom Saracen, the head of Task Force Stingray, track down the Melbourne Shooter. After Ben's murder, her head of department had insisted she take extended leave and although Jane still did the odd lecture and worked with the doctoral students and kept an office, she had never fully returned. Private practice was easier to manage, though she did that working from home, resisting establishing rooms and hiring an assistant. She enjoyed appearing in court as an expert witness, a forum in which she excelled. Her father could never understand why Jane had been so adamant she wouldn't follow him into the law.

Nicholas Mandel welcomed Jane into his office in the History Department. An academic in the English eccentric tradition with a fondness for dates and numbers, his lectures were more like sermons, his wit so dry it had elbow patches.

But no one knew more about medieval history. His books on the subject were revered around the world.

"Ah, the Judas cradle and the rack—or more correctly, the ladder," exclaimed Nicholas with delight as Jane showed him the crime-scene photos. He frowned, wiggling a disapproving digit at a photo of the rat cage beside a diagram to show how it had been fixed to Bernero's body before the rats gnawed through the twine. "But that's wrong. That's never combined with the ladder. Never. Someone hasn't been doing their homework."

"Both victims had connections with the Catholic Church," Jane said. "Do you think that's significant?"

"Secular torture was widely used in the Middle Ages but it was the Roman Church who perfected it. The Dominicans in particular, and the Franciscans. Masters of their trade. Anything of any moment back then was generated in the name of God."

"Why were the Catholics so committed?"

"Well, I could blame it on a climate event—the Medieval Warm Period from 950 to 1250—but it was probably the Crusades. In the High Middle Ages, the Church was terrified by a resurgence in heresy so they thought they'd get in first and terrify everyone else. Torture was never about the victim: it was there for the greater good, as a warning to the wavering believer."

"Is that what's going on here, you think?"

"You tell me, you're the shrink."

"How many people were tortured?"

"Too many to count, but it wasn't the main cause of death. A peasant's life expectancy was twenty-five to thirty years. Longer if you were a woman."

Jane was astonished. "Women lived longer?"

"They didn't go to war. Thirty percent of soldiers died in battle as opposed to twenty-five percent of women dying in childbirth. These were precarious times. Dysentery and primitive medicine. Mental illness was relieved by boring a hole in the head. Not to mention the bubonic plague, which killed sixty percent of Europe."

"When did torture end?"

"With the development of humanism in the seventeenth century. Trial by jury put an end to circumstantial evidence and the Bill of Rights did the rest; 1689, if you're taking notes."

"Though I believe the Church persisted?" Jane said to show she had done some reading.

"Napoleon tried to stop it when he conquered Spain in 1808 but it continued for twenty years. The office of the Universal Inquisition still exists though it's changed its name a couple of times. It is currently called the Congregation for the Doctrine of the Faith."

"What can I read? What's the best reference for torture?"

"Try this." Nicholas plucked one of his books from the shelf, wrote Jane a copperplate dedication with his fountain pen, and ticked off the chapters she should read. "I wanted to write about the Knights Templar but my publisher wanted something she could sell."

Though a former colleague from Jane's time as a member of the tight-knit university fraternity, Nicholas didn't ask Jane about the murders. Or how she was adjusting to living alone. He would have found it too confronting. He was happy to live in the fifteenth century with all the comforts of the twenty-first. Renaissance man with guaranteed tenure, time to write and enough superannuation to attend the opera for the rest of his life.

"You can't codify the transgressions of the human mind,"

he said. "You can record what they did and where they did it and the reasons they gave at the time. And what other people said about it. To go further than that isn't history, it's fiction. And that's another department."

Jane thanked Nicholas for the book and headed back to the present. A parking ticket, dog shit on her shoe, and the tedium of cooking for one while they were doing it so much better on reality TV. At least there was no bubonic plague.

Jane changed for bed, made a green tea, and curled up on the couch with Nicholas's book.

The range of tortures was horrendous.

They hanged them by the thumbs, or by the head, and hung fires on their feet, recorded one old English chronicle. They put knotted strings about their heads and writhed them so that it went to the brain. Some they put in a trunk that was short and narrow and shallow and lined with sharpened stones, wherein they pressed the man so they broke all his bones.

Thumbs, fingers, feet, and heads were crushed in iron presses and limbs smashed with heavy mallets. Eyes and tongues were cut out and teeth, fingernails, and toenails removed with red-hot pliers. There were tabillas, turkas, gresillions, and tortillons—the latter for squeezing and mutilating genitals. A metal device called the pear of anguish was inserted into vaginas and expanded by means of a screw. There were Spanish boots and brazen bulls and iron maidens. Gossip bridles and scavenger's daughters. Even, to Jane's dismay, a Halifax gibbet—a kind of medieval guillotine.

People were burned at the stake, boiled in water, and flayed alive. There were wedges and skewers and breast rippers and cat's paws to tear the flesh. And intestinal cranks for removing the innards while the victim was still alive. There was no limit to their cruelty or invention: people were hung upside down and divided in half with a two-man saw, starting at the crotch.

Once accused, the die was cast. If you confessed you'd be executed. If you did not, you'd be tortured until you did. Either way, misery and death were inevitable. And all because someone accused someone else of heresy without evidence, due process, or motive (unless they wanted the land and property of the accused, though that was a supposedly secondary reason).

Jane read an account of one unfortunate victim—a heartbreaking letter to his daughter on the eve of his execution.

Many hundred thousand good-nights, dearly beloved daughter, Veronica. Innocent have I come into prison, innocent have I been tortured, innocent must I die.

I will tell you how it has gone with me. When I was the first time put to the torture, Dr. Braun, Dr. Kötzendörffer, and two strange doctors were there. Then Dr. Braun asks me, "Kinsman, how come you here?" I answer, "Through falsehood, through misfortune." "Hear, you," he says, "you are a witch; will you confess it voluntarily? If not, we'll bring in witnesses and the executioner." I said, "I am no witch, I have a pure conscience in the matter; if there are a thousand witnesses, I am not anxious, and will gladly hear them."

Now the chancellor's son was set before me and afterward Hoppfen Elss. She had seen me dance on Haupts-moor. I answered: "I have never renounced God, and will never do it." And then the executioner put the thumb-screws on me, both hands bound together, so that the blood ran out at the nails and everywhere, so that for four weeks I could not use my hands, as you can see from the writing.

Thereafter they stripped me, bound my hands behind me, and drew me up in the torture. Then I thought heaven and earth were at an end. Eight times did they draw me up and let me fall again, so that I suffered terrible agony.

When at last the executioner led me back into the prison, he said to me: "Sir, I beg you, for God's sake confess something, whether it be true or not. Invent something, for you cannot endure the torture which you will be put to; and, even if you bear it all, yet you will not escape, not even if you were a nobleman, but one torture will follow after another until you say you are a witch."

And so I made my confession, but it was all a lie.

Dear child, keep this letter secret so that people do not find it, else I shall be tortured most piteously and the jailers will be beheaded, so strictly is it forbidden.

Dear child, pay this man for the letter as I have taken several days to write it and I am in sad plight. Good night, for your father Johannes Junius will never see you more.

July 24, 1628.

Jane started as her mobile jolted her back to the present.

"Hello, Jane. Is that you?"

Melissa Woods. Jane peered at her watch: it was almost midnight.

"You said I could call if I needed to. Everyone's out at a

family gathering, but I didn't think I could face it." Jane could tell she'd been drinking.

"Hello, Melissa. How have you been?" After her frostiness at the funeral, Jane was intrigued.

"Fair to suicidal. But my bottle keeps me warm. So, he's done it again?"

"He?"

"Whoever did what he did to Nigel. The press aren't saying too much, but it's not difficult to draw conclusions."

Melissa Woods was clearly after information, but that's often a two-way street. Alert to the opportunity, Jane kept the mood conversational.

"Let me get myself something as well," she said as she headed across the room for a bottle already open. "That way we can drink together."

"Widows in their cups." Melissa chuckled, though Jane could have done without the reminder.

"Did Nigel know Franco Bernero?"

"I doubt it," said Melissa. "Wasn't he dodgy and Labor?"

"They didn't meet through the Church?"

"Nigel wasn't an active Catholic. His knighthood was a reward for his charitable works. And Bernero, by all accounts, was a political bagman." Melissa's disdain for the billions-deprived was showing.

"If we could make a connection, it could be useful . . ."

"The Ferraro Foundation's not a charity like ours. If you ask me, the whole operation's a sham."

None of which was news to Jane, but at least Melissa was talking.

"Chin," said Jane.

"Bottoms up," countered Melissa. "I hope you've got more than this Catholic thing?"

Jane didn't and neither did the cops. Two weeks of investigating the business dealings of Nigel Woods and Associates had provided very few leads. But she wasn't about to tell Melissa.

"Do you think another woman's involved?" Melissa said.

The suggestion was so leftfield, Jane didn't see it coming. "Why do you say that?"

"I'm not naive. People lead double lives. Nigel was an attractive man. Powerful, admired, younger than me. I wouldn't have blamed him."

"Melissa—"

"For God's sake, call me Mel."

"Mel, this crime wasn't committed by a woman. She wouldn't have had the strength—"

"I'm not suggesting a woman did this directly. But what if someone—a woman—committed the crime in the first place, committed the betrayal that drove the murderer to do what he did? You're the psychiatrist, Jane. Aren't crimes of passion at the heart of all cruelty and revenge, the most selfish and most obscene of all?"

For someone who'd had too much to drink, Melissa was making more sense than might be expected. Or was it more sense, thought Jane as she pondered the possibilities, than Melissa intended? "Another woman." "Crimes of passion." "At the heart of all cruelty and revenge." Jane added the words to her profile working sheet, wondering if they would help. Or were they merely the ramblings of a widow unable to make any sense of her husband's pitiless death and suffering? The circle in the center of the page remained stubbornly empty of any conclusions.

At this early stage in the investigation, divining for motive was like divining for water but without a magic stick. Why hadn't the murderer left some clue or made some statement? They usually do. Why go to all this trouble with so much premeditated cruelty only to keep your reasons obscure? If the killer had a message, his opacity wasn't helping his cause.

Jane had to acknowledge that the inventiveness with which the murderer had re-created his tortures was truly remarkable. But his purpose, if there was one, had been lost in the process. Or was this sadism, pure and simple? Extreme cruelty for no other reason but the perpetrator's grim satisfaction?

Yet for all the obscurity, links were beginning to emerge as Jane drew lines between words and highlighted others. Medieval torture. Charitable foundations. The Catholic Church. A Papal Knight and a low-level bagman. Pain and inevitable death. Unspeakable suffering. And now some new additions offered up by the first victim's widow.

If Jane ever wondered why she did this work, she only had to look at her scribblings. She was at the beginning of a very long process and she was hooked.

6

Jane pressed the intercom at the gate and looked into the camera.

"Can I help you?" said a voice that wasn't Melissa Woods's.

"Jane Halifax. I've come for coffee with Mel."

"Was she expecting you?"

"Yes. We spoke last night. She said any time after ten."

"Just a moment . . . I'm sorry. Mum's not feeling well . . ."

"I've brought tarte tatin from Babka," said Jane, holding up the Brunswick Street bakery's pièce de résistance.

More muffled irritation and a grudging concession as the lock went *click*. "Push the gate."

By day, the grounds of the mansion were immaculate: groomed lawns cut in two directions, sculptures and a fountain, rows of fragrant flowers and flowering natives; a professional gardener's labor of love.

Jane was met at the door by Charlotte, Melissa's frazzled daughter, a toddler adhered to her leg.

"Sorry. Mum forgot. But I'll take the opportunity to do some shopping, if that's okay. She's through in the kitchen." Charlotte scooped up the child and headed for her Porsche Cayenne Turbo GT, leaving Jane to orienteer the way on her own. The foyer seemed barren without *The House of the Stolen*, not that Jane was surprised to see it gone.

Melissa Woods was at the coffee machine, weary and unapologetic. In the yard beyond, a man was using an oxyacetylene torch to cut up the sculpture for ease of removal. Melissa couldn't look at what the workman was doing; Jane couldn't look anywhere else. Melissa plated the tarte and they carried their coffees through to the conservatory so the vandalism could continue unwitnessed.

"I know the sculptor. Does he know about this?" said Jane.

"Yes, and he offered to buy it back. But it wasn't about the money. I never liked it in the first place. And I didn't want it becoming famous for all the wrong reasons. The artist offered to remake it into something else, even pleaded to take the scrap, but I didn't trust him for a moment. And it isn't my problem. He could always make something else."

Jane found the destruction of *The House of the Stolen* shocking. Melissa had made it sound so easy, but Jaroslav Petranovic was in his seventies and not strong enough to wrestle steel anymore, not on that scale. His prize-winning monument to his adopted homeland, the crowning glory of a long and storied career would be no more. Was the destruction a by-product of Melissa's desire to protect her husband's memory—or a glimpse into some inner ruthlessness she worked very hard to conceal?

Jane watched as Melissa collected up some discarded toys and retrieved the cushions which had been made into a fort. She looked like any grandmother who disapproved of her daughter's laissez-faire approach to parenting, but this was no ordinary woman.

"I'm sorry about last night," said Melissa as she struggled in her fog. "To be brutally honest, I don't even remember calling." She sipped her coffee with a steady hand. There were no signs of a long-term alcohol problem. To abuse alcohol after her husband's brutal murder was understandable and something Jane had done herself. She recalled with some embarrassment how the head of faculty at her university had come to rescue her from a bar one night when she'd needed help getting home. But Jane never drank to the point of amnesia and she doubted that Melissa had either.

"You didn't sound that drunk," she said with a laugh, trying to put Melissa at ease. "From my own experience, alcohol is not the solution. There are antidepressants I could give you that would be a lot easier to manage." As a physician, Jane genuinely wanted to help. As a forensic psychiatrist, she was visiting for another reason: to take full advantage of the opportunity of a meeting with Nigel Woods's widow.

"So, what did I say?" asked Melissa. Jane suspected it was less an attempt to recall the conversation than to assess what she had made of it.

"You were worried about another woman."

"What other woman?" Her tone said she wanted more information but feared what she might hear.

"You thought Nigel might have been killed because of a crime of passion, that behind it all, there was a woman who was really to blame."

"Well, I must have been drunk to say that."

"Mel, was Nigel having an affair?"

"No."

"Would you know if he was?"

"Did you?"

It was a sharp and brutal reminder of what Jane had endured when Mandy, her husband's ex, had been charged with Ben's murder. Along with all the other details, their affair had been splashed across the newspapers for every-one to savor. Nothing like a juicy murder mystery involving well-known identities to spice up the drab lives of others.

"No, I had no idea my partner was having an affair with his former wife."

"I thought that's what came out in the trial," said Melissa, feigning sympathy. "Maybe I had that in the back of my mind last night."

Jane took Melissa back to the previous night's ramblings to try and get her affirmation of her suspicions of an affair, but the widow deflected and dissembled as if Jane had been talking to someone else.

"I phoned you because I wanted to know what the police knew about this latest murder. I wanted to know if they thought there was any connection. I wanted to know if they were any closer to identifying who had committed this outrage against humanity. Or why. I wanted the world to make sense again, that we were not on the edge of oblivion."

All of which was perfectly plausible. So why didn't Jane believe her?

———

"The other woman" was still on Jane's mind as she returned to police headquarters. As was usual in serial killer cases, sepa-rate pods had been established within the team to quarantine the investigations. It was important to run each killing to earth without evidence being contaminated by the other homicide. Ray Cheung's unit focused on Nigel Woods and Showbag's led the team investigating Franco Bernero. The exception to this was forensics, where crossovers and matches were crucial, so physical evidence was coordinated by Nita Marino. The only other time the pods came together was in the muster room for daily briefings.

When Jane popped her head into Ray Cheung's office, he was taking Ringer through his rogues' gallery—photos of people with a grudge against Woods, some arrived at through their own inquiries, others suggested to the police by Nigel Woods's personal assistant. Pride of place on the wall was a photo of Isaac McLaughlin. The police had been given an avalanche of emails from McLaughlin to Woods that were laced with threats and menaces, and Cheung's own inquiries had confirmed him as a principal person of interest.

"Good afternoon, Jane," said Ringer as he glanced at his watch.

"I've been having coffee with Melissa Woods. She phoned me last night to tell me there was usually 'another woman' behind these things. But when I followed it up this morning, she didn't remember making the call. She said she'd had too much to drink."

Ringer turned to Cheung. "Have we come across anything suggesting Woods was having an affair?

"No."

"What about his assistant?" asked Jane.

"She used to work for Melissa Woods at the charitable foundation, one of the few women Melissa trusted to work with her husband. According to those in the know, it was Melissa who got her the job."

Jane could only agree with Cheung that it was very unlikely the assistant was involved. "Melissa Woods certainly lived in fear that someone might lure her husband away. She seemed to believe his billions made him irresistible."

Ringer told Cheung to follow up on a possible affair, grabbed a stack of documents from the table and asked Jane to come through to his office. He closed the door and dumped the documents on his desk.

"This is Maurice Engels's idea of cooperation, contracts from Woods's empire with so many redactions they barely make sense. It's to do with a start-up Woods acquired from Isaac McLaughlin and how ugly things got about price. But there are so many deletions they're meaningless. Well, stuff him—I'm getting a warrant."

"Careful, your prejudices are showing. And you know as well as I do where that will end: in court."

"Let him do his worst. I know a cover-up when I see one."

"And what do you think they're hiding?"

"I've no idea. But for two men to die in the way they did, I'd say something pretty serious, wouldn't you?"

Jane knew they were jumping at shadows so when she called by Showbag's office for an espresso from the Giotto Cronometro she had noticed he kept in the kitchen, she half-expected more of the same. And indeed, the senior sergeant was dancing with specters of his own.

"Can you imagine this prick?" said Showbag as he tossed a photo in Jane's direction. It was of a developer called Jimmy Khan, one of Bernero's regular clients. "Double shot or single?"

"Single."

"Pretends to be a good mate while bad-mouthing him behind his back." There was a pause in the conversation as he flicked on the grinder: Toby's Estate, Woolloomooloo, roasted, as per recommendation, two weeks prior to use.

"Bernero did everything to get this arsehole's development across the line, despite an adverse ruling from council, the Department of Planning and the minister no less. And how does he thank him? He cancels Bernero's presale on the penthouse and repudiates the contract."

"Great coffee."

"If it was me I'd have a macchiato."

"Spoils the crema."

"Bernero was a fixer. He didn't make waves, he floated in the lagoon. Waves weren't in his best business interests. He did lunch and got things done. And I know I can't say this in the current climate, but this Paki jerk—" Showbag jabbed his finger at the photo for emphasis.

"You're right. We don't say that anymore."

"Jerk or—"

"Oh, jerk's okay."

"So this . . . 'jerk' got sick of Bernero complaining but Bernero just wanted his fee."

"In the form of a discounted penthouse?"

"Or the monetary equivalent thereof."

"More than reasonable under the circumstances."

"But the jerk says no. You took too long to get the approval and I've lost my profit before I start. Whereupon, an unholy war breaks out."

"Whereupon?"

"Can I finish?"

Jane sealed her lips.

"So, Bernero threatens to use his friendship with the minister to have the entire development revoked because 'it didn't comply with the bushfire regulations.'"

"That old trope . . ."

"And that's when the jerk threatens to put out a contract on Bernero. But now for the fatal flaw in the case against the jerk."

Jane had to confess to her inner-self she was thinking of lunch. Or having a pedicure. Or euthanasia.

"He's Muslim."

"Thanks for the coffee, Showbag. Gotta go!"

"Muslims cut off hands or do decapitations. Or blow people up with explosive vests. They don't stretch victims on racks. As you've said all along, that's Catholic."

Jane smiled to humor him and edged for the exit. To distract Showbag from his racist rant about Jimmy Khan, she asked him how he was going with the rats from the crime scene.

"What do ya mean?"

"Well, the killer took his time to catch them and starve them and put everything in place."

"Yes . . ."

Jane struggled to keep a straight face. "So, if you could catch some of those rats—maybe you could learn something about him?"

"Like?"

"I'm not a zoologist, but I suspect rats are territorial. Maybe there's a way of doing a dissection to find out where the killer lives."

"You've been watching too much CSI," said Showbag, convinced Jane was having a lend of him yet strangely attracted to the possibilities.

Jane gave a "who knows" shrug, but she was in too deep. How could she tell him it was only a joke, that you couldn't dissect the gut of a rat to determine its postcode any more than you could a human's.

"Anyway—I hope you get your man," she said as she finally escaped, leaving the policeman utterly confused in her wake.

It would have been quicker to have grabbed a coffee across the road.

7

Jane had resisted having an office at the police center but Ringer had insisted. He hoped it would keep her closer to the action. In the past she had found not everything was close at hand when she ran two offices, books and papers being inevitably split between the two. When she worked at the university, she kept everything there and let Ben use the office at home. Now the office in her apartment was where she kept her resources, everything filed and shelved and cataloged like the Virgo she was. Jane enjoyed the flexible hours a home office allowed.

Or was that her insomniac's excuse?

But her office at the Homicide Squad had an advantage her home office didn't: the computer was linked to the interview rooms and she could watch interrogations. An important one was about to begin. Jane closed the door, angled the venetians so the light level was low and settled into her chair. She flicked on the screen and put on her headphones. Ringer had wanted them to watch the interview together, but Jane didn't want his commentary to cloud her assessment; analysis is a solitary occupation and requires focus and concentration.

It takes a particular man to walk into a police station without representation, and Isaac McLaughlin was such an individual. Forty-eight years old with prematurely graying hair tied at the back. His jeans were expensive, his collar unbuttoned. He still had the bearing of a self-made man but for the sadness in his eyes.

As he took his seat and helped himself to a glass of water, Nita Marino turned the recorder on and introduced herself and Ray Cheung.

"Thank you for coming in, Mr. McLaughlin. For the record, could you confirm that you've been advised that you are entitled to legal representation, but declined?"

"Correct. I've nothing to hide."

"How long have you known Nigel Woods?"

"Longer than I wish to remember. Since 2001. Just after 9/11. I'd developed a credit start-up and was looking for a backer. Unfortunately, I chose the wrong person."

Jane watched as McLaughlin recounted his story, riveted by a man whose scars seemed as raw as the day they'd been earned.

"We were both pretty young back then, Nige a few years older than me but still in his early thirties. I'd just invented Afterpay before Afterpay was thought of. But it was more than that, with a kind of blend of subprime bundling to lay off the debt and use syndicates to carry the risk. Twice the fees, twice the profits, half the exposure."

Jane was impressed by his schtick, his ability to make banking sound sexy.

"I took the proposal to Nige, who was so leveraged to the banks that he could only get out of the shit he was in by taking on even more risk. It was a partnership made in heaven. Or hell, depending on your perspective. So, he had the documents drawn up by his lawyer—"

"Maurice Engels?"

"Oh, you've had the pleasure?" said Isaac, sounding as

if he hoped Marino would confirm his opinion of the man, though the detective gave nothing away. "Morrie was supposedly acting for us both. The joint venture was paying his fees but he only ever answered to Nige. Morrie was and is risk averse, but in awe of the gambles Nige would take, and I have to confess, so was I. Big balls can do a lot for a man."

Again, not a flicker from Marino, but Ray Cheung, who Jane already knew had a secret fantasy to be an entrepreneur, seemed entranced.

"So, we hired more people to refine the product and took on more debt and put it out to the highest bidder. None of which Nige accepted. He just used the frenzy to raise the price and hold out for a bigger payday. And all the while, Morrie was using his drafting skills to migrate the risk to my forty-nine percent and none of it to Nigel's fifty-one."

"Why did he have fifty-one?"

"According to Engels, it was a taxation thing. If Nige had technical control he could write off his risk. The irony being he had no risk. Not by the time he finally sold the IP and left me holding the baby."

"But as partners, didn't you know what was happening?"

"You know how lawyers work . . . maybe you don't. They swamp you with documents so dense they put you to sleep. This one to transfer debt to new lenders; this one to minimize tax; this one to make sure windfall profits go through tax shelters overseas. Morrie would restructure the venture as frequently as he traded up to a new model car. As he liked to brag, he 'needed the fees to pay for his lifestyle'. But he was an amateur compared to Nige. Nige would take a life preserver from a drowning man and sell it as a souvenir."

"Mr. McLaughlin, did you know how to gain access to Mr. Woods's home when he wasn't there?"

"Yes. After I went bankrupt he used to pay me to clean his pool."

Jane wondered if he was joking.

The detectives looked at each other. "When was that?"

"Five years ago. When he still had me convinced bankruptcy was just a tactic, that my payday would come soon enough. Before things fell apart."

He wasn't joking.

"But it didn't?" Ray Cheung asked.

"No."

"And you stopped cleaning his pool."

"Yes."

"Though you still had the code to his keypad?"

"I had the opportunity to kill him, if that's what you mean. And the motive. But not the imagination."

Marino said she didn't understand.

"Whoever designed the way Nigel Woods died deserves a bloody medal."

The team assembled in Ringer's office.

"Do we know what McLaughlin was doing on the day Woods was killed?" asked Ringer.

"Fishing," said Cheung, who had checked before the interview.

"Can he verify that?"

"No. He was fishing on his own."

"You're assuming it matters what he was doing. McLaughlin could have ordered the killing. He didn't have to do it himself to be guilty." Showbag had a point.

"Then what do we think?" asked Ringer.

"I think he's being cooperative," said Marino. "He's not pretending he doesn't have a motive."

"Anyone else?" Typically, Ringer was keeping his views to himself.

"It's too pat for me," Jane offered. "Too rehearsed. But then I'm suspicious by nature. Showbag, make me two flat whites. Let me try it from another angle."

"Nita, are you okay with that?" asked Ringer.

Jane knew as well as Marino did that her boss was only asking to be polite. It's called chain of command and if it comes from above you take it as read and don't argue. And apart from a passing dent to her professional pride, Jane knew the senior sergeant was as curious as anyone to see what she might achieve.

———

Jane backed in through the door to the interview room with a coffee in each hand.

"I've taken a total punt on this but I figure you're a flat white. Am I wrong? I'm a forensic psychiatrist, the 'non-copper' on the team. But I source very good coffee. So, I thought I'd take the risk and say hello. Hello. I'm Jane."

McLaughlin took the coffee, immediately on the back foot. "What makes you think I'm flat white?"

"I wasn't being determinist," she joked, offering to take it back.

"Flat white's fine. I'm Isaac."

"I know. I've been watching you on the telly." Jane indicated the camera.

"Isn't that an abuse of my personal rights?"

"Only if I put it on YouTube."

Her humor had an immediate effect. Showbag's coffee was helping as well. McLaughlin relaxed.

"Your story was very affecting. I don't know how you recover from something like that. Something you've given your life to."

McLaughlin was silent.

"Must have been hard on your family?"

"My father pretends everything's fine but I know what he really thinks, that bankruptcy's almost as shameful as Sandpapergate, but who gives a shit about cricket? My mother doesn't go out anymore and has stopped playing bridge with her friends. All they wanted to hear was the real dirt, the stuff they couldn't get in the papers. Some friends."

"What about your wife?"

"What makes you think I've got one?"

"Maybe the ring on your finger?"

"She killed herself."

"Oh, Isaac, I'm so sorry."

A steel wall descended, blocking all emotion apart from the desolation in his eyes. There were no tears.

"In the beginning, Nige and Mel were probably our closest friends. My Nessie was asthmatic and on bad days the pollution in the inner city was more than she could take. But the Woods had a place at Portsea and suggested we try living there. It was a classic Aussie beach shack with a lean-to kitchen and a million-dollar view, back in the days before they acquired all the neighbors' properties and built Hyannis Port. I was working ridiculous hours and the drive was a pain in the bum but Nessie loved it and when Nige bought the place two along the street in order to pressure the folks in between, we saw the Woods every weekend."

"That's close," said Jane. "More than a business relationship."

"We were going to conquer the world. Mr. Forty-Nine and Mr. Fifty-One, but who cared about two percent?"

Jane smiled. Her instincts had been right. There was more to his relationship with Nigel Woods than business.

"We were on the IVF program and it wasn't working, but Mel was fantastic. The power of positive thinking: fitting out the nursery, developing a fitness program, watching the food Ness was eating. And just like our dreams for the business, it seemed only a matter of time. Keeping fit, a surf every day before work, only drinking weekends. We didn't have much but if dreams were enough . . . Then it all went to custard.

"It started with the GFC and Morrie's 'creative documentation'. He had become a Portsea person too like the true sycophant he is—had to be up Nigel's arse every hour of the day. Then we got pregnant with twins and lost them. Then pregnant again, same result. Then Nige finally got the last property from the hold-out neighbor and brought in the dozers. So, we had to find somewhere else.

"Like the high-flying tech developer I thought I was— well, I was certainly rich on paper—I borrowed a motza and we bought a mansion on the bay. And a Falls Creek ski lodge and a place at Port Douglas. After three years, we had to sell them all in a falling market and we were back to renting again. Then pregnant again and another failure. Triplets: third time unlucky."

"And the Woods? Did they stand by you in all of this?" asked Jane.

Isaac stifled his reaction. "By then I had my own lawyers to challenge Engels, which only made things worse. Nige saw that as my final betrayal."

"Your betrayal? Getting a lawyer to protect your position?" said Jane.

"He sold the whole thing to the Yanks, who folded it into another product. I still don't know what he got. Except his share was profit and mine went to pay debt. End of venture, end of story."

"And Mel and Ness? Did their friendship survive?"

"Mel made Ness feel like a failure. Always talking about her children. Always thrusting them in her face. Ness had given up her job as an architect to have children and now she had neither a job nor a family. And her husband was broke and pathetic and dependent on his parents. So, this gentle soul who would not harm a fly bought a gun and blew out her brains."

"Do you still have the gun?"

"The police took it away."

"Yes, until the coroner had completed her inquiry. After that, they would either offer it back or arrange to have it destroyed."

Isaac was silent for a moment. "Yes, I've still got the gun."

"Why did you keep it, Isaac?"

"And several boxes of bullets. I take it with me when I go fishing and loosen off a few shots. One for him, one for her, and one for him again. I wanted them to die like Ness did—but someone beat me to it. I guess I should be thankful, though they only did half the job."

"Let's give the gun to the police, shall we, Isaac? And start some healing, which is long overdue. I have an excellent person I can send you to who helped me when I was lost. What would Ness want? You're still a young man."

"I feel as old as Methuselah."

"If that's the case, you've got nine hundred years to go." Jane took Isaac's hands in hers and let him feel her humanity was more than just words.

Jane had rightly sensed that he was hiding things, but he wasn't the killer.

————————

"You should give lessons in interrogation," said Ringer afterward, impressed by Jane's techniques.

"It's easier when you're not a cop. I guess I have more license. I'm a behaviorist, not an investigator."

"Makes for a bloody good team."

Ringer had a habit of making comments that made their relationship seem more than just professional. Or was Jane being oversensitive to their past? She wanted to warn him he was pushing boundaries, but didn't want to look like she was overreacting. The behaviorist and the detective, she overanalyzing every possibility while he hid behind his charm and played everything close to his chest. It was obvious he liked her, but that was hardly a crime. He never mentioned the past, never implied it gave him some kind of access, never suggested it might give them a future. Jane had to admit that she was as attracted to him as he was to her, and there was nothing wrong with that, a fact of life in a situation where coworkers could be friends—even very close friends—and abide by all proprieties. Maybe Jane needed to examine her own feelings and not speculate on Eric Ringer's? To admit that the real reason for her reluctance was the commitment she still felt for Ben.

Sigmund Freud would probably have blamed her father.

8

The low eastern sun flooded in through the window, making her bed a cocoon. If it had been Saturday, Jane would have opened the balcony slider and stayed in bed with the newspapers the concierge dutifully left at her door. But it wasn't. It was Tuesday and the long week still stretched ahead. Jane forced herself into the shower and dressed in the clothes she'd selected the night before, one less decision to make while half asleep. She missed the mornings in the big Brighton house where she and Ben had lived, Ben cooking a breakfast for everyone only he could face while chasing Zoe out of bed, where she would have stayed until noon if given the chance. Noise and contention as father and daughter transacted their morning ritual while Jane watched on, nurtured by the predictability of family.

Her family now was a clutch of cops with private lives they seldom shared; the task at hand too overwhelming.

Ringer called the briefing to order and went around the table. First up was Nita Marino, who gave an update on the physical evidence. With two extensive crime scenes to manage, the detail was hard to retain. Fingerprints, DNA, CCTV, logs of comings and goings, crime-scene photographs and videos, diaries of known events before and after the murders, related parties: family, neighbors, friends and enemies. And crucially, anything the crimes had in common.

"Both crimes were committed between dusk and midnight. Both victims were high profile in their particular worlds, probably not known to each other. Both victims were married. Bernero was having at least two affairs. As far as we know, Woods was not."

Jane interrupted. "I'm sorry, Nita, I haven't had a chance to tell you this, but Melissa Woods did mention 'another woman'—then retracted."

"Let's put that up on the whiteboard, shall we," said Ringer. He had dismissed it as drunken ramblings, but if Jane thought it important, he would back her.

Jane crossed to the Venn diagram on the whiteboard. Woods's wheel was on the left with its spokes of relevance, Bernero's to the right. Jane looked at the markers and pondered the relevance the new entry deserved.

"Rub out Isaac McLaughlin and put it there," suggested Ringer.

"Color?"

"Yes. Make it red."

Jane was pleased Ringer rated the idea that highly. She certainly did. So up it went on the board, sharing prominence with the other key words in that color: Torture, Detailed Planning, Premeditation, Extreme Violence, Sadism, The Catholic Church, Pre-Crime Surveillance, Dusk to Midnight Window and Telecom Man. Jane added a question mark to "Other Woman." A red flag but not one with any certainty.

"There's some evidence that the lock on the service gate to Woods's house has been tampered with," Marino continued. "That may be how the perp gained access. We're having it tested to determine when that might have occurred, but this is hardly carbon dating. At best it will be an intelligent guess."

"Thank you, Nita. Okay, Ray, you're on." Ringer couldn't wait for this one. Despite an eleventh-hour appeal from Maurice Engels, Ringer had obtained his warrant, which Cheung had executed, removing dozens of boxes of files from Nigel Woods and Associates.

"We've had to bring in consultants on this. Lawyers, taxation people, forensic accountants. Let me read what one of them has written. *The deals are complex and onerous and always in the principal's favor. The pattern is predictable. A honeymoon stage where targets are set in an atmosphere of high hopes and optimism. An extended period of due diligence and documentation. Then several months later, the start of some modest development funding from Woods secured against the other side's stake in the venture. Plus interest, some might say 'excessive interest,' when the venture fails to deliver on dates that were never realistic in the first place.*"

"Sounds like a form of mercantile torture," said Jane, realizing as soon as she said it how apt the metaphor might be. The point wasn't lost on the others.

Cheung continued, "Apart from the threats from McLaughlin we knew about, we haven't found anything else. Though it's fair to say the ratio of satisfied to unsatisfied clients would be no better than fifty-fifty."

"What a prick of a way to make money," offered Showbag from the peanut gallery.

"All right, sergeant, you'll get your turn," said Ringer, suppressing a grin. "Any questions?"

"Have your consultants signed confidentiality agreements?" asked Marino.

"Of course," answered Cheung. "Why do you ask?"

"We wouldn't want any of this stuff leaking out. The boss got a warrant to investigate a murder, not run an inquiry into how Woods did business—however dodgy it was."

Jane glanced at Ringer. Marino had a point, but he didn't rise to the bait.

"Unless the two things are connected," he said without missing a beat.

"Agreed." Marino wasn't trying to ruffle feathers, simply warn where things could go wrong.

"Okay, big boy—what have you got?" Ringer asked Showbag, leaving the best till last.

"An ex-pollie who lived at Wood End,

"Did his best to be everyone's friend,

"A glad-handing chappy,

"Who kept everyone happy,

"It was too much of a stretch in the end."

"There're not many workplaces where you could get away with that," observed Jane as the laughter subsided.

"I'm not sure he did," said Ringer.

Showbag didn't have a lot more to offer beyond his limerick. His investigation was still very new and, unlike Woods, Bernero was generally liked. He had looked into Bernero's relationship with Jimmy Khan and found nothing there but bluster and empty threats. The state opposition thought Bernero was a bit of a clown, which he was, but his backroom deals were so blatant and public that it was difficult to take offense. Sure, the planning laws were bent from time to time to accommodate his clients' desires, but he wasn't the only lobbyist doing that. The nexus between developer and party donor was something only legislation could outlaw but neither side of politics had the stomach to do it.

"I don't think our physical evidence is as good as it should be. We still don't have a comprehensive list of everyone with access. There're too many volunteers who knew where the keys were hidden and Bernero's lady-friends are trying to outdo each other as to how upset they are, so I'm not getting sanity from either of them. I'm heading back to the crime scene this morning for another squizz. I don't think access to the building is as material as who could drive that forklift. It's got levers missing, it's held together with wire and has to be put on charge every fifteen minutes. I reckon the perp would have had to recharge it at least once, which means the victim could have been there for more than an hour."

Despite the jokes, Showbag was a smart and intuitive detective, and as the briefing ended and the others dispersed, Jane hung back to talk.

"You want a signed copy of me poem, don't you?"

"No, Showbag. But you can take me with you when you go to the crime scene? I need another look myself."

———

Working on a violent case like this could be a somber affair, but Showbag always kept the mood buoyant. As Jane sat beside him in the unmarked police car, he pondered out loud whether to turn on the flashing lights and siren to clear a path through the traffic, but Jane knew he wasn't going to do it.

Showbag loved to give people nicknames, many of which were obscure. Ding Dong for Ringer was obvious. Others, like Stretch for Franco Bernero and Kebab for Nigel Woods, though of dubious taste, were also easy to understand. But Jane needed help with the others.

"Why do you call Ray Cheung 'Gary'?"

"Because he's garrulous."

"What's Marino?"

"Neuter. Cos she'll take your balls as quick as look at yer."

Jane raised an eyebrow. "And why do you call Maurice Engels 'Rimmer'?"

"Because he likes to lick arse."

"So, what do you call me?"

"Campbells."

"Why Campbells?"

"You'll work it out."

"Okay, Showbag," said Jane, lining herself up for the big one. "Why do they call you Showbag?"

"You're winding me up?"

"No, I'm not."

"You know what a showbag is?"

"Of course. Those bags you buy at the Royal Melbourne Show?"

"Yeah, full of novelties and samples. They used to give them away. Now they sell them for thirty bucks."

Jane was still none the wiser. "So . . ."

"Well, the contents haven't changed. They're still show-bags. Full of shit."

Jane was still laughing when they got out of the car at North Melbourne. She knew her mirth was not a good look for the young constables who guarded the crime scene, but when you get the giggles, they're hard to stop.

———

Jane and Showbag stood in the middle of the deserted building. Although the body had been removed, everything else was still in place. The chains and the shackles, the forklift and its container still parked on the ramp by the fire hose. Without the distraction of the corpse, it was easier to notice other things, like how high the windows were and how thick the walls; how screened the building was from the street and its immediate neighbors. After Mary McCluskey had puttered off home, the killer could have done what he wanted with Franco Bernero with little risk of being disturbed—provided he had removed the keys that were kept in a place everyone seemed to know about. But if he did that, then why would he put them back? How the killer gained access to Nigel Woods's house was a mystery still to be solved. This location had the opposite challenge—reducing a long list of people with access to the one that mattered.

The inventiveness of the killer was again on display. At Nigel Woods's house, *The House of the Stolen* with its long central spear combined with the mechanism that raised and lowered the chandelier was ready made for purpose. All the killer needed was a harness, or did he use Nigel's trousers and belt for that? But here, his version of the medieval rack had to be invented from scratch. The chains and the shackles had been dragged in from the yard at the rear of the building, retrieved from a pile of discarded scrap that dated back to when the building was a foundry. The forklift and the container of clothes and blankets were already there inside the building—but what kind of mind had the inspiration to park it on the ramp and add water to gradually increase the weight?

"Did the killer bring anything onto the site?" asked Jane.

"Yes, funnily enough: the compression sleeves he put underneath the chains. They were brand new. Why he bothered, I don't know. He could have used the sleeves from any of that." Showbag indicated the piles of recycled clothing awaiting sorting.

"Can you trace the compression sleeves?" asked Jane.

"Probably not. It's a popular brand sold in most sports stores and he had the nous to remove the labels. But we're trying."

"He thought of everything, didn't he?" said Jane, trying not to sound too impressed.

"Why go to the trouble? With the compression sleeves, I mean?"

"If the chains tore the skin there was a danger the limbs could separate, which is not what he wanted. He wanted to leave the body intact."

"But why?"

"To maximize the agony? To stop the victim bleeding out and dying too soon? To mimic the Crucifixion?" Jane stopped as if something had gone click in her head.

"The guy's a nutcase."

"Probably not. That would make catching him easy."

She needed space to think and wandered off to see if the location offered up anything else. Crucifixion? Certainly Bernero's body had been left in that position, but why? Both victims had links with the Catholic Church and both had been tortured by means perfected by Catholics in medieval times. Nicholas Mandel had established the historical link between the Church and torture, but it was difficult to relate that to these crimes. It gave theme and subject matter but not motivation, a means and a method but not an MO. The killer's motives were still impossible to see.

When she returned, Showbag was busy erecting something by the kitchen.

"What are you doing, Showy?"

"Building a trap."

"Do you think it's big enough?"

"It's not for the killer."

"Yeah, I didn't think so," said Jane. "Then for what?"

"Rats."

Jane went to laugh it away as another of Showbag's jokes but the sergeant was deadly serious.

"Wasn't it your idea in the first place?" he said.

Jane watched as he put the finishing touches to his construction, attaching a narrowing chicken-wire cone inside the only access to the cage to prevent the rodents' escape. With some out-of-date food from the kitchen fridge as bait, the task was complete.

Yes, Jane had indeed made the suggestion, but she didn't dream he'd take it seriously.

9

Jane whipped up her version of aglio e olio with anchovies and Japanese panko. With gluten-free pasta and a glass of New Zealand Black Peak pinot noir, it was a tasty accompaniment to the evening news, which did nothing to improve her appetite. The war in Ukraine continued to dominate the headlines and the deficit the federal government had plundered to keep things afloat during Covid was beginning to come home to roost. Social media influencers competed with off-season rugby league stars for "Dick of the Week" while real estate continued in its parallel universe and was clearly controlled by Martians.

But Jane's thoughts were with the killer. Religious hatred or religious mania? Terrorist or martyr? Or just a heartless sadist without any purpose beyond his own base gratification?

The mind diviner, Ben used to call her. The analyst who couldn't switch off. As Jane liked to say, "Everyone's more or less sick." Maybe her obsession with the criminal mind was her affliction?

Poor Ben. He'd deserved a longer life, but there was no point dwelling on that. They had enjoyed a long time together and the memories were strong. That would have to do for now.

Her mobile rang.

"I suspect you've opened a bottle of red, so I'm heading in your direction," Ringer said.

"How do you know I'm not with someone?"

"Sorry. I should have asked."

"I'm not. And you're welcome. I could even make you some pasta."

She could tell from his failure to reply that he was feeling under pressure.

"Has something happened?" she asked.

"I've just left the minister's office. I'll tell you when I see you."

───────

"Wow, this is nice," said Ringer as Jane let him in. "Are we paying you too much?"

"Save your prejudice for the billionaires. The middle class is doing it tough."

Jane's apartment was impressive. With the proceeds from the sale of the family home, she had decided to reward herself. She and Ben had worked hard to put the Brighton house together and she wasn't going to slum it now. She had forsaken an apartment with a view of the bay to avoid the bite of the western sun. This one looked out to the east across the Botanic Gardens and was close to the bikeway along the river that kept her fit. On a clear day you could see all the way to the Dandenong Ranges. There was an indoor pool, a sauna, and a gym, with basement parking for two and extra provision for guests. But she still let Ringer park in the street. She could only imagine what Pol Pot might say about so much parking in the heart of the city.

Jane and Ringer sat in the dining area with bowls of pasta

and glasses of the 2018 pinot noir. The open doors to the balcony allowed a cooling breeze to temper the warm night air. As the traffic streamed silently below, Jane admitted she loved her aerie and the sanctuary it provided away from the city's bustle.

"So tell me about the Minister for Police."

"No prizes for guessing. He wanted to know why I needed a warrant."

"I was wondering when that little time bomb might blow."

"You know who's behind it, don't you? Maurice Engels."

"Rimmer."

Ringer looked confused but continued. Clearly not all of Showbag's nicknames had percolated that far up the chain. "What Engels failed to achieve in court, he's attempting to achieve through his mates. Woods might have been a big party donor, but he's not a protected species."

"What did the minister expect you to do? Withdraw the warrant?"

"Limit my investigation to matters directly connected with the murder. Which I assured him I was doing."

"So Marino's instincts were right."

"You don't have to be a bloody genius to work that out." There was a tinge of bitterness in his comment, but Jane let it pass.

"You think something's being covered up?"

"I don't know, do you?"

"It's possible. Or they think you're opening a can of worms that's better left buried."

"They're terrified we'll come across something dodgy and tip off the tax department. Or the Anti-Corruption Commission."

"Well, wouldn't you?"

"Yes, but not officially. It's the hypocrisy of the man I can't abide. When I asked if I should treat the other investigation the same way he said, 'Of course not. Bernero's Labor. Go for your life.'"

Ringer was taken aback when Jane started to laugh.

"The hypocrisy of politicians? What about the hypocrisy of cops? Don't you see you're doing the same thing? Doing nothing on an official level but leaking like a sieve behind the scenes?"

"My commission is to uphold the law."

"Then don't make it a vendetta."

"Is that what you think I'm doing?"

"You're only human. I don't like billionaires either."

Twenty-three years had done nothing to change the ease they felt in each other's company. In that sense, nothing had changed—except twenty-three years of caution and callus and a sense that some things are best when they're kept in the past.

"This is bloody good wine."

"It's from Central Otago. If you promise to be a good boy I'll open another bottle."

Jane liked him and not only because of his Hollywood smile. He was a committed investigator who led from the front and demanded excellence from his team. He was a cop with strong opinions who did nothing to hide his politics and never took a backward step. There was a lot to admire. But Eric Ringer was divorced, and that raised a range of questions. Was it him or had it been her? Was he the one to stray or did she? Or was it neither of those possibilities? The computations drove Jane and her analyst's mind to distraction. She wanted to ask but knew she'd be entering a minefield where her own flanks would be unprotected; you can't ask someone about past relationships unless you're prepared to talk about your own. And she wasn't ready for that. It was still too raw. It was easier to drink and make jokes.

So they laughed and drank long into the night until Ringer had to uber home. He left his keys with Jane, who'd bring his car into work in the morning. The evening had been a welcome break from the intensity of two terrible murders, but it would all resume the next day. Jane knew Ringer felt exactly as she did: that the killer was out there planning his next move and that every time they took a break, they were handing him the advantage. It's called the Investigator's Curse: it consumes every waking hour and much of your sleep. And never lets go until it's over.

Ringer thanked her for the wine and pasta and she walked him to the lift. As he got in he smiled like Curly from Oklahoma and raised his hand in farewell.

"Good night, Ding Dong," she said.

But the doors had closed and he hadn't heard a thing.

A man's car reveals a lot about its owner. The Chrysler SRT had all the detritus of a teenager taxi. Cricket balls and ancient footie records, an aroma of chlorine-soaked Speedos, abandoned socks, and corn chips. Whatever the state of his relationship with his ex, Ringer spent plenty of time with his sons. Evidence of his daughter, a solitary bobby pin, was harder to find. Maybe she went with a lighter step.

Showbag was in the carpark unloading something from the boot of his car when Jane pulled in alongside.

"Morning, boss," he said without looking up from a cage seething with *Rattus rattus*.

"Morning, Showbag. You've been busy."

The sergeant's Jack Russell pride evaporated as his mouth dropped open like the entrance to Luna Park.

"Can that boss of yours drink," she said for added impact as she headed for the lift. She was still laughing as she checked herself in through security.

Jane delivered the car keys to Ringer, who was in his office with Marino. DNA matching was taking too long, but as Marino explained, the process was complex and the number of samples enormous. Ringer offered more troops if she needed them and Marino left to check with the lab. But it was more hours in the day she needed—not more technicians.

"Thanks for last night," Ringer said to Jane. "I'm typically not one to invade people's private time."

Jane smiled, remembering their late-night meal at the Magic Mountain Saloon had happened only the week before. It was already becoming a habit.

"I've got a meeting with the commissioner, who wants to know what the minister said. She's probably had pressure herself. If they've nothing to hide, they're doing everything they can to create the wrong impression. What about you?"

"Me? I'm going to church."

The last time Jane had been to St. Patrick's, the cathedral had been filled with Nigel Woods's mourners. Today it was almost deserted apart from those who came to pray.

Jane made the sign of the cross and sat in a pew toward the back.

A man slipped in to kneel behind her.

"I didn't know you were Catholic."

"I'm not. It was a sign of respect. Did I get it right?"

"You're supposed to join the first three fingers to symbolize the Holy Trinity, but close enough."

"As a kid I wanted to be a Catholic," confessed Jane as they headed outside. "Either that or Jewish. The Presbyterians were too austere. The Jews and the Catholics understood majesty and ritual. Bringing a loaf of bread or a box of Weet-Bix to church for Harvest Festival didn't have the same grandeur. I told my mother I wanted to convert but she said it wasn't that simple. Then my best friend at school, a Catholic, had her confirmation and said she couldn't speak to me anymore. I've been atheist ever since."

Father Kevin Keely chuckled at her tale of nonconversion and suggested they walk the Pilgrim's Path with its meditative flowing water. Kevin had been one of Jane's doctoral students before he joined the Jesuits. It was a late-in-life return to his faith—his conversion "on the road to Deniliquin" as he liked to call it. There wasn't enough mystery in forensic psychiatry: he had found that in the Church.

"It's great to see you, Jane, but why are you here?"

"To pick your excellent brain over the murder of two rather prominent Catholics."

Jane wanted to know what Kevin had made of the victims' connection to his faith. Nicholas Mandel's history of torture had only gone so far: Jane was looking for something deeper.

"I'm not sure I know what you mean?" asked Kevin.

"Nigel Woods and Franco Bernero were Catholic, but beyond that had little in common. I guess I'm looking for some kind of connection, some key to the killer's mind."

"Are you sure you're asking the right person? I completed my course in forensic science but, as you know, I've never practiced."

"But you loved its philosophy."

"Which you told me would get me nowhere."

"I think what I said was that your thesis on Criminal Symbolism was taking a narrow view."

"I was only doing it for the study. I was a perennial student back then."

"Kevin, you're the only person I know who really understands the Church and I think there could be a connection. Both victims were prominent Catholics and both were subjected to torture which could only be described as medieval—like that perpetrated by the Church in the Middle Ages. I can see what the killer is doing—but not what he's trying to say."

"Maybe he's trying to put things right, for past historical wrongs."

"I don't think it's an intellectual concept driven by history. It's far more visceral and personal than that. Something hateful and vengeful and passionate."

"Passionate? That's a strange word to use," said the priest.

"Absolutely, though not in the nice sense of the word. But believe me, this is done with a singular and terrible commitment. Has the church received any threats recently?"

"No."

"Would you know if it did?"

"Yes. They would come to me."

"When Nigel Woods was murdered, did you think it could be an attack on the Church?"

"No. Why would I?" Father Keely paused and thought for a moment. "The Church has let me down in so many ways, I had to embrace it or walk away. But I can see how someone else could take a different path. Faith and the meaning of life are big concepts, and if they get shattered, anything is possible. Your murderer could be doing this not because he hates the church, but because he loves it too much and feels it isn't living up to his ideals."

"That's a fairly broad concept," observed Jane with some frustration. "Where do I start with that?"

"Maybe with Voluntary Assisted Dying. There's a schism in the Church about that. Between those—namely the majority of our parishioners—who want VAD introduced and the Vatican and the bishops who vehemently oppose it. You could describe it as the last great fight of the Middle Ages."

"Why is the Vatican opposed to VAD?"

"They see life as a gift from God. It's not for us to decide when it ends. And if it ends in suffering, then that puts us in oneness with Christ on the Cross, our suffering, like his, redeeming our souls."

"Do you believe that?" asked Jane.

"No. I'm a Jesuit. Then, so is the Pope."

"You'll forgive me if I'm confused?"

They had reached a large bronze bowl, the origin of the water that ran down the center of the walk. It contained a submerged golden image of the Lamb with verses inscribed from the Book of Apocalypse around its rim. Water cascaded down from the bowl on to a seven-stepped structure beneath.

"What's this?"

"The Apocalypse Bowl. You'd know it as Revelation, the last Book of the New Testament. If you're looking for symbolism, this could be it. Apocalypse is big on the number seven."

"You think there'll be five more murders?"

"I'm not saying that. In Jewish numerology, seven is a symbol of wholeness. Catholics believe the Second Coming will bring about the fullness of the reign of God. Others believe it will be the final and eternal judgment of God, resulting in the glory of some and the destruction of others."

"You think these murders could be based on the Book of Apocalypse? That the end of the world is coming?"

"It's possible. Forty percent of Americans believe Jesus is likely to return by 2050."

Kevin was not giving Jane any easy answers, not that she found that surprising. The Bible could be interpreted in too many ways.

"What about the Royal Commission? Did you encounter anyone there who could have committed these crimes?"

Father Keely had joined the Jesuits at a time of crisis and attended most of the Royal Commission into Child Abuse. After it was over, he had helped establish a unit within the diocese to try and make sure it never happened again.

He looked a little shocked by her question. "Among the victims?"

"Well, we know the perpetrators are unlikely to have done it, given their psychosexual immaturity."

"It's possible. I sat through most of the hearings and the trauma was overwhelming. I've worked with refugees in war-torn Africa, but the scars of child abuse are the worst I have seen. Combine that with a loss of faith."

Jane weighed what he was saying.

"I'm not being very helpful, am I?"

"I'm just trying to get my bearings, Kevin. Sense the possibilities and see where they take me. Not jump all the way to the end."

"Triangulation. I remember that from your lectures."

"Lick your finger and read the wind. People's psychologies will out."

"Sounds suspiciously like a faith."

"No, Father. Science, pure and simple."

They continued in silence across the lawn to two sculptures

of the patron saints of Italy, St. Francis of Assisi and St. Catherine of Siena.

"They're by a local sculptor, Louis Laumen," explained Kevin. "Aren't they beautiful."

But Jane could only think of Jaroslav Petranovic and the destruction of *The House of the Stolen*. At least the Church, whatever its failings, would never have done that.

Jane looked at the sculptures and thought about what Kevin had said. When faith is shattered, anything is possible. Passion and the Catholic Church—but was their perpetrator for it or against it? Anti-Christ or Christ? Did the killer hate the Church so much he wanted to defile it? Or love it so much, if love's the right word, to make human sacrifices in its name? And why, she asked herself once again, did the killer keep his motives so hidden?

———

When Jane returned to the Homicide Squad, she was met in the corridor by Ray Cheung. He was in a state of suppressed excitement. There would be a briefing in fifteen minutes. He couldn't share the details, but there had been a major breakthrough.

Jane entered the muster room and took a seat at the back. She was pleased for the police. They'd been working hard for little return. The public was scared, the press after blood, even the minister had an agenda. The cops didn't work in a vacuum and they took it personally. No one wanted this killer more.

The room hushed as Ringer marched in with Marino, Cheung at her side to present the visuals.

"All right, ladies and gentlemen, some good news, we think. And not before time. I'll let Nita explain the detail—but we think we have a suspect. A DNA match from the Franco Bernero crime scene. Nita." Ringer moved to the side to give her the floor.

"Sergeant Gawler thought the forklift might be a point of interest, so had forensics prioritize their tests on that."

Cheung put an image of the forklift up on the screen.

"As he said in previous briefings, it was held together with wire and would have presented the killer with more than a few challenges—unless he knew how to drive it."

The next slides were closer shots of the forklift. Marino used a pointer to identify the detail.

"The hydraulics—here—had a tendency to blow and someone has struggled to reattach this hose—here—and cut themselves in the process. This is oil but this"—she moved the pointer with emphasis—"is blood. So, we took a sample and ran it through the database—and came up with a match."

The next slide was a mug shot of a man in his early twenties, beside a later shot of the man some years later.

"Tomas Henrich Kurtza, aged twenty-three at the time of his arrest and thirty-eight upon his release from prison."

Jane stared at the images. Was this their killer, a young man hardened by prison life, a sadist, merciless and cruel?

"Convicted in 2007 for twenty years for the violent rape and kidnapping of a female university student, he was released six months ago after serving fifteen years and, despite parole's best efforts, hasn't been seen since. Our task is to find him."

In his office, Ringer complimented Marino and Cheung on their presentation and Showbag for his initiative. But he couldn't help but notice that Jane was unusually quiet. "Do you have a problem, Jane?"

"No. But I've got some questions."

"There'll be plenty of time for that."

"Is that his prison file?" she asked, indicating the lever-arch folder on Marino's lap.

"Yes."

"Thicker than normal, wouldn't you say?"

"He rebelled to begin with but ended up a model inmate."

Which made Jane even more intrigued. "Then he comes out of jail and does this? Could I take that home overnight and have a read?" She could tell Ringer wasn't happy. She was raining on their parade. But something didn't add up.

"But of course," said Marino, handing it over. "Whatever floats your boat. There's a microfiche version if you want one, which has the essential documents."

"No, this will be fine," said Jane, feeling its weight. "Nothing like going to the source."

The cops grinned at each other like coppers do, as if to remind Jane who the outsider was. She didn't react and promised to bring the folder back in the morning.

10

The prison file sat unopened on the dining room table. Was Jane anxious about what she might find inside, or waiting to savor it later? Maybe a bit of both.

She changed into her pajamas, cobbled together a meal and made herself a hot drink. A quick glance at the late-night news, then at last she took up the file and headed for bed. It's not everyone's idea of late-night reading, but Jane found the moment compelling. This wasn't fiction: this was real. A man the police had already launched a search to find, so present she could almost touch him.

The file was roughly chronological so she started at the back, exhuming each page like an archaeologist. *Aggravated rape and kidnap.* No mention of the victim, but Jane remembered Marino's summary—a young student aged twenty-one, held hostage and brutalized for almost three days. *Prisoner's sentence: twenty years with a nonparole period of fifteen.*

The next pages were to do with discipline and rule compliance, withdrawal of privileges and time spent in solitary confinement. He had endured a rough induction. Things settled down after a year, though there were still a number of prisoners from whom he had to be separated. Not that this could be guaranteed and "incidents" (prison jargon for bashings) persisted, though less frequently than before. The violence Kurtza had meted out to his victim was coming back with interest, but not as a form of vengeance. It was simply the way the inmates regulated their world, how stability was kept within that unseen Plimsoll line that kept the ark afloat. Brutality as a way of life.

During the third year of Kurtza's incarceration appeared the first of several reports from a prison chaplain, a man who took an interest in the prisoner and encouraged him to study. Australian history to begin with, then the history of the two World Wars. Then the American Revolution followed by an unlikely diversion to the Middle Ages. *I think Tomas has found his passion at last in the Reformation.* But was that the pastor's view of the world—or Kurtza's? Then as quickly as the reports appeared, they stopped and the chaplain disappeared without explanation; retired, deceased, or defunded. Had this been the beginning of a dark obsession with torture and the Catholic Church? Or was it nothing more than coincidence?

In the years that followed there was nothing much apart from requests for educational books and materials. Then, suddenly, a new direction as the prisoner joined a drama group run by someone called Cayden Voss. Voss started filing reports that were even more effusive than the chaplain's, though it was hard to tell if he genuinely held these views or was more concerned about keeping his funding alive. *Tomas Kurtza continues to amaze me. He is a gifted actor and a natural mimic. I have no doubt that a career in this field awaits him upon his release.*

The mimic in Kurtza certainly took flight as, once again, he earned the displeasure of the prison authorities. After disguising himself as a guard, he almost escaped from the prison by attempting to leave with a group of visitors. Remarkably, he seemed to have achieved this deception by simply putting on a prison guard's jacket. As punishment he had his privileges removed and spent a month in isolation. But as far as the acting teacher was concerned, it only confirmed Kurtza's brilliance: *His ability to change his voice and his posture, to inhabit his character so completely you forget it's a performance, is as unique and skilled as anything I have seen.*

The bulkiest part of the file was correspondence, mainly from fans who came to see the prison plays. Some of it was genuine but many of the letters had been heavily censored by the authorities. Offers of friendship, declarations of love, much of it clearly pornographic, if the blacked-out lines were anything to go by. Jane was familiar with hybristophilia, where women are attracted to men who commit violent crimes, especially of a sexual nature. Some want to save them, some see them as the perfect boyfriend because their incarceration guarantees their fidelity, some read and reread the correspondence and use the paraphilia as a way to achieve orgasm. All have low self-esteem.

Dear Tomas, I believe people change and I know you are no longer the person you were . . .

Sweet Kindred Spirit, when I saw your performance tonight, I shuddered. You have changed my life. It was like you were talking to me and there was no one else there . . .

My love, you are a beautiful person and a unique human being and I want you to ▮▮▮ *me for the rest of my life.*

The final section of the file was dominated by appearances before the Parole Board as Kurtza applied for early release. Though described as "a model prisoner" who had studied hard and prepared himself for a life outside, he was not recommended for parole. Then a lawyer got involved and it all got contentious and the Parole Board washed its hands of the matter. It wasn't up to them anymore.

The final entry had been completed on a printed pro forma: prisoner released with Parole Board conditions, his address a halfway house in Footscray supervised by the Salvation Army.

Jane closed the file and looked at Kurtza's mug shot, a young man of twenty-three accused of a brutal and violent crime. But the psychology of a rapist seemed a long way away from what they alleged he'd become. You don't study the Middle Ages and become a heartless sadist. You don't train as an actor in order to disappear. Or do you?

Jane stared at the photo, searching the young face for its secrets. Why was she so attracted to this man and his transgressions? Why did the criminal mind hold such allure?

Jane was well aware of the theory of the wounded therapist, that many people enter the mental health field because they or a family member had a history of psychological difficulties. Her father's suicide while she was still at high school had affected her deeply, as had her mother's failure to cope. But she liked to think it gave her an empathy and a depth of understanding beyond the normal person, a special sympathy and insight into the transgressive mind. Her father had wanted Jane to be a lawyer but she disliked the courts and the adversarial system of justice. It seemed too much like a debate with winning and losing overly dependent on the skill of the advocate and the resources of the client. Jane trusted science more, though she was well aware her specialty was considered less scientific than most. Nicholas Mandel wasn't alone in his opinions that psychology and psychiatry were too aligned to witchcraft—an ironic attitude for a man whose connection with the fifteenth century bordered on the obsessive.

Jane didn't look at the criminal mind like the police or lawyers did. She had no absolute concept of right and wrong, just shades of gray on an endless scale that sought understanding, not judgment. Which was why she chose to walk on the dark side where all was uncertain and nothing was safe. Even the worst of criminals, for all their sins, were human, just like her.

Tomas Kurtza had been imprisoned for his transgressions. What would Jane need to do to expiate hers?

11

Jane popped her head into Ringer's office. She was carrying the prison folder, but that's not why he wanted to see her.

"What did you say to Showbag when you returned my car?"

"I might have said something about drinking too much."

"Why would you want to say that?"

"Because I didn't want people thinking it was something else."

"If you and I weren't working together—" he began.

"I don't even want to go there, Eric," said Jane as Marino knocked and entered.

"I can come back later . . ." she said, picking up on the tension in the room.

"No, Nita, let's get this done." Ringer closed the door as Jane and Marino sat down.

"Are you any the wiser?" Marino asked as Jane handed her the folder.

"It's a prison file. It raises more questions than answers."

"Like what?" asked Ringer.

"Like how a man convicted of a violent crime against a woman became a sadist whose victims are men. They are two quite distinctive psychologies. I'm not saying it couldn't happen, but there are no clues in his prison records."

"How are we going with the search?" Ringer asked Marino.

"Not well. He had his parole officer bluffed from day one. Kept making excuses and changing addresses, then disappeared altogether. The police were alerted but they couldn't find him. He used a number of aliases as well as many personas—"

"What do you mean by personas?" interrupted Ringer.

"He seems to take delight in reinventing himself. In changing his backstory and disguising his appearance."

"In making the police look like monkeys?"

Jane listened, leaving the commentary to Ringer.

Marino continued, "He odd-jobbed at the Victoria Markets for a while, but no one dobbed him in. He was popular, a natural comic who made people laugh. No one knew where he lived. On the streets, they thought. He worked for cash and spent it at the pub. Then he'd disappear for weeks until he came back in another guise. As a Polish immigrant, or an Irish laborer. Until they tumbled to the fact it was Kurtza again, having a joke at their expense."

"A useful skill for a wanted man. How do we come up with a photo fit?" said Ringer.

"All we have is his photo on his release from jail but from all accounts he doesn't look like that anymore. He's even been known to have disguised himself as a woman."

"When he worked at the markets, did he ever drive a forklift?" asked Jane.

"I don't know," admitted Marino.

"Then you'd better find out," ordered Ringer.

Jane sensed something between Ringer and Marino, something she'd detected when Ringer let Jane take over Isaac McLaughlin's interrogation. While never disrespectful, there was something about the way Ringer and Marino related to each other that implied things unresolved, some mutual wariness or rivalry that bubbled beneath the surface. Jane watched as she always did. You didn't have to be a suspect to experience the profiler's stare.

"Thanks, Nita. Keep up the good work."

Marino left and Jane was about to follow.

"Do you know Ravi Patel?"

"Yes, I do. I've appeared for him as an expert witness. He's a very good senior counsel."

"Then why don't you come along and make the introductions. He was Tomas Kurtza's lawyer and got the Parole Board to change its mind."

———

Ravi Patel, SC, was a prominent member of his chambers and a rising star of the Victorian Bar. His specialty was administrative law and human rights, his ambition unbounded. A man with more than a roving eye, he had curbed his behavior in recent years as the MeToo movement outed the most blatant abusers.

"Hello, Ravi. This is Inspector Eric Ringer, who's handling the torture killings."

"You are a lucky man, Inspector, to have someone like Jane on your team." The senior counsel directed them to chairs around a coffee table and took off his gown and jacket. Barristers love to parade in their full regalia between the courts and their chambers and Patel was a natural peacock. "Jane is my favorite expert witness. The last case she helped me with, I couldn't have won without her."

"All I had to do was show your client had borderline personality disorder. It wasn't exactly a stretch," said Jane.

"How are you, Jane, after the shock of Ben's terrible death?"

The sudden gravity of his question took Jane by surprise, but she wasn't going to bare her soul, not here. And certainly not in front of Ringer.

"Well, as you can see, Ravi, I have lost myself in work. It's the only therapy I know."

Patel's eyes smiled at her irony and searched Jane's face for evidence of the truth behind her mask. It was difficult to know what he wanted. Surely not tears? And if he did, did she have any left to shed? As usual, she kept her feelings to herself. Displaying vulnerability to men following Ben's death too often elicited offers of company she didn't want.

"Can we talk about Tomas Kurtza?" said Ringer, throwing Jane a lifeline. "We've found DNA which puts him at one of our crime scenes."

"DNA, Inspector? Now there's a pit of snakes. I could take DNA from the headbands elite tennis players throw into the stands at the Australian Open and give you Roger Federer as a plausible suspect."

Jane knew Ringer didn't like barristers any more than he liked billionaires. Their air of superiority offended his egalitarian sensibilities and their habit of lecturing people irked him.

"Ravi, we just want to ask some questions," said Jane to prevent the bulls from locking horns. Their territoriality was palpable.

"You realize he's a former client?"

"And don't do the confidentiality thing. This is all off the record. No one's taking notes, nothing's being recorded. I apologize in advance for using the word, but there's a 'lunatic' on the loose out there and we need to stop him before he does it again."

"Can you see why she's so good in court?" It was another strut, as if Patel was asserting Jane as his expert to show his claim was stronger than Ringer's.

Men, thought Jane. They're still in the jungle. Why does everything have to be a contest?

Patel smiled, his domain secure. "What would you like to know?"

"We're dealing with a sadist," Ringer began. "Someone who likes to torture his victims and watch them suffer. His methods are literally medieval. It's an extremely unusual MO and, in thirty years of policing, not something I've seen before. So, I guess my first question is this: Is it something you can see Kurtza doing?"

Patel weighed the policeman's question, aware that Jane would judge his response, and tucked his thumbs behind his waistcoat.

"Kurtza's an interesting man, Inspector. He would have been released a whole lot sooner had he showed the Parole Board some sign of contrition. But he argued he no longer recognized who he was back then, that to say sorry now was fatuous because he had become a different person."

"So, for a point of principle he would rather stay in prison?" said Jane in disbelief. "I hope you didn't put him up to it, Ravi."

"Of course not, that's not what I do. The man had rehabilitated himself and the board was being pedantic. They were fixated—it was all or nothing. Either show genuine contrition for a crime you committed fifteen years ago in a drug-addled state or you're not fit to reenter society."

"Wouldn't it have been easier to say sorry?" reasoned Jane.

"He didn't see himself anymore as the man who'd committed that crime. It was as if he would be apologizing on behalf of someone he no longer knew."

"Then stay in jail," said Ringer, making it clear where he stood. "I'm with the Parole Board."

"But it's not their role, Inspector. They are there to assess the prisoner and take everything into account. Good behavior. His preparation for release. His rehabilitation. They're not there to set arbitrary conditions."

"So, what did you do?" asked Jane, intrigued. "You can't appeal a Parole Board's decision."

"No, you can't and I didn't. I took out a writ of habeas corpus. A judge had sentenced him to a period of years with discounts for good behavior. And his good behavior was uncontested. So do it. Don't set specious conditions. Deliver up the body."

"I'm sorry, I'm a humble copper. Do you think Tomas Kurtza is capable of these crimes or not?" asked Ringer.

"No, I don't."

"Why?" The simplicity of Jane's question gave Patel pause.

"He had discovered he had a talent as an actor. An acting coach . . . I can't remember his name—"

"Cayden Voss," prompted Jane.

"Yes, that's him. I believe he found him to be remarkable. There was even a film lined up for him to do."

"Then why go on with this nonsense about whether he was contrite or not?"

Patel's gimlet eyes locked with Ringer's. "Inspector—"

"Eric," interrupted Ringer to jag his rhythm.

"Eric. Some people put great store by these things. What you dismiss as nonsense, others see as principle, a position with which the court agreed."

"You won the case?" said Jane, surprised.

"The judge reserved her verdict and sent the parties back to mediate. And we found a compromise."

Not exactly a win, but Jane didn't press the point. They weren't going to get what they wanted from Patel by offending his professional pride.

"How did you find your client?" she asked.

"Principled. But I've already said that. Intelligent, respectful, extremely well read. 'A model of rehabilitation,' as I think the pleadings put it. But there was mischief there too. He had got the governor offside."

"When he tried to escape?" said Jane.

"Except he didn't, did he? Maybe all he was doing was revealing the weaknesses in their procedures."

"Man of principle, as you say," said Ringer with barely veiled disdain.

Jane gave him a warning glance. His commentary wasn't helping. "Did Kurtza ever talk about the Catholic Church?"

"No."

"Or the Crusades? Medieval torture? Or Nigel Woods?"

"Not to me, but why would he?"

"Excuse me for asking, but how could someone like Kurtza afford your fees?" This time Ringer's question was helpful.

"I did it pro bono. For the principle."

"But who brought you the case?"

"The instructing solicitor."

"But who instructed him?"

"Her."

"Who brought the case to her?"

"Well, not that we ever met, but as I understand it—his wife."

Ringer looked at Jane as if she'd been withholding information. But Jane had been blindsided too. There'd been no mention of a wife in the prison file. In fact, she distinctly remembered the summary page inside the cover had listed his status as single.

"Kurtza has a wife?" asked Jane.

"Apparently."

"Excuse me, I need to make a call." Ringer pulled out his mobile and headed out to the anteroom.

"I'm sorry, Jane. Did I say something wrong?"

"No, Ravi. Not at all. You've been very helpful."

———

As Jane and Ringer headed out into the street, Marino returned Ringer's call.

"Sorry, boss. I missed your call."

"Did you know Kurtza was married?

"He's not. His record says he's single."

"Well, someone calling herself his wife was behind the proceedings against the Parole Board. Maybe it's de facto. Get on to the instructing solicitor and see who she is."

By the time they'd returned to the office, Marino had a name and address.

"Her name is Ela Bey, a librarian, aged thirty-nine, lives in Richmond. She told the solicitor she was Kurtza's wife, so she took her at her word."

Jane went through the prison file and extracted Ela's letters. There was nothing unusual, nothing personal, certainly not much that required the censor's black pen. Just recommended books and reading lists and confirmation of sporadic payments into his prison account for purchases from the commissary. Everyday housekeeping stuff as you might expect from somebody's wife. If that's who she was.

12

Showbag headed his car for Richmond with Jane at his side.

"We're becoming a team, you and me." He grinned. "The brains and the brawn."

"Which one am I?" mused Jane. "I can bench press a third of my body weight."

"How much is that?"

"None of your business, Brawny."

They pulled up outside a red-brick block of six apartments in classic 1960s style overlooking the railway—if style's the right word for what Melburnians call a "six pack."

Ela showed them into her neat and ordered unit, the restrained décor revealing little about its owner. If anything, you'd think it had been furnished by someone older than a woman in her thirties, though her conservative Turkish heritage may have had something to do with that. She offered tea or coffee but her guests declined and sat in the lounge with its view of the Alamein Line.

"Ms. Bey, we are trying to locate Tomas Kurtza. Have you any idea where he is?"

"No, Sergeant, I don't."

"Have you seen him since his release from prison?"

"No."

"Or talked to him on the phone?"

"Wouldn't you know if I had?"

"Not without a warrant, no."

Ela smiled her disbelief.

"How would you describe your relationship with Mr. Kurtza?" Showbag asked.

"Extremely close."

"Do you consider yourself 'married' to Mr. Kurtza?"

"Who told you that?"

"The solicitor you instructed on his behalf."

"She had no right to tell you anything."

"I don't think she's breaking confidences, Ms. Bey. Either you're married or you're not."

"There's been no formal ceremony."

"Would you describe yourself as de facto?"

"No."

"Then what?"

"Common-law wife."

It was at times like this Jane wished she was a sworn officer. Her status as an adviser to the police didn't allow her to formally interrogate, but Showbag's by-the-book approach was not going to get what they wanted. She would have preferred a more conversational approach rather than the distancing formality of a policeman's inquiries.

"It must be hard on you, Ela. Not to have heard, yet knowing he's out there."

Jane's empathy had an immediate effect.

"Yes, it is," said Ela, pressing back tears. "It's been a long wait."

"Would you be more comfortable talking without the sergeant present?"

"No. I've nothing to hide."

"Actually, I've got a message to phone the office," said Showbag, picking up on Jane's cue as he fumbled unconvincingly with his mobile. "I'll pop outside and make the call."

"I will have that coffee," said Jane as Showbag departed.

"Turkish?"

"Of course."

The 10:57 to Camberwell rumbled by as Ela boiled the cezve and poured the sweetened liquid into two cups. She was already more relaxed without a man in the room.

"I believe Tomas is a talented actor."

"Oh, yes," agreed Ela proudly. "He's going to make a film."

"Is that why he's lying low?"

"I'm not going to help you catch him."

"Catch him? For what?"

"For breaking his parole. You'll send him back to jail."

"If breaking parole is his only problem, there are other ways to handle it. The longer he eludes the police, the worse it's going to get."

Ela sipped her coffee.

"What I can't understand is why Tomas didn't stick to his parole conditions after fighting so hard to get them."

"I've got nothing to say."

"Because you're worried about what he might have done?"

"Because I think you're here to trick me."

"Then I'll be as open and honest as I can. And it may be for your own protection. We want to question Tomas about what he might know about two very violent murders."

Ela closed her eyes as if she was closing her ears as well.

"If he's nothing to hide, the sooner we speak, the better for everyone, including you," said Jane.

"I knew it would be something like this."

"What do you mean—something like this?" Was this an admission?

"I want you to go."

"If they think you're withholding information, Ela, you'll be arrested."

"Get out of my house." Ela was screaming now and Showbag was at the door.

Jane stood and placed her card on the table. "Ela, I know you love him. That's not in dispute. But I want you to think about this very carefully. With so much to look forward to—including yourself—why is Tomas risking everything by not coming forward?"

Ela opened the door defiantly and turned her head away.

Jane could tell Showbag wanted to arrest the woman and take her back to headquarters for further questioning, but Jane thought there were better ways to go. "Thanks for the coffee. You can phone me if you change your mind."

As he drove back to the city, Showbag was concerned they had done the wrong thing. But Jane had planted seeds of doubt and was playing a longer game.

"You can question her all you like, but I don't think she knows where he is. But how can she admit that as his common-law wife?"

"Whatever that means."

"It means the same as de facto, but she obviously doesn't like the term."

"Common-law wife. Who's she kidding?"

"Probably only herself. But she's not alone. There were letters in his file from dozens of women. It's not uncommon. The more violent the criminal, the more prolific the correspondence."

"What's in it for him?"

"Well, there's no YouPorn in jail. You need something to pass the nights."

"So what do we do?"

"Keep an eye on her in case he makes contact, not that I think he will. Get that warrant you mentioned to tap her mobile. And wait for her to phone me."

"And why do you think she'll do that?"

"Because I validated her feelings and I doubt if anyone else ever has."

"We should have brought her in."

"Showbag, if Ela Bey's your only way to Tomas Kurtza, you may as well toss in the towel. How many cops in Victoria Police?"

"About twenty-two thousand."

"Then have a little faith."

"Thank you, doctor, for your vote of confidence."

But he wasn't convinced. Neither was Jane. They traveled in silence for a while.

"Oh, they looked at the guts of the rats I caught," said Showbag.

"Showbag, I'm really sorry—"

"No traces of Franco Bernero. At least not in the ones I got."

"I should never have made the suggestion."

"And nothing to indicate where they came from."

Now Jane was really embarrassed. "I never thought you'd take it that far."

"They had blue feet."

"Say again?"

"The rats. Their feet were blue."

Jane wanted to laugh but Showbag was deadly serious. She turned away and stared out the window, wondering how much time and resources her passing remark had wasted.

"Toorak."

"What?" Jane looked at Showbag.

"Well, that's where the blue bloods come from, isn't it? Though God knows what that tells us."

"Could we not talk about rats anymore?" said Jane. Had he seen through her from the beginning? Was this whole thing some elaborate prank?

"They reckon in any city there's four rats for every person. That's a lot of rats."

"Showbag . . ."

"And only one Tomas Kurtza. And not a bloody clue where he is."

As if Jane needed to be reminded.

13

Jane had been out with her girlfriends at Society, embraced by the city's diners as the epitome of post-Covid emancipation. Grazing on orange roughy and minute steaks with elegant cocktails and fine wine by the glass, the restaurant's Lillian Brasserie was a restorative escape from the pressures of the day. The others had talked about work and families, it was only Jane who had little to say. Elizabeth was a litigation lawyer who worked on high-end insurance claims; Jasmine was a midwife and mother of five; Virginia, who had once been kidnapped and held to ransom, had worked with the Red Cross in Africa. Their banter was insightful and hilarious. Jane didn't mention her semi-estranged stepdaughter, or the cop from her past she was working with again, or a woman in love with a sex offender, or a suspected sadist who tortured his victims. No wonder she preferred the company of cops during an investigation. Everyone else asked too many questions.

It was 10:30 p.m. when Jane called by the Homicide office to collect her books and papers. An insomniac needs something to read to get her through the night. Marino and her team were heading home after burning the late-night oil.

The lack of a credible trail was beginning to erode their confidence.

"What kind of a man has no bank account or credit card? Or even a driver's license? Who has never used his Medicare card?" Marino said to Jane.

"Someone who doesn't want to be traced," answered Jane rhetorically.

"Was he planning all this in jail?"

"Nita, I wish I knew."

"This is a man with no known links to either Nigel Woods or Franco Bernero."

"Maybe his victims aren't important. A sadist is all about self."

"A man who disguises himself on a daily basis."

"He doesn't want you to catch him."

"Because he's the murderer?"

"Possibly. You'll have to catch him and see."

Marino looked weary and defeated. "I'm going to the Magic Mountain. Wanna come?"

"I've eaten, but I'll have a nightcap and keep you company."

From the sublime to the ridiculous, from one of the best eateries in town to a cheerful all-nighter patronized by shift workers and millennials. But Nita needed the company and Jane wasn't going home to sleep.

Marino ordered pad thai with prawns and a beer; Jane, a vodka and watermelon cocktail called The Jig Is Up. They riffed back and forth about the case and were still there three drinks later. Not catching villains was thirsty work.

"What is it between you and Ringer?" asked Jane on a whim. "Seems more than professional rivalry?"

"I think he's a prick. Good cop, but a prick. In fact, a bloody good cop. Why do you ask?" Marino grinned. "Idle curiosity? Or personal interest? I heard he spent the night at your place."

Showbag had been spreading rumors.

"He did not spend the night at my place. He had a drink and ubered home. So I brought in his car in the morning. Why do you say he's a prick?"

"Because he is such a fucking boy. A total fucking misogynist, though too cool to let it show. I think he preferred the old days when women did 'community policing.' Or ran the Sexual Victims Unit, which is where he thinks I should have stayed. He probably feels Homicide's too frontline for menstruating women. It's operationally inefficient."

Jane had to laugh. Marino was on a roll.

"He prefers the company of men. Or blonds with good legs."

Jane wondered if Marino was describing her.

"If you're an overweight dyke, you're a threat to his manhood, which he wears like a pistol in his pants."

"I wouldn't call you overweight."

"And I wouldn't call me a dyke."

The mood was becoming personal. You can only blame alcohol up to a point.

"Time to go, I think," said Jane, placing her credit card on the bill. "And this will stay in club, Nita. That I can promise. But just for the record, I like Eric Ringer. He's not put a foot wrong with me, professionally or otherwise. Let's agree we are all stressed and drunk. And with no one to go home to."

"How do you know that?"

"Because we're sitting here in the Magic Mountain Saloon at one o'clock in the morning."

"And we've got to get up at seven," said Marino.

"I think you're a bloody good cop, Nita. I think the prick's lucky to have you."

Marino shrugged in gratitude. It had certainly helped to talk. She was stressed and exhausted and wanted to catch her man, maybe more than anyone, since she was the one who'd been tasked with the problem. "It's hard not to take these cases personally," she said.

Jane took her hand and squeezed it. "It's impossible."

Jane got up at six thirty and went to the gym. She felt as she deserved to feel, dusty with an unsettled stomach. She doubled her repetitions and resolved not to drink during the week anymore. She failed to bench press anything close to one-third of her body weight and had to admit that the last time she did, she was four kilos lighter and Ben was still alive, in the days when she had a full-time job and a family life and a proper regime. She hadn't adapted to life on her own. She missed Ben every day. She envied Zoe for being brave enough to start a new life in New York and felt she had let her down. Her step-daughter had lost her father, her mother was in jail, and she and Jane were barely speaking. Zoe was looking forward, Jane was looking back, replaying the last seventeen years with Ben as if she didn't exist without them. Grief wasn't that terrible moment in time with Ben's blood and brains on her face, grief was a gnawing ache that reminded Jane of her own mortality and the shocking brevity of life. Only work could staunch the pain. She couldn't get to the Homicide Squad soon enough.

Ray Cheung presented his map of Kurtza's confirmed and projected movements. From Nigel Woods's mansion in the east to Footscray in the west, the focus of the search would be an area with a radius of 7.5 kilometers. The Salvos' half-way house, the Victoria Markets, Franco Bernero's foundry in North Melbourne. All color coded and marked with dates and times. The map almost made the task seem manageable. It was only daunting if you were there on the ground in the midst of the teeming city.

Cheung's photo fit was graphical rather than photographical though it included an insert of Kurtza's prison mug shot. But height and build were more significant, the things disguises couldn't hide. Telecom Man's blurred CCTV image was another insert, which matched the height and build elements of the main description. Both the map and the photo fit would be circulated to all stations in the area.

As Jane left the briefing, Ringer suggested coffee, but she was already running late.

———————

"One of you might be the next Cate Blanchett. Or maybe," the presenter added with measured irony, "the next Geoffrey Rush?"

His audience glanced at each other, unsure how to react.

"But the moment you think like that, you're dead. Irrelevant. Inauthentic. Untruthful. Trying to be someone you can never be—somebody else."

Jane had slipped into the back of the studio, a converted warehouse south of the city. Cayden Voss knew she was coming, but his performance wasn't only for her. Ostensibly directed at the fifty students who had parted with twenty dollars for one of his drop-in classes, the presence of the forensic psychiatrist gave Voss something to work with and, like the exhibitionist he was, he was milking it for all it was worth.

"If you're playing a violent criminal, don't play Ivan Milat. The backpacker murderer was never like you. You have to find your performance in here." He touched his heart like he hoped he was touching theirs.

Cayden Voss was tall and angular, in his late fifties, Jane thought. He prowled the stage like he owned the place—and he did. He and a former lover had originally bought it to convert into a theater restaurant. Its heritage listing prevented demolition and kept the developers away, and long before the boom took off, they had got it for a steal. Then his partner left for a younger man, and neither could afford to buy out the other. So Voss turned it into an actors' studio and Stages In Acting was born.

"Let me give you a little exercise," Voss continued. "Turn to the classmate beside you and make them afraid by channeling your own darkest thoughts. Let them see the bad side of you. It's not that hard to do. One seldom remembers one's triumphs in life. The moments you never forget are regrets—something you wished you had never said, some cruelty committed as a child—like putting a spider in a jar and blowing it up with a firecracker to display your omnipotence, your power over life and death. Focus on some half-forgotten disgrace, a shame so profound it must never be mentioned. Then use it and meld it into a terrible power and show it to the person next to you."

Jane looked at the young man beside her and tried to gesture *I'm not an actor*—but the young man was already channeling his inner demon. He looked like someone who urgently needed to go to the toilet but Jane managed to keep a straight face. Maybe she could act after all?

Voss waited as his class tried to execute his task before dissolving into embarrassed laughter.

"I think we might end things there—though that's not where I intended to take you. This session was called

Channeling the Inner-self—not Clowning Around. There are refreshments in the foyer. If you've enjoyed the class, please come again."

The students showed their gratitude with obedient applause and filed for the exit, deluded Cates and Geoffreys for whom fame was all but guaranteed. A bargain at half the price.

Jane moved forward to introduce herself and Voss led her through to his office. The walls were hung with photographs of famous actors, some standing with Voss, others inscribed with messages of affection. Voss's reputation as a teacher of acting was once international. His three-day seminars were not as celebrated as Robert McKee's on writing for the screen, but his withering gossip about the frailties of the A list were worth the fee on its own. He hadn't toured for a number of years and his routine needed freshening up. Young people these days want the goss on Margot Robbie and the Hemsworths and Voss's targets were starting to age. But he had discovered Tomas Kurtza and that was all Jane wanted to hear.

"How did you meet him?" she began.

"Quite by chance. Some of my students were doing a play set in a prison and I wanted them to perform it in front of an audience where they had nowhere to hide. One of them, as you might expect, was utterly overawed and pulled out, so we had to ask for a volunteer to do a cold read. And that was Tomas. It was a minor part, but he walked away with the show. I'd never seen anything like it. His voice, his presence, the way he moved his body. I couldn't look anywhere else. After the show he said he wrote a bit and asked me to look at his plays. I usually leave hyperbole to my classes, Jane, but he had the most remarkable talent I had ever met."

"Did he realize how good he was?"

"I don't think he gave it a thought. When you're in a place like that for that many years, you do things to fill the time."

"How well did you get to know him?"

"We were never friends. Like a lot of prisoners, he kept his distance. But he was eager for advice and absorbed as much as he could. Why are you interested in Tomas Kurtza?"

"There are some questions we'd like to ask him, but he's broken his parole."

"Questions about what?"

"The torture murders." A trained investigator would probably have been more circumspect, but Jane wasn't a cop. And without giving too much away, she wanted to read Voss's reaction—psychologically.

"What would he know about that? Do you have some kind of evidence?"

"Now that's not a question I expected you to ask," said Jane.

"I'm just a little bit gobsmacked, Jane. The torture murders! And Tomas Kurtza!"

"Why do you find that so preposterous?"

"A man who's been in prison for twenty years—"

"Fifteen."

"And never wanted to see the place again. What on earth do you think his motive is?"

"If he's a sadist, maybe nothing more. Did you ever see that side of him?"

"No."

"Or strong attitudes about the Catholic Church?"

"I'm an acting teacher, Jane. We talked about the craft."

"What were Tomas's plans when he got out?"

"We were going to make a film. My concept, his script, me directing, him playing the lead."

"And what happened?"

"I couldn't raise the funds. End of story. For better or worse, I'm a teacher, Jane. A cobbler should stick to his last."

It was an odd expression for a man of his generation, like something Jane's father might have said.

"How many of your students would have understood that expression?" she said, not unkindly.

"Probably none of them," sighed Voss. "Maybe it's time to give it away."

Jane gave him the space to elaborate and he seemed to deflate.

"It's a tough business, Jane. Sometimes I feel like a fraud. The actor who couldn't act who becomes a teacher. To pass on what he's never done to students who'll never make it."

"Surely some of them do?"

"The greats have got it in them. In fact, it's got nothing to do with greatness. It's an aura, a God-given gift to the genetically blessed."

"Which lesson is this one?"

"Knowing when to quit."

"You're acting."

"I'm sorry?"

"You've had a bad day. Look at that stuff on the wall. Are you saying those photos are fake?"

Voss roared with laughter. He'd been sprung by an expert. "Someone told me I was an introvert masquerading as an extrovert."

But that was not what Jane was seeing. She had seen Voss in action and the performance had enlarged him. And however much he pretended otherwise, he was high on adrenaline still. This was a man who had built his own cult. His momentary disdain for his students had been unconvincing and delivered for effect; Jane doubted he gave them a second thought. She knew a narcissist when she saw one, and every-thing he had said about Tomas Kurtza needed to be filtered through that reality. It was like the photos on his wall, a form of self-congratulation.

He had discovered Kurtza, *he* had nurtured his nascent talent, *he* had declared him to be a star. She'd rather have Ela Bey screaming at her to leave. Cayden Voss didn't want to talk about Kurtza—he wanted to talk about himself.

This was not a nut to be cracked in one visit and Jane arranged to see Voss again. She asked if he had copies of Kurt-za's plays and was pleased he was happy to lend her some DVDs.

Or would the performances he'd chosen only serve to show Jane how astute and insightful Voss was?

The man's putty nose dominated his face, making his eyes seem small. His skin was gray and blotchy, his teeth so yellow his mouth was a hole.

"I got this new cream, Rejuvenator. I rub it all over my body. It don't work but it's nice to be slippery. Gotta look after yourself in here."

His audience laughed, some of them guests, a few of them warders, most his fellow inmates.

"I'm also taking hormone supplements, which can be problematic. Stuffs the libido but I'm growing breasts. I'll take the good with the bad."

Jane and the police weren't laughing as they watched their prime suspect perform. With a prosthetic nose, a crudely made bald cap, stained teeth and a facial wash made from newsprint ink, Tomas Kurtza had transformed himself into an old lag who looked twice his age. Whether or not Cayden

Voss was taking the credit for his discovery, Kurtza's powers of transformation were remarkable.

"I've been wasting my time," groaned Cheung, defeated. "We're looking for a chameleon."

"At least he's not taller or fatter," said Marino, trying to stay positive.

"Not in this performance, he's not." Ringer looked at Jane, knowing as well as she did what this man was capable of doing. The digital world was their usual way of finding a suspect, through bank accounts or mobile phones or other things they could track. But this man didn't dwell in the modern world, he lived in one of his own invention. He didn't need new tricks when the old ones were serving him just fine.

They played the other recordings, but it only made things worse. Tinted contact lenses, heavy-rimmed spectacles, false facial hair, denture molding paste behind the upper lip to give the appearance of an overbite. Platform heels and a scoliotic stoop to change his height and a Falstaff suit to change his girth; his techniques were as old as Shakespeare.

Jane and Ringer retreated to his office. The search for Kurtza was stagnating. They had to find another approach.

"We're missing something, Jane."

"Like what?"

"His modus operandi. Not his pattern of operation but his pattern of *thinking*."

"Don't you think I'm trying?"

But Ringer wasn't laying the problem on Jane. He didn't have to; Jane was doling enough of that herself. It was up to her to find a solution, psychologically. It was why she was part of the team, and she had barely scratched the surface.

"I'm going home to my books and to look at these discs again."

"I'll let you know if anything breaks."

"Like another killing?" She was giving voice to their darkest fear.

"We'll catch him, you know. It's a matter of time."

"Yeah. How much of that have we got?"

"*There's a dark side to every time in history, but perhaps none darker than what the unfortunate few experienced during the Middle Ages.*"

An overweight American tourist wearing a Stetson and Hawaiian shirt was reading from a brochure advertising a medieval castle near Ballarat that featured jousting contests and a torture museum. The tourist considered taking the ninety-minute trip by train but knew the museum would be disappointing. He had studied the Middle Ages in depth and torture was his specialty. And the photo of a victim laid out on his back was unconvincing. After all, he had seen the real thing.

"Can I help you, sir?" asked the attendant. "Are you thinking of Kryal Castle?"

"Well, no, it's probably too far away for the time we've got," he replied in a Midwestern drawl. "I'm looking for a map of your tram routes. I need to get to Fitz Roy."

"Fitzroy," corrected the attendant unnecessarily and handed the tourist a map. "Can I help you with anything else? There's so much to do in Melbourne. The Arts Centre and the National Gallery. Have you managed to see anything yet?"

"Alls we did is go down to the river, but thanks for your help with this." The tourist waved his map in gratitude and, keeping his head down and away from the security camera, waddled off on his sore-footed way.

When he got off the tram at Nicholson and Argyle, the Stetson had been swapped for a baseball cap and the tourist now walked with ease. He had replaced the loud shirt with a simple black hoodie. At Kerr Street he stopped, as if lost, and pretended to consult his map.

Across the street, a man in his seventies with thick silver hair and an unhealthy pallor emerged from a house with a shopping trundler and set off down the footpath. The tourist checked his watch, making a mental note of the time, then followed the old man to a supermarket in a shopping mall. Entering behind him, he watched discreetly as the old man shopped from a neat handwritten list, then followed him home via a liquor store where the old man purchased a bottle of shiraz labeled *Cat Amongst The Pigeons*.

The old man had no idea he was being followed. He had no idea of his stalker's connection with cruelty, of his need to consummate his carnal desires.

What do you do when the only thing that has meaning is to cause pain and suffering to others—when the only thing to make a dead heart dance is to commit crimes beyond redemption?

The old man headed home with his trundler, arriving as he always did before the nearby school released its children in the afternoon. *I do like a man with clear routines*, thought the tourist with a secret smile. *Makes everything so much simpler.*

He could have been describing himself.

14

Jane went home and rewatched the DVDs. Was there a hidden message in Kurtza's plays? Did his impersonations hold some clue to his motives? Or was he simply a gifted actor displaying his craft?

She froze the image and retreated to the kitchen to make a pot of tea. Her mobile rang: "caller unknown." She usually never took these calls. Too many telemarketers had her number. Or was it another random survey? But in case it was someone from Homicide, she pressed accept.

"Hello," she said without giving her name. The line stayed silent as Kurtza leered from the screen across the room. "Hello. It's Jane. Who's this?"

The line went dead and she went straight to Cheung in her speed dial.

"Hi, Ray, it's Jane. I've just had a call from someone. Can you trace it for me, please?"

Cheung rattled his keyboard and came back with the answer in seconds. "The phone belongs to someone called Ela Bey."

At ten the following morning Jane mounted the steps of the State Library and headed straight for the catalog. Scrolling through Medieval History and the Catholic Church, she selected a title and filled out a request.

Ela Bey was sitting behind a counter marked "Ask a librarian" and didn't look up until she took the slip.

"Hello, Ela."

"What are you doing here?"

"It's a public library."

Ela looked at the requested title. *Death, Torture, and the Broken Body.*

"You usually have to wait for a request like this. But if you find a seat in the reading room, I will go and get it for you."

Jane found a desk and a silky oak chair and gazed at the dome five stories above. Inspired by the British Museum and the Library of Congress, the State Library was one of her favorite places. That Ela Bey was fetching her request only confirmed its magic.

When Ela delivered the book and turned to leave, Jane knew she only had one chance.

"Ela, please. Can we talk?"

"I'm on a break in an hour. I'll meet you in the foyer."

Jane paid more attention to her watch than the book as the minutes dragged by and was at their meeting place early. They agreed to stroll in the Carlton Gardens, away from the city's hum.

"Did you find what you wanted in your book?"

"Not really. But then, I'm not sure what I'm looking for."

Ela didn't reply.

"Did you grow up in Melbourne?"

"Yes, in Dallas. Little Turkey. It had its ups and downs. I always felt safe, if a little smothered. If I ever did anything wrong, three aunties would phone my mother before I got home."

"Community's important."

"Especially if you're Turkish and Muslim."

"But you moved away?"

"My father had expectations. To marry someone in the community. His values belong to the 1970s when he first arrived in Australia, but I wanted something else."

"And?"

"I fell in love. And out of love."

"Someone broke your heart?"

"That's none of your business."

"I'm sorry, Ela, I had no right—"

"I shouldn't be so sensitive."

"You phoned me, didn't you? What did you want to say?"

"It doesn't matter. It won't help him or me."

Jane knew she was close to something but needed to take her time. "How did you meet?"

"I did some work at the prison as an interpreter. Then joined a voluntary group that helped with education. Tomas was studying and I helped him with his books."

"Medieval history?"

"That came later. It started with the World Wars."

"Is Tomas Muslim?"

Ela laughed. "He's a committed atheist."

"A former Catholic?"

"No. He's totally Christopher Hitchens. I think he always has been."

"How often did you see him in jail?"

"Every week. On Sunday mornings."

"For how many years?"

"Seven."

"And did you . . . ever do more than that?"

"They don't allow conjugal visits, if that's what you're asking. And if they did, we wouldn't have done it either. Not till we're properly married. I come from a traditional family. I'm loyal to my faith and culture."

"Did Tomas ever talk about Nigel Woods?"

"No."

"Or Franco Bernero?"

"No."

"Or the Catholic Church or torture . . ."

Ela gave a long-suffering smile as if another "no" was superfluous.

"So what was his interest in the Middle Ages?"

"The Reformation."

"A committed atheist. That doesn't make any sense."

"He wanted to learn. He didn't care what. He wanted to expand his mind."

Jane was stumped and Ela a resolute witness.

"Do you worry Tomas is so far out on a limb he doesn't know how to get down?" Jane's question was a calculated risk: 20 percent actuarial and 80 percent speculation. But she was down to flying kites.

Ela looked at Jane as if she were reading her mind. "He's suspicious of everyone. Totally paranoid. I know he's making things worse. He's a private man in real life. The court case was such an ordeal. He hated the scrutiny, being examined. Laid bare for everyone to see."

"But you supported the case. Didn't you pay his solicitor?"

"We didn't think it would get that far. His barrister was so convincing. But once we started we couldn't stop."

"I thought the barrister did it pro bono?"

"Only when he knew I couldn't pay."

"Yes, I know Ravi Patel. A man of principle," said Jane, chuckling to herself.

"But the solicitor's costs went on and on. I had to get a loan on my unit."

"Didn't Tomas know his case would attract publicity?"

"No. We didn't think it through."

Jane was struggling to understand and said so.

"Tomas loves being an actor, but hates being himself. I think it's why he's so good. He immerses himself in his roles. He told me once he hides in his characters because he doesn't like who he is."

"And since getting out of jail, he's never been to see you?"

"How can he when he knows you're watching?"

"Ela, until two days ago, the police didn't know you existed."

"He hasn't done these things."

"Then he needs to come forward and tell us."

"And even if he has, it doesn't change a thing."

"I'm not sure I know what you mean."

"I love him, Jane, whatever he's done. It's unconditional."

And with that, Ela smiled her certainty and hurried away.

If Sunday mornings had been visiting days for Ela, they were bike riding time for Jane. The city was ringed with cycle tracks and Jane's favorite ran along the river. Today she'd headed in the other direction along St. Kilda Road to shop at the Prahran Markets. But as she cut through Fawkner Park past the Quidditch Pitch she was stopped in her tracks by a high-flying body in motion—the unmistakable and surprisingly athletic form of Eric Ringer. Moving backward, he had reached up high and away to his left and taken a screamer.

Teenage boys and three girls, all dressed in whites, were playing cricket. The batsman had hit a risky six to bring his team to the cusp of victory, but it was Ringer's catch beyond the boundary that brought cheers and laughter from the small group of supporters. It was one of those reflex things that people with great hand–eye coordination do without thinking. Jane was transfixed though she knew nothing at all about cricket. An onlooker explained there were three balls to go and that five runs would win the game.

The next ball was edged for one but the new batter was small, with none of his partner's swagger. A swing and a miss and a suicidal run—but somehow they made their ground. The taller batter returned to the crease and needed four off the last ball to win. The bowler ran in with a wild full toss which came off the keeper's gloves and raced away to the boundary. Ringer jumped in the air and pumped his fist as if his team had won the Grand Final.

Jane stood with her bike and watched as the teams mingled with parents and friends. She could have been in England, a perfect oval surrounded by trees, children playing in the filtered light. Ringer was with the confident batsman, who looked like his son, and Jane suddenly felt like an intruder. But as she mounted her bike to escape, her movement caught Ringer's eye.

"Jane," he called. "Is that you? What are you doing here?"

"Not watching cricket, you can be sure of that, but I take it your team won?" She felt exposed in her cycling gear. Lycra wasn't her favorite look. Her Sweaty Bettys with the foam-padded bum weren't something she'd wear to work. Ringer looked great in his muscle-fit shirt and clearly spent more time in the gym than she did. He looked like someone who could race his son in the pool and leave him two lengths behind.

"I was on my way to the markets when I saw you take your catch. Hello, I said, that show-off is someone I know."

Ringer laughed and tossed his head and became even more appealing. It was good to see him away from the office and taking a break for once. It reminded Jane there were other things—like family. It reminded her of what she had lost.

"Come and meet the kids," he insisted, waving them to come and join them.

The two boys headed over. The older one was thirteen, his brother about eleven.

"This is Tom, the batting hero. This is Jane from work, but she's not a cop, so don't hold that against her."

"Don't you like cops, Tom?" said Jane.

"I like them better when they live in Melbourne."

Jane could feel the bond between father and son and why Ringer hadn't stayed in Canberra.

The younger boy was loaded up with his brother's cricketing gear.

"And this is Edward. He's a cricketer too."

"Not playing today, Edward?"

"My team plays on Saturdays."

"Not a game I understand," said Jane as she looked across at a young girl aged nine with her head buried deep in a book.

"Caroline. Come and meet Jane."

Ringer's daughter closed her book, keeping her finger marking her place.

"Hello, Caroline. I'm Jane. Did you enjoy the game?"

"I can take it or leave it."

"Yes, you and me both. What are you reading?"

"*Raising the Sun.*"

"I'm guessing it's not about cricket?"

"It's about a girl who lifts a curse on a town where the summer has gone away."

"So you know how it ends?"

"Oh, yes, I've read it three times already."

"Caroline's the brainy one," said Ringer. "She gets it from her mother." It wasn't meant as a put-down, but Caroline seemed hurt by the comment. She clearly didn't have the sporting bond Ringer enjoyed with his sons.

"Speaking of which, we'd better get moving. Your mother said not to be late. See you tomorrow, Jane. Enjoy your ride."

As Ringer herded his kids toward his car, the boys waved goodbye. Caroline's nose was already back in her book.

Jane turned her bike around and headed for home. She didn't feel like the markets anymore. Meeting Ringer's kids had affected her in a way she wished it hadn't. She and Ringer were coworkers, colleagues. His family was private and none of her business. But if his personal life didn't matter, then what was this knot in her stomach? Was she annoyed at herself for invading his world or angry she'd been lying to herself all along? That her resolve not to reengage with this cop after all these years was a paper-thin overreaction? That her insistence that she felt nothing at all for Eric Ringer—not back then and certainly not now—was nothing but self-delusion, as irrational as Ela Bey's?

When Jane got home she stood in the shower for fifteen minutes. She knew it was bad for her skin but she needed to clear her head. She knew who she was and she knew her weaknesses and she didn't need a degree in psychiatry to figure them out. Jane was a rescuer, as fabled as the Flying Doctor Service and every bit as reliable. She knew what had clinched her relationship with Ben: Zoe, his six-year-old daughter. Up until then she had wanted kids of her own, but suddenly here was a possibility, almost new and ready to go. Why wait for someone she was yet to meet? Was her womb better than anyone else's? Did the perfect man or the perfect child even exist?

She got out of the shower and, still wrapped in a towel, juiced up a storm. Beetroot, apple, carrot, and ginger. She had to stop this storm in her head.

She felt sorry for Ben, he'd deserved to live longer. She wished they'd had their own child together so more of him remained. She resolved to phone Zoe when the time zones were right. She resolved to phone her mother. She wondered how Melissa Woods was doing. And Ela Bey. She wished she'd done law like her father had wanted. She wished she wasn't so obsessed with the mind. She wished she wasn't alone.

———

When she had dressed, she flicked on the telly, but there was still a disc in the player and up came Tomas Kurtza. He was portraying a Sam Shepard cowboy, with a Texan drawl and Sam Elliott mustache. It was hard not to be impressed.

The dining table was strewn with books and images of the Catholic Church and the Middle Ages. *Death, Torture, and the Broken Body*? Somewhere she would find the key. Jane had to laugh at herself. Was this the only time she was sane, matching her wits with the diabolical, trying to make the irrational make sense? Was work her only salvation?

She spread out the latest Homicide chart: a printout from the whiteboard. It was after one of Ringer's better sessions—The Case Against Tomas Kurtza—and why he should not be their primary suspect.

1. The fact they couldn't find him proved nothing—beyond the fact they couldn't find him.
2. He had no known links to Nigel Woods.
3. He had no known links to Franco Bernero.
4. The DNA linked him to the forklift but he could've been a volunteer. It was the kind of work he did. It didn't make him the murderer.
5. Men who rape women have a different psychology to men who kill and torture men. (This point was attributed to Jane.)
6. He was a model prisoner who had a future as an actor.
7. He had sought early release to make a film.
8. Nothing in his prison record suggested a capacity to commit these crimes.
9. There was no evidence he hated the Catholic Church any more than any other religion. He dismissed them all.
10. Studying something—e.g., The Medieval—is not of itself incriminating.

Jane remembered the session clearly. It was a timely challenge from a clever detective to get his team to look elsewhere. Whatever his failings might have been as a husband, Eric Ding Dong aka "The Prick" Eric Ringer was a consummate investigator.

Jane needed to clear her assumptions. She was as guilty as anyone of being in the Kurtza tunnel, though in fairness she had queried him more than most. But if it wasn't Tomas Kurtza, who was it? And how would they find him? And stop him before he did it again?

15

Michael McGill had nothing in common with the other two victims, apart from being Catholic. And even that was debatable since he'd been defrocked in 2003. The former priest had neither Nigel Woods's wealth nor Franco Bernero's affability. As a registered sex offender, he kept to himself and stayed away from children.

He rented a sleepout behind an old woman's house and looked after her garden. She let him grow vegetables, which he always shared, but she never asked him inside. At night he would listen to classical music and watch television, reflected without sound on the old woman's window. She would hang out her washing on the rotary clothesline with her underwear on the inside. Not that it was likely to rouse him: nothing much did anymore.

He kept a journal for his sanity, to remind him he'd been born. He hardly remembered his mother anymore but his father's rage was indelible. He remembered praying to a God who never came, he remembered being alone. He remembered the cold of a bluestone orphanage and the warmth of the house father's bed. He remembered the joy of the seminary, and the pride of being ordained. He remembered every court case and every witness and every statement he'd made to the police. He remembered the shame and the misunderstanding. Didn't they know he would never do harm, that he only had love in his heart?

He remembered his years in prison, as cold as the dormitory of his bluestone youth. He remembered the violence and the humiliation; the rape and the mortification.

He remembered his faith, which had never left him. Its glory and its power to heal. Without God, he was an empty vessel. And he knew God loved him still.

It didn't take the killer long to figure out Michael McGill's routines. He always took the long route to the shopping mall, avoiding the primary school. He liked to go to the garden center but it was next to a children's playground, so he had to choose his times. He bought his liquor from a discount shop, but never the alcopops or malternatives favored by the young. He liked to go to the cinema, but the film had to be R 18+.

He would do the old woman's shopping from a list she provided and leave the bags and change by the door. He would go to church on Sundays, never for Mass but between the advertised times. He loved to work in the garden, but it was always weather dependent. His favorite days were when the old woman visited her sister and he could have the place to himself. If the sun was shining he would take off his shirt and wipe his hands on his singlet. It seemed to give him validation—like he was a toiler in the fields.

"I'll be back before dark," said the old woman. "Make sure you feed the cat."

"Take your sister some runner beans," he said, handing her a plastic bag he'd already packed. "I am particularly proud of my crop this year—though they grow as easily as weeds."

Michael McGill took off his shirt and felt the embrace of the sun on his neck. For a moment he considered removing all his clothes and dancing with garlands of beans. But a sex offender understands perceptions and the cat would not approve. He looked at the cat and the cat looked back: you can tell when a feline's not happy.

He heard the gate swing open and shut. It was the old woman returning for sure. She had a habit of forgetting her specs and Michael was pleased his fetishes were confined to his thoughts these days and that the runner beans remained on their frame.

But the woman that rounded the house was not his landlady, perhaps not a lady at all, with a formless dress on a manly body and pancake that failed to conceal a five o'clock shadow.

"Hello, Michael," she said in a baritone voice. "It's time you lost some weight." She flicked open his knife. "I have a device here that's tried and true—or should I say, sharp and to the point."

The knife slipped into the right side of Michael's groin with such precision that pain held its breath. The incision continued in a half moon below his belly and up to his ribs on the other side. The killer lifted the flap of his stomach and Michael's innards fell out as if from a ruptured piñata. The failed priest could only watch and wonder.

As Michael collapsed to the ground, overwhelmed by shock and still waiting for the pain to come, the killer crossed to the garden hose and disconnected the device that kept it coiled. Then, grabbing a section of Michael's intestines, she started to crank them on to the drum, separating them from the mesentery until the reel could hold no more.

"I'm nearly done," said the killer, "or maybe not. It's hard to say in this haphazard world."

But her victim wouldn't live to share his words and Jane would never hear them.

But Jesus did. And Mother Mary. And a Host of Heavenly Angels. But what could they do? After all his prayers, they couldn't even save a believer, their devoted Michael McGill.

16

Jane sat silently beside Ringer as his car was waved through the checkpoint. Crowds were gathering at both ends of the cordoned-off block in Kerr Street that contained the crime scene, animated by rumors that the torture killer had struck again, this time in their neighborhood.

Marino was in the front room with the old woman, still shaken by her encounter with the fleeing perpetrator—which was nothing compared to the shock of what she found in her back garden, an experience that Jane and Ringer were about to have for themselves.

Like the two victims before him, Michael McGill's earthly remains had lost any semblance of being human. His body reclined against the garden shed, attached to a mechanism that looked for all the world like some sort of life-saving device. The tubes that ran from the hose reel into his body seemed like they were trying to prolong his life and compensate for the liters of blood on the ground. His skin was pallid, his expression perplexed, his hands upturned to heaven.

Ringer had already been informed that the victim was a registered sex offender, but it didn't make the scene any less distressing.

"It's much less sophisticated than the others. It appears much less planned, almost ad-libbed," Jane said.

"Do you think he's feeling under pressure?"

"I would have said the opposite: almost overconfident."

"An escalation?"

"Or a deviation."

Marino joined them. "Got to love this work," she said, "every day something new. This time he was disguised as a woman. The landlady met him coming round the side of the house when she came home early. She was halfway to her sister's when she received a text asking her to come on another day. So she got off the bus and caught another one home. She almost caught the killer in the act."

"He was disguised as a woman?" repeated Jane.

"If 'disguise' is the right word to use. He was wearing a dress and exaggerated makeup, but it wasn't designed to fool anyone."

"A drag queen?" postulated Ringer.

"Well, not a self-respecting one."

"Unless it's not him at all." Jane's suggestion stopped the others in their tracks.

"A copy-cat?" said Ringer.

"What better way to conceal your crime than making it look like the torture killer? As I understand Tomas Kurtza, he takes great pride in his transformations. They are skillful and thoughtful, not shove on a dress and some lippy."

"You don't think it's him?"

"If Kurtza committed the first two murders, he's significantly changed his MO. In which case, that is interesting in itself."

Marino was staring at the body again. They all were, as if the answer was under their noses.

"How do you think he died? From his intestines being removed?"

"I doubt it, Nita," said Jane, "you can survive that for some time. Though I haven't examined the body, it looks like the killer severed the external iliac artery—either deliberately or accidentally. He would have bled to death in three to five minutes."

"That's quicker than the others," noted Ringer.

"Yes. Another distinction. No requisite period of pain and suffering."

A young constable emerged from the house and crossed to Ringer.

"Excuse me, boss, but there's someone outside asking for Dr. Halifax. A Father Keely."

Jane made her way outside. The rubberneckers were building. It's a community thing in Fitzroy—any excuse for a street party. Jane was surprised there weren't balloons.

Father Keely looked pale and somber as he waited at the checkpoint. Jane was pleased to see him and signed him through.

"Did you know the deceased?"

"Oh, yes," said Kevin. "I got to know him fairly well during the Royal Commission."

"And what did you make of the man?"

"He was doing his best to make his peace."

"Remorseful, do you think?"

"Repentant. There's a subtle difference. The trouble with this kind of offender is they struggle to see the harm."

"Though harm they do."

"Unspeakable harm. Is that what you think happened here?"

"We have no idea who did this, Kevin. Though we will interview all McGill's victims."

As they entered the house, Jane cautioned Kevin about what he was about to see. She even suggested he might like to wait for a more opportune moment in a different location, but, unable to give the last rites, the good Jesuit still wanted to bestow a proximate blessing.

The others retreated to give the priest some privacy, though Jane remained nearby. Kevin did his best to disguise his shock but Jane could see that he was shaking. It only emphasized how much she and the police accepted these things as routine. She hated that she'd become inured and wondered at the cost.

Kevin turned away and crossed himself and said another prayer. Maybe this one was for him. And Jane.

"I would like to take the body when it's available." He knew forensics and pathology were ahead of him in the queue.

"Yes, of course. But the police will want to ask some questions."

"Yes, I know."

"It's none of my business, Kevin, but what will you do with the body? Will it rest in consecrated ground?"

"Probably not. He'll be cremated and since the church won't look after him, I will. I'll take the ashes back to Northern Ireland, to the town his great-grandfather came from as a ward of the state. I'll sprinkle some of them on a hill overlooking the church and the rest I'll take down south, to The Burren where my people come from, and fling them into the sea like the pagans did and howl at the wind. Though only on my day off."

Kevin Keely knew tonight would only be the beginning and that in the days that followed he would have to relive the pedophile's transgressions all over again.

Marino took him aside for a preliminary statement. He would tell her that of McGill's many victims, there was no one in particular who came to mind as someone who might be capable of such an atrocity, though it wasn't Michael McGill's victims who were at the forefront of his mind right then, but the image of a hose-reel bound tightly with the dead man's entrails, a sight he would not unsee for the rest of his days.

———

Ringer called it quits at 12:45 a.m. and sent his team home. They had a big day ahead. As Jane got into his car, she was aware of Marino and Showbag watching. The rumors had taken root but she was too tired to change their minds and have someone else drop her home.

"They think we're having an affair," said Ringer, grinning as he turned his car toward the city. He seemed pleased by the innuendo.

With Jane it had the opposite effect. That they were attracted to each other was undeniable. But why did he bother with remarks like that when they both knew nothing could or would happen?

"What did you learn from your Jesuit friend?" Ringer asked.

"That even sinners can be saved," Jane said.

Ringer gave her a sideways look, surprised by her sardonic tone. "Can he give us a primary suspect?"

"He can give you hundreds and jam up the system if that's what you want."

"McGill abused that many people?"

"Not personally. But there are survivors out there who see McGill as representative. The killer mightn't need a personal link. This could be a crusade against kind."

"Is that your latest thinking?"

"My latest thinking is I need to go home to bed."

There she was, blurring the lines again, saying things any

red-blooded cop could be forgiven for taking the wrong way. Thankfully, Ringer wasn't any old cop and let her comment go through to the keeper.

"I'm glad you met the family the other day."

"Nice kids," said Jane, not wanting to pursue the subject.

"Though Caro's a bit of a bookworm. It's all she wants to do."

"Reading's not a bad thing."

"I don't think she's handled the split very well. Doesn't like being away from her mum."

Jane didn't respond. She didn't want to tell him how much Caroline reminded her of Zoe, how much she missed the ceaseless curiosity of a young female in the house.

Jane smiled at Ringer to show she wasn't troubled by his banter even though she was. She noticed his jacket on the hanger behind him. She liked how he always took it off to prevent it from being creased. She looked at his long, slim hands caressing the steering wheel like a man who enjoyed his car, how he drove with the rhythm of the traffic and not against it, how his eyes glanced between her and the road and the rear-view mirror like someone who liked to keep things in balance.

She turned to look out the window and caught her own reflection. She wondered if things would be different with the case behind them, if she would relate to him any differently. But why was she even thinking like this while Ben was still so present and real?

They continued on in silence until he drew his car up outside her building.

"Thanks for the lift," said Jane.

"I wouldn't say no to a drink."

"Not tonight, Eric. Maybe some other time when we're not so distracted." She smiled her thanks and got out of the car. She imagined him watching as she crossed the street and thinking what a great arse she had. For once she hated that the lights were so bright, that the streetlights that kept her safe at any other time only illuminated her problem: her unerring ability to say the wrong thing.

The concierge let her into the building and Ringer drove off into the night. As Jane got into the lift she looked at herself in the mirror, slumping as she replayed her lines. "My latest thinking is I need to go home to bed." And, "Not tonight, Eric. Maybe some other time when we're not so distracted."

If Jane was so clear about Ringer, why did she think he had beautiful hands and that the way he removed his jacket from that long, straight back was, well, kind of sexy?

Jane opened the door to her apartment, flicked on the lights and dumped her keys on the table in the hall. Another mirror and another Jane staring back as if to challenge herself with the question: If you think these things, is your subconscious trying to tell you something?

Jane headed though to the loungeroom and poured herself a gin and tonic, grateful for the lack of mirrors.

17

A man wearing a beanie emerged from Flinders Street Station, walked up Swanston Street and caught a tram from Bourke Street that took him all the way to the corner of Nicholson and Argyle. From there the cameras lost him as he ducked through the back streets on his way to his destination, stopping somewhere along the way to change into his female guise. Jane and the others watched as Ray Cheung took them through the CCTV record of the killer's precrime progression. Cheung's team was still working on his route prior to emerging from the station and his progress after the crime. They had worked all through the night. Even with facial recognition technology, the task would be laborious. But it was more than they had for Franco Bernero and much more than they had for Nigel Woods.

Cheung showed how close-ups of the man in the beanie matched with Telecom Man, who had watched the Woods house the two Fridays before the murder. Bone structure and height were identical and, despite Beanie Man's backpack, their build was generally the same.

"The backpack is bulky, suggesting he used more than one disguise, though it would have been dumped at some point. The earliest image we have of Beanie Man is him emerging from the toilets at Flinders Street with the back-pack turned inside out. The last is getting off the tram at Nicholson and Argyle."

Ringer thanked Cheung for his presentation and opened the session for questions.

"So was it Tomas Kurtza or not?" asked Marino, wanting the uncertainty to stop there and then.

Ringer glanced at Jane.

"It's a reasonable assumption," Jane said. "Given Beanie Man, the copycat theory is looking thin. But with no CCTV footage of the faux woman, we've only got the landlady's description to go on. And she was obviously in shock."

"Then what's the female disguise all about?" asked Ringer.

"I wish I knew," Jane said, "but it won't be irrelevant."

"Like what?" asked Marino, her exasperation shared by the others.

"Maybe he was impersonating the landlady. From what she told you, Nita, it's clear she bullied her tenant—not letting him in her house, requiring him to do her shopping. Maybe he figured this out as he was casing the place and the costume was just for McGill. Or maybe he did it for his own amusement, probably to show us how easy it is to travel around the city, undetected, even with a bad disguise. Maybe he's enjoying himself at our expense."

"Telling us what, exactly?" Marino asked.

"How confident he is that we can't stop him until he's finished."

"Finished what?"

"His crusade against the church? I'm sorry, Nita, it's as close as I can get."

Jane felt she was letting the team down. It wasn't the time to remind them that psychiatry was an imperfect science, that it was hard enough to see into the mind of someone she could interview; almost impossible to deduce anything from the scraps of evidence she had. Conventional means of detection weren't delivering results. They thought they knew who their killer was but couldn't find him. Wasn't Jane there to join the dots, to provide answers to questions yet to be defined?

"Let's redouble our efforts to find Tomas Kurtza—to rule him in or out once and for all," said Ringer.

The briefing finished and the detectives dispersed.

"I'm missing something," Jane confessed.

"We all are," said Ringer, sharing the responsibility.

"Yeah. But I'm supposed to be the expert."

———

The paraglider wasn't responding. What in the hell was she thinking when she hired the thing? She had always been scared of heights. She pulled on the lines to slow her speed as a sudden alarm went off. She was stalling and falling to earth . . .

Jane woke with a start, her mobile ringing beside her bed.

"Hello, Jane. Have you read the morning papers?"

"No, Eric. I've only just woken up."

"Have a look and call me back."

Jane peered at her watch: it was 6:45 a.m. Didn't he ever take a day off?

Jane stumbled to the door, unsticking her eyes, and took up *The Sunday Age*. Is PEDOPHILIA THE CLUE TO THE TORTURE KILLER'S RAMPAGE? shouted the headline. Jane read the article with a sinking heart and opened the sliders to the terrace to clear her head. When she returned Ringer's call, he answered immediately.

"I can hear the minister now: 'So investigative journalists know more than you do.'"

"It's only a theory. They still aren't naming the killer."

"That will be in part two tomorrow. Meet me at Southbank for breakfast."

By the time Jane headed along the promenade, Ringer was on his second coffee.

"I blame myself," he said as she pulled up a chair. "Too obsessed with corruption and tax evasion, I didn't even look at the obvious."

"They're not saying Woods was a pedophile," said Jane as she ordered a long black, still feeling like she was falling to earth.

"No. But he spent a fucking fortune defending a young assistant from pedophilia charges, all the way to the Court of Appeal."

"Some people would see that as loyalty."

"Like a West Australian billionaire defending a VC winner? Rich bastards are all the same. And what about Franco Bernero attending soirees with fourteen-year-old girls? How come we didn't know about that?"

"The existence of a pedophile ring in high places is largely speculation," said Jane as she took up the menu. "The press have been banging on about it for years. I don't like conspiracy theories."

"Even if they are true?"

"I'm having the scrambled eggs."

"I'm not hungry."

"Then take a deep breath and calm down."

He ordered water and another coffee and poked at a piece of toast while Jane tried to enjoy her eggs.

"Okay, so it's all about pedophilia and the Catholic Church. Is that going to help you catch him?" asked Jane.

"You're taking this particularly well."

"I like theories that help us catch him. What do we do with

this? If there was any substance, the journo would have phoned you for a quote. And thanks for phoning at six forty-five on a Sunday morning."

"Sorry, were you in the middle of something?"

"Only a panic attack."

It was clear he didn't know how to take her. She didn't know how to take herself. Dreaming of going paragliding and dropping out of the sky? She hoped it wasn't Freudian.

After breakfast, they walked by the river. *The Age's* article hadn't been the only one to appear in the newspapers. The public was scared and the press was responding in kind. Three gruesome murders in less than a month. Politicians were frantic and eager for answers and the police were under the pump. Ringer wondered when it would end.

"I know *when* is your priority, Eric. I just want to know *why.*"

"So why don't you buy pedophilia?"

"It's too . . . esoteric. Unless he had a personal connection. Unless he was abused by all three."

"We're going nowhere fast."

"You're going to have to catch the killer, Eric. And when you do, I'll sit him down and tell you precisely what makes him tick."

"I was hoping you might be able to tell me that now."

"Which of course is the plan, as always." Jane was hurting as much over this case as he was, maybe more, but she wasn't going to jump at shadows. "There's some terrible logic behind this. There always is. What looks totally mad and unhinged on the outside will be crystal clear to him. I just have to find the key."

"Well, don't take too long."

"I'm trying, Eric. I truly am."

On Monday morning, Jane headed into the office tower in Southern Cross Lane that housed the Department of Justice and Community Safety and took the lift to the office of the Commissioner of Corrections. Serena Manzoufas was ten years younger than Jane, a bureaucrat who was going places in a government department with an annual budget of 8.5 billion dollars. Serena had worked in corrections for a number of years and had managed prisons throughout the state, but it was her one-on-one contact with Kurtza that had caught Jane's attention.

Serena made Jane a coffee as expertly as any barista and led her through to the boardroom. Jane could tell Serena's no-nonsense approach would take her all the way to the top.

"I saw on his prison file that you worked with Tomas Kurtza?" Jane said when they'd sat down.

"Yes. As a prison psychologist."

"So, obvious question first. How did you find him?"

"Where do I start? Complex. Funny—in a cruel kind of way. Intelligent, thoughtful. Anti-narcissistic and masochistic—"

"I'll come back to the antinarcissism," interrupted Jane, "but masochist? I expected you to say sadist."

"There's not much of an outlet for sadism in a jail. But his ability to endure pain was quite remarkable. He clearly provoked some of his bashings. At first I thought it was so he'd be sent to an isolation cell. But he would self-harm there as well to ensure his injuries didn't heal."

"Yeah, that's masochistic."

"Tomas was incredibly self-disciplined. We saw that when he studied, though he seldom followed the syllabus set by his supervising teachers and would go off on digressions of his own."

"Like medieval torture?"

"And the Holocaust, and Caravaggio, and Imelda Marcos . . ."

"So—talk to me about anti-narcissism."

Serena smiled. She knew it wasn't a popular term and that Jane wouldn't use it. "Jane, you have to understand I'm a bureaucrat these days. I haven't worked as a psychologist for years."

"And?"

"Antinarcissist—as opposed to a grandiose narcissist. Someone who's fulfilled by their failures. Someone who self-sabotages to prove how worthless they are. Someone who seeks obliteration as a self-fulfilling fantasy."

"Did he ever attempt suicide?"

"Not to my knowledge."

"And he's hardly doing that now. He's suspected of killing three people."

"Yes."

"What do you think he's trying to do?"

"I've no idea. And I've thought about it long and hard ever since the police asked for his file."

"Had Kurtza ever been the victim of pedophilia?"

"Not to my knowledge. He'd had a rough childhood, but never that. Unless he kept it hidden, as people often do."

"Tell me about his acting. Did you see his plays?"

"Oh, yes, and he was extraordinary. He had this ability to become someone else. Not only to get into their body and their mannerisms, but seemingly into their mind. I think it's called method acting, but this was another dimension. It wasn't as if he was possessing his character, it was as if the character was possessing him."

"You mean like 'antiexorcism,'" said Jane, unable to resist the opportunity.

Serena laughed at herself. Her terms were crude and approximate, but as she had said, she didn't do this work anymore.

"What about the Catholic Church. Did that ever come up?"

"Not while I was treating him. His time with the prison chaplain was some kind of intellectual game. He delighted in challenging the poor man's faith and in the end, the reverend gave it away. He was a volunteer and semiretired and as he said in his letter of resignation, Kurtza had 'exhausted his benevolence.'"

"Tell me about the court case?"

"That waste of time."

"Did Ravi Patel put him up to it?"

"I've no idea."

"Or his wife?"

"Wife? Which one? He had a virtual harem. No, I think it was Kurtza's idea. His resentment of the Parole Board system. His fury you couldn't appeal its decision."

"And he nearly won?"

"No, he didn't. They wasted so much time in the courts, it amounted to the same result. The board was never going to go to the wall over remorse. They actually had some sympathy for his argument—that after all these years he was no longer the twenty-three-year-old who had committed the original crime."

"Ravi made it sound like a victory."

"For Ravi's vanity, maybe. But it was a total waste of money for us—and no doubt a waste of Ravi's time."

"Anything else?"

Serena deliberated for a moment. "His sense of humor. And politics."

"Okay," said Jane. "Let's take those one at a time."

"His sense of humor was legendary in the prison. And he was very funny. But at times I found it cruel. A mask for his beliefs."

"Which brings us to politics."

"I can't say he was an admirer of Trump, but he shared

many of his negative values: his resentment, his intolerance, his desire for revenge. His desire to punish people for real or imagined wrongs."

"And if he's the killer—is that what he's doing now?"

"I don't know, Jane. If you ask me, what the killer's doing is beyond comprehension."

Which Jane knew more intimately than anyone. "I hope I don't have to see any more crime scenes," she confessed. "When this is over I suspect I will be spending quite a few sessions with my analyst to decompress."

"Don't you miss the academic world?"

Jane was momentarily taken aback. "For a pen-pusher, you show a lot of insight."

"That's what's good about an organization as big as this one. After you've served your time in the prisons, they move you on to something less confronting. I must say I am utterly in awe that you're still out there in the field."

"I used to say it was because I'm good at what I do. These days I'm not so sure."

Jane thanked Serena for her time and waited for the lift. She had gained an insight into Kurtza—antinarcissist or not. Sadism and masochism are intimately connected and she now had a new way to look at his crimes. Was Thomas Kurtza their killer? Was he putting himself in the place of his victims? As distressing as the concept might be, was he really torturing himself? Or was it toxic Trumpian revenge against some real or imagined enemy?

As the lift arrived, Jane got in, not realizing she had pressed the up button by mistake. To avoid embarrassment, she rode the elevator to the top before plunging down thirty-nine floors to the street below, effectively falling 160 meters in a matter of seconds. She wondered if she would dream about it in the morning.

For now, her mind was on other things.

18

Jane hadn't dressed up like this since Ben had died. When she'd been out with her girlfriends, it had been no more than a tidy-up after work. It wasn't good that she had fallen out of the habit of shopping, but her Zambesi fitted dress with the twist side was never going to go out of fashion and with the Art Deco drop earrings Ben had given her for her fiftieth, she knew she looked sensational. You need to when you're invited to Vue de monde at $320 a head plus wine.

The restaurant was almost as elevated as the Department of Justice and the maître d' led Jane to the prime corner table by the window looking out at the city thirty-one levels below. Melissa Woods was already there and Jane had to disguise her disappointment that Maurice Engels was with her. That hadn't been the arrangement, to have Melissa's lawyer at "an informal chat over dinner."

But Engels got to his feet as Jane approached and gathered up the documents sitting on the table. "Good evening, Dr. Halifax. I'm not joining you, if that's what you think."

"That's all right, Mr. Rimmer, I'm the guest in this situation."

"Engels."

"Pardon?"

"You called me Rimmer."

"Did I? I must have been thinking of someone else." Jane secretly cursed Showbag for his wicked nicknames.

"Thanks, Mel, I'll leave you to it. Enjoy your meal, Dr. Lancaster," he said as he took his leave, clearly thinking his Second World War aircraft reference amusing.

"Goodnight, Maurice," said Jane as the maître d' pulled back her chair. As she sat down and felt the unwelcome warmth of its previous occupant, she couldn't help thinking a truly classy establishment might have thought to bring a fresh seat.

Melissa Woods looked well coifed but tired. As usual, her diamonds stole the show, but Jane noted she hadn't bothered to get a manicure. She was drinking Perrier water. It seemed her excessive consumption of alcohol was a passing aberration, but Jane was not going to take her lead on that and ordered a glass of Riesling, the Grosset Polish Hill.

"We need to talk about these appalling rumors in the press," Melissa began. "Nigel might have been interested in many things but pedophilia wasn't remotely one of them. He had a young employee of whom he was particularly fond. Clever—I might even say brilliant—but like most of us, fatally flawed. He was the pedophile, Jane, not Nigel. Nigel's sin, if you can call it that, was loyalty."

Jane sipped her wine and listened. They had only just been served the first of the twelve degustation dishes. It was going to be a long night.

"In the beginning, Nigel was convinced his employee had been framed by a business rival, so he went nuclear. Private detectives, PR consultants, and the best lawyers money could buy. Do you realize the risk he was taking? A Papal Knight, defending a pedophile?"

Normally Jane would interrupt at this point to suggest that Nigel might have been defending the reputation of Nigel Woods and Associates, but tonight Melissa Woods was paying to be heard and Jane would allow her platform.

"I thought he was overreacting, but when Nigel gets the bit between his teeth—when Nigel got the bit between his teeth," she corrected, "he was not to be stopped."

"I am not sure why you're telling me this," said Jane, not unkindly.

"Because this ridiculous vendetta against him has got to stop. A pedophile ring? Involving Nigel?"

"Mel, I have no influence over the press."

"But you do have influence over Inspector Ringer. I've watched how he defers to you."

"Mel, that isn't true—"

"He's driving this investigation and the press will take their lead from him. Tell him to go after taxation matters or other irregularities if that's what he wants to do. Maurice will tie the taxation department up in the courts for years until they settle, as they always do. But these allegations besmirch Nigel's memory. For pity's sake, Jane, at least leave him with his reputation. It was his employee who was the pedophile. And even then, he was only guilty of possessing images, he was never actively involved."

Jane resisted telling Mel of the extreme harm done to children whose images were used in child pornography. She was still more interested in why she'd been invited to dinner.

The sommelier suggested a wine to match the West Australian marron curry, but Jane declined.

"You are supposed to taste a different wine with every course," Melissa explained. "Just leave what you don't want: they'll take it away."

Jane was familiar with fine dining, but Melissa's approach

was on another level. She could only imagine what Eric Ringer would have said. She decided to change the topic.

"How are you doing, Mel?"

"I'm putting my affairs in order, Jane. I am going to sell the house. I was looking at the video tour we made last year. If we edit out the sculpture, I'm sure it will do."

"Video tour?"

"It's what the market expects with trophy homes: this one is from the interior decorator's website. Nigel disputed his fee and as a compromise, we let him make a video. I never imagined it would help me sell the house." Melissa stopped talking. "Is something the matter?"

"There's a video tour of your house on the interior decorator's website?"

"Yes. Is that a problem?"

"It might explain how the murderer was so familiar with the detail. It hasn't been clear until now how that was the case," Jane said gently.

The use to which the sculpture had been put had always puzzled Jane. It had never seemed improvised, but she hadn't been able to work out how the killer could have had such an intimate understanding of a work that had been in private hands since its creation. To adapt it into a Judas cradle took forethought and preparation.

Melissa was aghast. "Oh my God," she said as the realization sank in.

But Jane only saw the opportunity. "Maybe the police will be able to tell who's accessed the website. Maybe it's the link we're after. Maybe he used an intermediary. Do you mind if I make a call?"

Jane slipped away to phone Ray Cheung and when she returned, she found Melissa staring out at the city.

"I lied to you, Jane. It wasn't Nigel who disputed the interior decorator's bill. I was the one who felt his charges were outrageous, I was the one who forced him to cut his bill in half and agreed he could make the video as some kind of consolation. I was the one who made our private lives public and gave the murderer his unspeakable idea. It was me."

"Don't punish yourself. It's only a theory. It could have been anyone who visited the house." But Jane knew she wasn't helping.

"We have so much money, Jane, one would think we wouldn't care. But you'd be surprised how many people try to take advantage, how many people think of a figure and double it to see how stupid we are. A billion dollars is a curse, not a blessing. If I could only have a normal life like anyone else . . ."

They plowed on through the degustation, though Melissa never finished any of her courses. Each dish was exquisite in every detail. It wasn't the amount of food but the richness that tested Jane. The seven glasses of wine—most of them untouched—didn't help and by ten o'clock, Jane was ready for home.

"I don't know how I'm going to survive without Nigel."

"You have four children. Think of them."

"They don't need me anymore. I'm just an obstacle between them and their inheritance."

"Are you seeing a counselor, Mel? I can recommend a very good one."

"Oh, yes, I'm seeing Beverley twice a week. We're doing mindfulness and meditation. I have so many tapes with running water, I think the house has sprung a leak."

"Joking about it is good."

"When I go to sleep at night, I hope it will be forever. The most distressing part of the day is waking up."

"Now you are making me worried."

"How did you get through it, Jane?"

"By acknowledging grief and not pretending it away. By putting one foot after the other. By replying to people who'd sent me condolences. By looking at photos and remembering the great times we had. By being with friends and making sure I wasn't alone."

"Basic stuff."

"Utterly basic stuff."

"Just take this pedophile thing away, Jane. Tell Inspector Ringer, tell your friends in the press, Nigel was a hard man but he wasn't that. Or if he was, then everything's a lie."

Jane studied her host. Melissa Woods liked to make speeches and had a habit of saying too much. The last time it had been about the "other woman." Was she allowing now for the possibility her husband had been a pedophile after all?

Nothing was making sense. The abundant food and the excessive wine, the sublime restaurant suspended in the sky, the widow and her ever-attentive lawyer putting her affairs in order, diamonds on unmanicured fingers. Sometimes all Jane had was her gut, and her gut was telling her to be watchful, that whatever Melissa Woods was trying to project, the truth was somewhere else.

It was nothing she could share with the cops. This wasn't police work and it certainly wasn't forensic psychiatry. But it was like the dance the guilty do when they try to play the victim. And Jane's instincts were primed.

———

When Jane headed into the Homicide Squad early the following morning, others had arrived before her. Animated voices coming from Ringer's office were not unusual, but on hearing herself as the subject of the conversation, Jane quickly diverted in that direction.

"Since when have you taken orders from Jane Halifax?"

"Boss, it wasn't an order," said Showbag.

"Did you intend to discuss this with me?"

"I'm doing that now."

Jane appeared in the doorway with a breezy good morning. "Something I can help you with?"

"No, Jane. This is between me and Showbag."

But Jane wasn't going to go away.

"I've just been advised that Ela Bey's house wasn't searched."

"Yes, Eric, that was probably my suggestion," admitted Jane in an attempt to deflect Ringer's anger away from his sergeant.

"Maybe it was," said Ringer. "I don't have a beef with that. You can suggest whatever you like. But I didn't send one of my detectives to the suspect's wife to have a cup of tea." Ringer's gaze hadn't moved from Showbag. "Get a warrant and search the place. And put her under surveillance."

"Yes, boss," said the chastened detective as he headed off to comply.

"I wanted to keep the channels open," said Jane. "I'm trying to keep Ela on side."

"And what's that called? 'Investigation by being friended'?"

"I'm sorry."

"You're a consultant. You can act any way you like. But I expect my cops to be cops."

Jane hadn't seen Ringer this angry. The pressure of suspecting who the murderer was and not being able to find him was beginning to tell. In these days of enhanced surveillance and digital tracking, locating suspects was not supposed to be this hard. Persons of interest were not supposed to be able to move around a defined inner-city quadrant without being detected. To make things worse, mobile phones and personal computers could be incriminating records and Showbag had left Ela's without them.

"I know you say 'wife' but she isn't the only one," Jane said.

"Then let's search them as well."

Only a change of subject was going to calm him.

"I saw Melissa Woods last night. She took me to dinner. Wanted to assure me that Nigel wasn't a pedophile." Ringer looked like he was about to reach boiling point. "But I think I learned something else: how the killer cased the Woodses' house. There's a video tour on their interior decorator's website. I phoned Ray Cheung last night and suggested he check who might have taken a look."

"But Kurtza doesn't use a computer."

"Maybe he had someone do it for him."

"Let's hope it wasn't Ela Bey," said Ringer bleakly, as if to reinforce what Showbag's sloppy policework might have cost them. And Jane's role in that decision.

"Sorry," she said again as the point sank in. It was all she could say.

19

Jane had arranged to meet Cayden Voss at the Script Bar and Bistro attached to the Southbank Theatre so she could return the DVDs of the prison plays, which the police had copied. Voss had just finished lunch with a journalist friend and was in a state of some excitement.

"Can you believe it, Jane? I've been asked to write an article about my discovery of Tomas Kurtza." He offered her a glass of champagne from the bottle left over from lunch but Jane settled for coffee.

"A little premature, don't you think? He's only been described as a person of interest." It seemed macabre to be talking about making money off a serial killer—if that's what Kurtza was—before he was caught, but nothing about this case surprised Jane anymore.

"Oh, it won't be published until all this is over, but my friend is a feature writer and thinks it could be serialized over a number of parts—and could be made into a podcast as well. Do you think Inspector Ringer would agree to be interviewed?"

"Not at this point in the investigation," Jane said, masking her distaste. "What angle are you going to take?"

"Oh, it will all be about the acting. His ability to change his appearance and your inability to catch him. Is it true he threw in a bad disguise of a woman just to have fun?"

"Who told you that?"

"My journalist friend. He got it from Police PR, though they told him it was not for publication."

"Which also means not to be shared with anyone else."

"Oops!" said Voss, though it was obvious he didn't care.

"So you think Kurtza committed these crimes?"

"Don't you?"

Jane didn't answer. She didn't need to. She refined her questions.

"Assuming it's Kurtza, what do you make of his female disguise?"

"Classic. He's showing off. Even with a deliberately clumsy costume, you still can't catch him."

"Are you writing about the murders as well?"

"No. It's not my field. It will be more about my discovery of a uniquely gifted actor, languishing in prison, and the career he could have had."

"And the film you never made?"

"I won't be writing about that."

"Why not?"

"Too painful, Jane. Too many disappointments, too many what-might-have-beens."

"So—how do you think this will end?" Jane asked, not wanting to pander to his ghoulish enterprise.

'You won't take him alive." Voss's certainty and self-satisfaction was disarming. "He made one thing clear: he was never going back to jail."

"Did you know he was going to commit these murders?"

"No. How could I?"

"Then why did he tell you he was never going back to jail? What made him think that was even a possibility?"

"You'd have to ask him."

"His statement didn't strike you as strange at the time?"

"We're not all forensic psychiatrists, Jane. It was simply something he said. That he hated the place and that he was never going to go back. I'm sure a lot of people think that about prison."

"Not to the point of taking a bullet."

"Well, maybe you'll catch him and prove me wrong," said Voss but he wasn't making a concession. Quite the opposite.

Jane watched as he sipped his champagne. All she could see was his smugness, his belief that his assessment of the situation was correct and allowed for no other interpretation. And such certainty in people always put Jane on guard.

But in case Voss was right, she would warn Ringer of the possibility. For if Kurtza was their killer and intended to go down in a hail of bullets, the police had better be prepared.

When Jane returned to the Homicide Squad, the materials seized from Ela Bey's apartment had been laid out in the muster room and Showbag and some young detectives were examining what they had.

"I need to apologize," said Jane as she entered.

"No, you don't. It wasn't your call." Showbag was taking Ringer's admonishment on the chin. "The boss will calm down—by Christmas."

Jane grinned. "How did Ela take it?"

"Not well. They seldom do. She said there was nothing to find and I think she's right. Bills, tax returns, family correspondence ..."

"Letters from Kurtza?"

"No."

"How well did you look?"

"We didn't rip off the gyprock or dig up the garden."

"Sorry, I didn't mean to criticize. But I expected you to find correspondence with the man she loved. Maybe it's on her computer."

"Nope. The team has already checked."

Jane was stumped. "They've been writing to each other for seven years. She would value every word he sent. The letters must be somewhere. Did you check the ceiling void?"

Showbag looked mildly insulted. He didn't need tips on searching from Jane. "We planted cameras in the apartment. If she goes to some secret hiding place, we'll see it."

Ray Cheung entered with Ela's computer and mobile and handed them to Showbag. "You can return these now. We've copied the files and linked them into our system so we can follow any usage. Have you got your iPad handy?"

Showbag took up his device.

"Open it for me," asked Cheung.

Showbag did so and handed it to Cheung, who typed in a few commands. "Now you can look in on the cameras too— though our people are monitoring 24/7."

"Thanks, Gary," said Showbag as he took a quick tour around Ela's unoccupied apartment. At this time of day, she would be at work.

Jane watched on like the supernumerary she was. So, this is what modern surveillance had become. She certainly hoped it was legal.

Jane went to Ringer's office to pass on Voss's warning that Kurtza would not be taken alive. It didn't come as any surprise: with serial killers, it's standard to presume resistance and prepare for the worst. She was pleased to see Ringer had calmed since the morning's disagreements. He seemed more anxious about something else.

"Caro's refusing to come for weekend access."

"Why's that?"

"She says she's sick of watching cricket."

"Fair enough."

"But she doesn't. She reads her books."

"In order not to watch cricket."

"She always reads her books, even when we go skiing."

"Have you thought of having her on her own?"

Ringer balked. "Who'd take the boys to cricket?"

"Their mother. Or their mother's boyfriend?"

Ringer seemed stumped.

"Do you even know what she likes to do? Apart from reading?"

"I'm a weekend father, Jane. And sometimes not even that."

"Which makes your time with Caroline even more important. Give her one weekend in every three."

"Is that how it works?"

"It doesn't work, Eric. Divorce is a compromise, especially for kids. At least you've come back from Canberra. So now push on to the next level: father and daughter time. Maybe take the boys to cricket, go somewhere with Caro and pick them up when the game is over."

"But they like me being there."

"Are you really that scared of girls?"

"No. Just a bit out of practice."

"Then one week in three. It's my best offer."

"Okay. Then next week's for Caro."

"Well done."

"Though I'm more secure catching villains."

Jane managed a smile and hoped that this one wouldn't be the exception to prove the rule. Or that Eric Ringer wasn't agreeing to spend time with his daughter in order to make an impression. Or that maybe Marino was right: that her boss was "a boy" after all.

———

Everyone was silent as they filed in for the briefing. There were too many jagged edges between the team, too much front-foot aggression, too little generosity for those who had put a foot wrong. It wasn't her place, but Jane felt compelled to speak.

"As resident shrink, there is something I'd like to say before Nita begins. This crime is the hardest I've worked on. I just want you to know that in case those of you younger than me—which is most of you—are feeling particularly confronted. I think that's what he wants. He wants to take us down with him. And we don't know if he's finished or only starting. So, please, if anyone's feeling stressed, please come and see me and talk. And be kind to yourselves and each other, be careful and, most important of all, stay vigilant. Here endeth the reading of *The Book of Jane*, Chapter 12 . . ."

The assembly dissolved into laughter, which in itself was progress.

"Thank you, Jane," said Ringer gratefully. "Okay, Nita, what have you got?"

"We've been looking at evidence of pedophilia, and while we've found disturbing stuff concerning all three victims, there is absolutely no evidence of collusion or a ring. There's no evidence that the victims knew each other or exchanged images on the web.

"I'll start with the most obvious, Michael McGill. His

activities are well documented and at last count there are twenty-seven known victims, twelve of whom gave evidence to the Royal Commission. He has been carefully monitored since being listed as a registered sex offender and has not reoffended.

"Franco Bernero attended a number of sex parties thrown by a developer mate, Bobo Grimaldi. Several underaged girls were present, but there's no evidence Franco was involved. Or even Grimaldi, for that matter. There have been prosecutions but these involved the drug dealer who trafficked the girls.

"Which brings us to Nigel Woods, though the real person of interest here was Andy Palachik, aged twenty-eight. With an MBA from Harvard, this was a young man going places and when the initial charges were laid, Woods threw everything at his defense. Woods seemed to take it personally, seeing the allegations as an attack against his company. But Woods was wrong and Palachik was clearly guilty. He possessed more than forty thousand images of prepubescent girls and boys in sexually suggestive poses and was under investigation for pedophilia with a number of individuals when he broke his bail and disappeared, we think, to Africa, probably with Woods's assistance. Investigations are ongoing. Any questions?"

"Did you talk to the reporter who broke the story?" asked Ringer.

"Yes. And most of his information was correct. Just not the bit about the pedophile ring, that was pure conjecture, really, no more than a question to justify the headline."

"The minister is giving me grief over this. You can come with me when I see him again and rerun the presentation."

"Yes, boss."

"And the press are still stirring the pot even though there's nothing there," observed Ringer.

"Not that that would bother the killer," noted Jane. "If he's made the connection, the connection is there. It doesn't have to be rational."

"I'm not sure I understand what you're saying, Jane."

"If the killer thinks there's a pedophile ring it doesn't matter if that belief is true or false," Jane explained. "It could be a figment of his imagination, but feel real to him."

"Leaving us where, precisely?" Marino asked, sharing Ringer's frustration.

"Hopefully with an open mind. If Kurtza's our man, just don't assume he's thinking like we do. We are dealing with a very sick mind and we don't know enough to rule anything out. Let's keep everything on the whiteboard."

"Including a pedophile ring that doesn't exist?"

"That's your reality, Nita. And almost certainly the truth. But in case the killer thinks differently, we have to allow for the possibility."

"What? And look for possible targets? Where?"

"In fairness, that's not what Jane is saying," said Ringer. "But good work, good presentation. Let's leave the board as it is for now and get out there and catch this prick."

As the team dispersed, Nita Marino gave Jane a look that could have melted her teacup. She had worked hard to get her report together and clearly felt Jane had slighted her efforts. Which was far from the truth but yet another piece of psychological housekeeping that Jane would have to address. She was beginning to feel like a den mother. It didn't help when Ringer nodded at Jane to join him in his office. Coming to Jane's defense as he'd wrapped up the briefing would only feed the rumors that something was going on between them.

As Ringer closed the door behind her, Jane was wishing she had kept her mouth shut.

"Something the matter?"

"I'm tired, Eric. We all are. I was being pedantic about the pedophile ring. I should have let it go."

"Bullshit. And tiredness is no excuse. Nor are Marino's feelings, for that matter. They all need a kick up the arse."

"How hard can you drive them?"

"Wait and see. I've only begun."

He was talking tough but Jane knew he would lead from the front, not from above.

"We're working on tonight. I've ordered pizza. You should join us."

"Thanks, but my books and files are at home. I'll work there and leave you to it."

"Well, the pizza's not from Vue de monde."

Jane had to smile. He was a hard man not to like.

20

Down in the city in the fast-food cluster between La Trobe and Little Collins, the Deliveroo riders were gathering for the early evening rush. One headed into McDonald's to get his order and came back to find his helmet missing. A similar thing happened further along the street, although this time it was a reflective jacket that had disappeared from the back of a bike. Another rider suffered a more serious theft: his thermal backpack.

Tomas Kurtza, dressed in a Deliveroo helmet and reflective jacket with a thermal pack on his back, lolled in the mouth of an alleyway, sucking on a cigarette. Deliveroo riders were everywhere. He only had to choose the right bike. Electric, of course, with decent lights—the traffic out there was crazy. The experienced riders locked their bikes or chained them to a post. But there were others in too much of a hurry to make money and maximize their deliveries and he knew his opportunity would come.

Watching a rider leave his bike under a streetlight beside a bus stop, Kurtza killed his cigarette, waited a beat or two, then casually crossed the road. It was like taking candy from a baby.

Jane arrived home with Thai takeaway and made herself an enormous salad. Romaine lettuce, green apple, parmesan, walnuts, and her own special dressing. At least she was staving off scurvy.

Her books and papers were spread out on the dining table and on the coffee table in the lounge. She mirrored her latest photograph of the muster room whiteboard on her computer and opened a bottle of pinot noir from the rack. Her thoughts already lost in her work, she didn't even look at the label until she'd had her first sip. It was no surprise the Amisfield tasted so good. She'd been saving it for a special occasion. What the hell: if she was going to work, she would spoil herself without apology. She toasted the photograph of Ben on the mantel and remembered better times. They had ended too soon, but there had been some great adventures together. They'd laughed and argued with notable people—and their fair share of ratbags— all around the world.

Jane finished her Thai and salad and sat down to work.

———

Ringer sat down with Cheung and his team to review their surveillance procedures. The computer wasn't coping with so many images. They had to narrow the sample.

"Let's concentrate on the lesser disguises," he suggested. "Like Telecom Man and Beanie Guy. I think we're learning he makes changes all the time, but let's concentrate on the quick-change versions. False noses and the elaborate stuff takes time and he can't do that on the run. Let's assume he's hiding in plain sight. The woman was designed to throw us off the trail, so let's not take the bait."

Feeling superfluous to the computer reprogramming, Showbag grabbed a slice of cold pizza and wandered back to his cubicle. His iPad was on his desk so he took it up to see what Ela Bey was doing. Maybe she was rereading her hidden stash of correspondence from Tomas Kurtza. Wouldn't Jane Halifax be pleased to hear about that?

At first he couldn't orientate himself with the shadowy figure behind the glass or even work out which room the camera was in. They had been placed, as surveillance typically does, in the light-fittings that were already there—on this occasion in the hallway looking east and west toward the front door and bathroom, and in the living room with an ability to look in all directions. Was it the one in the hallway, Showbag asked himself, the one inside the front door? It didn't look like the back door though that camera would explain the frosted glass. Flipping between images, he wished Cheung had labeled the cameras. He scrolled through the sequence until he came back to where he started. The figure pushed at the glass.

Showbag froze as Ela Bey stepped out of the shower. Alone in her house, she had left the bathroom door open and the hall camera was looking at the shower screen and not the back door. Relieved it wasn't an intruder but unable to look away, Showbag watched as she raised her arms and used her towel to dry her hair. He felt like a voyeur although he knew he wasn't. He was a battle-hardened policeman on a high-level investigation tasked with catching a brutal and dangerous criminal. So why did he keep on watching, having established that the risk had passed? Why did he fight the instinct inside him that told him to look away? Is this where perversion begins, by looking at something when you know it's wrong, by watching because it's forbidden? If someone had reported an incident about a deviant and a hidden camera, Showbag would have been the first to make the arrest. Pervert, degenerate, deviate, pedophile— weren't they part of the same continuum? So why did he wait until Ela had dressed for bed and put on her robe before going to another camera and checking all was quiet outside?

He abandoned the thought and switched his focus to the street outside the apartment block. No one was there in the empty street but for a ubiquitous Deliveroo rider, determinedly pedaling his e-bike.

————

When her phone rang, Jane expected it would be Eric Ringer, home alone like her but with a much lesser wine. She was tempted to ask him over to share the Amisfield.

"Hello, Jane, it's Melissa Woods."

"Hello, Mel. How are you going?"

"How do you think? I thought you were going to help me. The articles are getting worse."

"Mel, we don't control the press. We've told them there's no pedophile ring."

"Yet they're running with the story anyway. And trashing my husband's memory."

Jane could tell Melissa was drinking again. Her voice was loquacious and slurred. Suddenly the Amisfield had lost its appeal.

"Mel, are you alone?"

"Oh, yes, I'm alone. About as alone as someone can get. My children want to send me off to a health farm or something. A sanatorium for the widows of pedophiles where they can't embarrass their friends. Trouble is, it's alcohol free. I wouldn't last twenty-four hours."

"Are you on medication?"

"Why?"

"You said you were seeing someone . . ."

"Beverley."

"Yes, Beverley. Has she been giving you something?"

"Only to help me to sleep."

"Which won't work well with alcohol. What's Beverley's name again?" Jane was already on Google looking for likely matches.

"I don't think she's got a second name. She's too alternative for that."

"Beverley Sharif?"

"God, she's not an Arab, Jane. Why do you want to know?"

"I know it's late but I'm happy to make a house call."

"Whatever for?"

"It's no fun to drink alone."

"Yes, it is. No one to tell me off and spoil my combinations."

Now Jane was really concerned. She gave up on Google and messaged Ray Cheung instead.

> Ray, can you get me Melissa
> Woods's daughter's mobile?
> I think her name is Charlotte.

"Do these sleeping tablets have a name, Mel?"

"There's two sorts she's given me. Mr. Green and Mr. Blue. That's the color of the bottle caps. The writing is too small to read."

> Charlotte Woods, married name
> Cockerel?

> Yes—that's her. Can you call her
> and keep her on the line? Say it's
> to do with her mother.

Phoning now.

"I can be there in twenty minutes."

"Where?"

"At your place, if you wanted company."

"It's too late, Jane. You had your chance at Vue de monde and you blew it. You were no fun at all."

Ray. Any luck?

Still trying. She's not picking up.
Should I leave a message?

Yes. Get her to phone me. Say I
am worried about her mother.

Should I send a patrol car?

Yes. But she probably won't let
them in. The place is a bloody
fortress. And send me Charlotte's
number.

"Hello, Mel. Are you still there?"

"Yes, but I need to take a pee."

"Okay, Mel. I'm holding . . ." But Jane was holding on by a thread.

The police computer was scanning more efficiently now with fewer images to target. Ringer was showing a test run to

Marino while Cheung messaged Jane. Showbag joined them with his iPad and a look of concern on his brow.

"I've been checking on Ela Bey. Take a look at this."

The image on Showbag's iPad was focused on the front door of the apartment block. A long cardboard box about 600 by 200 millimeters had been placed by the door so that it leaned against the letterbox for apartment six, Ela's unit.

"It just appeared there in the last few minutes."

Ray Cheung moved to the console and brought up the camera cluster on his larger screens. He zoomed in for a closer look at the package but could see no address or identifying markings.

"What's she doing?" asked Marino, pointing at the camera that covered Ela's balcony from across the railway track. Ela Bey was standing in the doorway. She had opened her dressing gown and unbuttoned her pajama top.

"I'd say she was trying to attract someone's attention," offered Ringer as Cheung focused on the street camera and rolled it back to check who had made the delivery. A Deliveroo rider powered along the street on his e-bike, a long cardboard box protruding from his thermal backpack. As the rider got off his bike and delivered the package, Cheung tried to get a facial match but the rider's helmet and visor prevented the computer from getting a read.

Ringer made a decision. "Nita, seal off the area. Give me a four-block perimeter. We're going in."

As Marino took command and Cheung instructed his computer to track the Deliveroo rider before and after the drop-off, Ringer and the others scrambled.

***

Jane was scrambling too. She had kept Melissa on the phone for as long as she could but Melissa's battery was running low. She'd gone to look for her charger and never phoned back. Jane managed to get through to Charlotte, who, like Jane, was now heading for Toorak as quickly as the traffic laws would allow. A police patrol had got there before them, but no one was answering the intercom.

Jane met the police at the Toorak mansion and tried the intercom herself. Maybe a friendly voice might have more luck. It didn't.

Charlotte's Porsche Cayenne turboed into view as her remote device opened the gates. They had barely parted as she swerved her vehicle in and up the long driveway, Jane and the cops running behind.

Charlotte punched the keyboard and the front door opened. They hurried inside and Charlotte called out to her mother. There was no reply.

Such a big house, so many rooms. Everyone ran in different directions.

Jane was the one who found Melissa, collapsed on the kitchen floor. Suddenly, the burglar alarm went off, its screaming siren making a distressing situation even worse. As Charlotte headed off to stop the alarm, Jane felt for a pulse. There was none. Nor any sign Melissa was breathing. Jane started CPR and shouted at the cops above the cacophony to get an ambulance.

Completing thirty chest compressions, Jane leaned down to give two rescue breaths. Pinching Melissa's nose with her thumb and forefinger, Jane sealed her mouth over the widow's cold blue lips and blew.

Marino radioed Ringer, confirming that her perimeter was secure. A helicopter circled overhead, scouring the streets with its powerful light. Confident no one could leave the area, Ringer sent in his troops, lights and sirens blazing. If Kurtza was there, Ringer wanted him to know, to feel that the noose was tightening.

Attracted by the commotion, Ela Bey came down to the front door along with other tenants. Dressed in her pajamas and robe, though suitably wrapped to the neck, she was confronted by Ringer and Showbag.

"Is Tomas Kurtza with you, Ms. Bey?" asked Ringer.

"No."

"We'll search the building anyway. I just needed to ask the question."

"Why do you think he'd be here?"

Showbag held up the package in his gloved hands. "This has just been delivered. It's addressed to you." He indicated her name and address, written in bold, neat handwriting.

"Would you open it, sergeant?" said Ringer.

Showbag did. Inside was an arrangement of flowers.

Ela gave a sad laugh. "That'd be right," she said. "Violets. The flowers of unrequited love."

"You can have the flowers, Ms. Bey," said Ringer. "But we're taking the packaging. Sergeant, can you get it tested immediately?"

Showbag arranged for the packaging to be rushed to forensics with a "must know now" designation.

"Okay, people. Let's do it."

As the assembled teams started to search the building, Ringer radioed Marino back at base to tell her the search had begun. Marino advised more backup was on the way. The police would door knock and search the entire sector in the hope that Kurtza could be found. The operation would last several hours.

In fairness, the police had come close. They found the abandoned e-bike. And Cheung's computers got a facial match. Kurtza had ridden into the area by e-bike but left by train after running through a barrel drain that led directly to Burnley Station.

It was 2:00 a.m. when Ringer received his "must know now" from forensics, but it only confirmed what he already suspected: that it was Tomas Kurtza's fingerprints on the sticky tape around the flowers he'd delivered to Ela Bey.

The perimeter remained in place for another twelve hours until Ringer was convinced Kurtza had escaped their net, though he had already come to that conclusion.

His mobile rang. It was Jane.

"How did you go?" she asked.

"Close but not close enough. How about you?"

"Melissa Woods has been taken to hospital after being worked on by a critical response team."

"Will she make it?"

Jane sighed. "Probably not."

It hadn't been their night.

21

The following morning, Showbag escorted Ela Bey through to an interview room where Marino was already waiting. The senior sergeant advised Ela of her right to remain silent and of her right to a lawyer, which Ela declined. For someone many would describe as unworldly, Ela appeared remarkably calm and self-possessed. Jane and Ringer were silent as they watched the interview on a closed-circuit screen in Ringer's office. Jane had already told Ringer she disapproved of his tactics, that Ela was a potentially helpful witness, if they could only win her trust. But now he had placed her firmly on the other side. Ringer was unmoved. So many questions needed to be answered, it was difficult to know where to start.

"Do you know the current whereabouts of Tomas Kurtza?" Marino began.

"No, I don't."

"Were you expecting him last night?"

"No."

"You hadn't been in contact?"

"No."

"Are you sure?"

"Check for yourself. You've had my mobile and computer."

"What were you doing on your balcony before the police arrived?"

"Nothing."

"The sliding door was open and you had unbuttoned your pajama top."

"It was hot. I was getting some air."

"Trying to attract someone's attention?"

"Well, obviously I was noticed by the police."

"I put it to you that you were trying to attract someone's attention—in particular Tomas Kurtza."

"Well, I wouldn't have minded if he was watching. But I don't think the police had any right."

"He's a person of interest, Ms. Bey, in connection with three very violent murders."

"A suspect. His involvement is yet to be proved."

"And if he is found guilty and you've assisted him in any way, you could be charged as an accessory. Do you understand that?"

"Yes, I do."

"And the seriousness of such a charge?"

"Yes."

"Have you been assisting him, Ms. Bey?"

"Only in spirit."

"Apart from sending him money from time to time in jail and funding his appeal against the Parole Board, did you provide Kurtza with any other financial support?"

"No."

Showbag continued the questioning, though he took a less direct route. "What about the flowers you received last night? Had Kurtza sent you anything like that before?"

"No."

"No gifts, messages, communication of any kind. Letters?"

"No."

"Though he'd written to you before?"

"Yes, when he was in jail, every week."

"And you to him?"

"Of course."

"An important and, shall we say, intimate exchange of correspondence?"

"Yes."

"Which presumably continued after his release?"

"No."

"You mean a seven-year correspondence suddenly stopped?"

"Yes."

"I find that hard to believe."

"That's your prerogative, sergeant."

"After all that time—not another word?"

"He was in breach of his parole conditions."

"How did you know that? If you weren't in communication?"

"His parole officer told me."

"Maybe eventually. But not the following week."

"I don't understand your point, sergeant."

"You say your correspondence stopped as soon as he was released from jail?"

"Yes."

"And, as you have just agreed, before you had any idea he was in breach of his parole? So why did the correspondence stop?"

For the first time, Ela's answer wasn't immediate. And when it came, there was genuine emotion in her voice.

"Because I was hoping my husband would come and see me."

"But he didn't?"

"No."

"And made no contact—of any kind—until last night, when he sent you flowers?"

"That's correct."

"And you expect us to believe that, Ela?" said Showbag with compassion.

"I don't care whether you believe it or not."

"These letters you exchanged with Kurtza every week for seven years. Fairly significant correspondence, wouldn't you say?"

"Yes."

"And important correspondence for you both. As you said, intimate?"

"I think that was your word, sergeant."

"Do you still have his letters, Ela?"

"No." It was clear she was lying.

"Why not?"

"I destroyed them."

"Why?"

"Because I didn't want anyone to read them. Because they're 'intimate.'"

"Your only real communication with your 'husband' and you didn't keep them?"

Ela Bey was silent.

"Please answer the question, Ms. Bey," said Marino.

"As you pointed out at the beginning of this interview, senior sergeant, I am not obliged to tell you anything. And as far as the letters are concerned, I am exercising that right."

In his office, Ringer was sharing his detectives' frustration. "Do you think she has the letters?"

"Of course," answered Jane.

"Then they must be incriminating. Or why wouldn't she give them up?"

"Oh, I don't think she's protecting Kurtza. She's protecting herself. It's probably all of him she'll ever have."

"Does she know that?"

"On a rational level, probably. But not in her heart."

Back in the interview room, Marino's questioning was becoming more direct.

"When Kurtza was studying, you would undertake research on his behalf?"

"Yes."

"Did you ever access an interior decorator's website that contained a video tour of Nigel and Melissa Woods's house in Toorak?"

"No."

"Did you ever undertake any other internet searches on Kurtza's behalf?"

"No."

"In particular to do with medieval torture or the Catholic Church?"

"No."

Marino slid a document across the desk. "This is a copy of a warrant executed this morning at your place of employment authorizing us to look at the computers there."

"Why did you have to do that?" asked Ela, suddenly distressed.

"So, I'll ask you again, did you ever access an interior decorator's website that contained a video tour of Nigel and Melissa Woods's house in Toorak?"

"No."

"Did you ever undertake any other internet searches on Kurtza's behalf?"

171

"I'll lose my job."

"In particular to do with medieval torture or the Catholic Church?"

"Why are you doing this to me?"

"I'll be honest with you, Ela. We think you know a lot more than you're telling us about Tomas Kurtza, in particular his current whereabouts. Or how to contact him. And possible details relating to his alleged offenses."

"No . . ."

"Ela Bey, you are hereby formally charged with being an accessory to murder, both before and after the fact, and will be presented to a magistrate in the morning to enter a plea. We strongly advise you to seek legal advice and can put you in touch with Legal Aid. The sergeant will escort you downstairs to take your photograph and fingerprints and we will present you or your legal representative with a copy of this recording. Do you have any questions?"

In Ringer's office, Jane was appalled. "You don't have enough to charge her on."

"Yes, we do. If we hadn't intervened last night, what do you think would have happened? That he would have delivered the flowers and left?"

"Isn't that what he did?"

"Initially. But maybe he was going to come back."

"And what? Murder her as well?"

"Then this is for her protection."

"Eric, have you lost the plot?"

"She knew Kurtza was coming."

"How do you know that? Because she was parading herself on the balcony? She probably does that every night."

"You think he went to all that trouble to deliver a bunch of flowers?"

"I wish I knew. And I really wish I could help you." Ringer's question only accentuated Jane's sense of impotence, that for all her investigation of their primary suspect, she still knew so little about Kurtza's motivation and psychology. "I will admit I'm missing something, Eric, but I don't think it's to do with Ela Bey."

"Call it my copper's gut, but she knows more than she's telling us. Maybe this will help change her mind."

"Well, that's one way to get to the truth," said Jane. "Or you could try waterboarding."

She headed out into the general office as Showbag ushered his prisoner toward the stairs. Jane hoped Ela might sense her sympathy for her predicament but it had the opposite effect—Jane looked like one of them, part of a law enforcement system that would put a woman whose only previous brush with authority had been for minor traffic offenses through the mortification of being formally charged as an accessory to three heinous crimes. An act which, despite Ringer's gut, would neither loosen her tongue nor be an experience she would easily forget.

Jane sat in her office, spooling through the surveillance tapes of Ela's house recorded before Kurtza delivered his flowers. Like Showbag, she mistook the figure pushing at the opaque glass door as an intruder trying to force his way in through the back door—until it was revealed it was Ela herself, emerging from the shower. She fast-forwarded through the sequence to allow Ela her privacy. Showbag knocked at the door and entered.

"You wanted to see me?"

"Are these tapes legal?" asked Jane.

"As in authorized by a warrant? Yes."

"Why did we need a camera watching the bathroom?"

"Don't ask me. I didn't put them there," answered Show-bag directly. "Their placement is usually dictated by where the light-fittings are. That's how they're hidden. That one was in the hallway."

"Looking into the bathroom?" asked Jane.

"Only because the bathroom door was open. That was never the intention."

"But you were watching. Wasn't it you who noticed that the flowers had been delivered?"

"Yes."

"You saw Ela displaying herself on the balcony?"

"Yes. And I watched her take her shower."

Jane found his honesty both surprising and revealing. "Did you watch it all the way through?"

Showbag's failure to answer amounted to an admission.

"Can I ask you why?"

"It's a question I've asked myself. Because I could? Because I knew it was wrong? If I'd found someone else doing that, I would have thrown the book at him."

"Well, I'm not going to make a complaint, Showbag. You were authorized to watch and you did. It's not for me to judge."

Jane tried to return to her task. Her complaint, if she had one, was with the person who had placed the cameras.

"But you do, don't you? Judge me. Well, no more than I do myself."

Jane turned to face him. If he wanted to confess, she would listen. At least she owed him that.

"I wonder what my wife would say if she knew? I can tell you, she'd be appalled. Perving on a woman in the shower? Leilani would be disgusted. She's Samoan. We go to church every week."

Jane listened to his confession.

"I pride myself on doing this job by the rules. Avoiding

excessive force. Not verballing people in statements . . . Then I go and do a thing like this and wonder who I am."

"A fallible human being, Showbag. No more, no less. And one decent enough to admit his failings. Believe me, that is rarer than you think. We all of us are made of clay."

Showbag frowned at the reference.

"Sorry, it's mythological."

"So—what are you finding here?" asked Showbag, uncomfortable Jane had returned to the tapes.

"Another decent person. I can't see her involved in any of this. And if Kurtza is our killer, I can't see him involving her either. Even a sadist has his limits."

"If all he was doing was delivering flowers, he took one hell of a risk."

"Yes, he did."

"But why?"

"I worry there's something fatalistic about Tomas Kurtza. Like Voss, the acting teacher, said, this isn't going to end well. And Kurtza knows that. He's putting his house in order."

"By torturing three men to death and sending flowers? It's a funny kind of love."

"I don't think the two things are related. It's called compartmentalization. It's how the sinner carries on."

"So, I'll leave you to it."

And, unburdened by his secular priest, Showbag left, gently closing the door.

Jane sighed. Would her pastoral work ever be done?

————

The Intensive Care Unit at Royal Melbourne was state of the art, with single rooms and glass that went opaque at the flick of a switch to provide privacy for its patients. Jane emerged from the lift on the sixth floor and was directed to the lounge for families near Pod B.

The persistent Maurice Engels nodded a cautious greeting but it was Charlotte who introduced Jane to her siblings. George, her brother from Melissa's first marriage, was two years older than Charlotte, though he didn't look his twenty-eight years. He had a degree in economics but had failed to complete an MBA and had been taken into Nigel Woods and Associates to continue his humiliation at the hands of his adoptive father. The other two children, Emma and Bill, were nineteen and eighteen, hurried into the world in quick succession after Nigel's business had made its first billion dollars. A double-nuclear family as befits the rich: four children, one mother and two fathers, though no one spoke of the first father anymore.

"How's she doing?" she asked.

"Not well," Charlotte said. "She's still on life support. They're concerned about the brain, of course, and quality of life if she survives. I still can't believe she did it, not after what happened to Nigel." All four children were looking at Jane as if she could provide some answers.

"I'm glad the critical response team got there as soon as they did," Jane said, though it had been Jane who had got Melissa breathing again.

Which to Maurice Engels seemed to be of lesser importance than the health of his client companies.

"I trust the cops might back off now, as if they haven't done enough damage already."

Some things never change.

"Anyone want a coffee?" asked George.

"Yes, please," said Jane as the others mumbled their orders.

"I'll come and give you a hand. How are you doing, George?" she asked as they headed to the coffee bar downstairs.

"Poor Mum. I'm not surprised she couldn't take it anymore. After losing my dad the way she did. He died in an office fire in what was supposed to be an act of arson—though they never found what happened. But to have two husbands die so violently. There's only so much you can take."

Jane didn't try to hide her shock. "Oh, George, I'm so sorry. I didn't know."

"Not many people do. We never talk about it as a family. Nigel thought it detracted from him. And of course, the Catholic Church and suicide . . ."

"Is that what they think your father did?"

"I don't know. I was four at the time. But Mum's attempt clearly was. Hopefully we'll be excommunicated."

As they carried the coffees back upstairs, Jane's mind was racing. A young man whose ambivalence about his adoptive parent and the Church was obvious; a matriarch who had been widowed twice in particularly violent circumstances; and an ever-present lawyer whose interest in his clients was all-consuming. Was there a pattern somewhere, a connection she couldn't see? Or was she simply, like Eric Ringer, tired and frustrated and out of ideas as a callous killer continued to roam the city?

———————

Jane powered her bike along Beaconsfield Parade, Ringer in hot pursuit. She needed to get the cobwebs out of her head and so did he. Jane had a better bicycle, Ringer was using one of his sons'.

But he had better strength and fitness, which his

competitive instinct could not suppress. By the time she got to Brighton he was waiting with restorative juices: watermelon, mint, and lime.

"Did you know that Mel's first husband died violently as well? In an office fire, suspected arson, though never proved."

"Meaning what? That she's a serial killer?"

"I don't think she lowered Nigel onto *The House of the Stolen.*"

"But you think she killed her first husband?"

"I'm not saying that either."

"Then what are you saying?"

"That it's unusual for this to happen to someone twice. And why is it that every time I see Melissa Woods, Maurice Engels is there?"

"Because he's an arse-licker? Or is he a serial killer too?"

"Can we take a look at the file on the death of Melissa's first husband?"

"No. We're the Homicide Squad, not the Cold Case Unit. Did I miss lunch for this?"

"I'm sorry. I thought you found the chance of a ride appealing."

"Up to a point. But I've got a real killer to catch. And I don't like being this far away from the office." Ringer radioed Ray Cheung. "Gary, have I got any messages?" he asked as he mounted his bike. "I'll be back in twenty minutes."

"Thanks for the juice," said Jane, feeling a little foolish.

"Thanks for the workout," said Ringer. "Maybe we should make it a regular thing." He smiled at Jane like he usually did, implying a more personal agenda. "And if you want that file, talk to Marino."

As Ringer stood on his pedals to build up speed and head back to the city, Jane stayed for a while to think things through.

Melissa wasn't the suicidal kind. Despite her double tragedy, she had too much to live for: children, grandchildren, not to mention $14 billion. And in the society pages, she was more of a fixture than Nigel had ever been. Popular, feted, the annual Nigel and Melissa Woods Foundation fundraising ball was an essential date with the glitterati. Which is not to say she didn't bruise like other mortals or hadn't suffered tragedy and genuine loss. But people who kill themselves usually do so without having someone else hanging on the other end of a phone for over an hour. And although she didn't have the conviction to say it to Ringer, Jane felt as if Melissa's attempt to kill herself had been an attempt to do something else. An ill-handled distraction to move people's focus elsewhere, not a cry for help as these things often are. A calculated stunt gone wrong.

Jane hated conspiracy theories, so why was she building one of her own involving Melissa Woods?

22

While Victoria Police was throwing its considerable resources behind finding Tomas Kurtza, Jane was taking the long way around. Forensic psychiatry was not a straight path, but a maze with many turns. Ringer had dropped the charges against Ela Bey, but her mug shot and fingerprints were in the system and Jane knew the librarian felt unclean. The library had shown understanding and offered counseling. There is something about people who work with books, something that sets them apart. An unspoken empathy that is almost tactile, like a turning page.

"Hello, Ela."

"I've nothing to say to you."

"I want you to help me find some newspapers. From 1998."

"I'll get someone else to assist you."

"Ela, please. Can we talk?"

Ela listened as Jane explained. How she had been against the charges, yet understood the police's frustration. That she knew how important it was to find Tomas to establish if he was the killer or not, that she understood Ela's conflict. That she knew Ela loved him and didn't want to do anything that might put him in jail.

"But what if there was a better solution for everyone—including Tomas?"

Ela's posture was still resistant, but she was listening.

"These crimes are inexplicable, Ela. They're not committed by a rational person. And if Tomas is involved, he needs help. That it may be in his best interests if he was placed in a facility."

"An asylum for the criminally insane?"

"We don't call it that anymore. The Thomas Embling Centre is a hospital run by people like me."

Jane could see Ela was tempted, but also that she wasn't ready to talk or forgive. Not yet.

"What newspapers do you want?" she said, changing the subject.

"Here. I've written them down." Jane handed over a list.

"You can wait over there."

"Thank you."

Ela disappeared and didn't return.

About ten minutes later a young man came and took Jane to a computer that had been loaded with the material she wanted to see. Jane resisted asking after Ela. She wanted to give her the time and space to come to her.

Jane started to scroll through the headlines: BUSINESSMAN DIES IN TRAGIC FIRE. ARSON SUSPECTED—BUT DEATH WAS ACCIDENTAL. BUSINESSMAN DIES LEAVING MASSIVE DEBTS.

Melissa's first husband was Stewart Vizor, an accountant who was trying to break into the nonbank mortgage sector. Raising money in volatile off-shore markets, his fees were as fat as his margins were thin. His partner handled the marketing, a man by the name of Terry Tressyder, who had a background in selling mobile phones. Tressyder was known for his lavish lifestyle, while Vizor, with a wife and two young children, worked long hours with minimal staff in order to keep things afloat. As the debts grew, Tressyder was constantly overseas, trying to secure fresh funding, leaving Vizor to face the music. As he often did, Vizor was working late at the office when the fire occurred. An accelerant had been spread around the office and his body was found by the fire escape door, which had been illegally locked after a number of minor break-ins. The coroner ruled out suicide and suspected that it had been Vizor's intention to destroy the records and that his death had been accidental. Vizor was thirty-nine at the time of his death, his wife Melissa was thirty-four and their children four and two.

A cold case, Ringer had called it, but it barely qualified. Arson and death by misadventure by a man who was drowning in debt. What was probably more remarkable was the fact Mel had remarried within two years. At that rate, Jane should have settled on Ben's replacement by now, though even the thought seemed absurd.

Jane made some notes, thanked the attendant and asked if Ela Bey was still there.

"I think she's gone home but I'll check if you like?" said the young man.

"That's okay. Just leave this thank-you note on her desk."

She left the library with an empty feeling. Her instincts were letting her down. Jane had joined the case with such high hopes and expectations that she could help, yet her profile of the killer was incomplete, his motivations as impenetrable as his many disguises. It was time to recalibrate and redefine. She could only hope that Ringer was having more luck.

Back at the police center, she slipped into the briefing and sat at the back of room. Despite near-misses and failures, the police had no trouble maintaining their focus. Why was Jane struggling to hold on to hers?

There was a spring in Cheung's voice as he began his CCTV presentation.

"Since we've dispensed with the more exotic disguises, we are getting more consistent readings. Before he stole the various elements of his Deliveroo garb, we traced him coming out of Melbourne Central Station, wearing a version of Beanie Man again."

"That's encouraging," said Ringer. "He's running out of ideas."

"Yes and no. After the incident in Richmond, we traced him from Burnley to Flinders Street wearing sunnies and a face mask. He had dressed himself in leathers, which he had in his thermal backpack, giving the impression he might have a motorbike somewhere. But at Flinders Street he changed trains for Footscray, which is where we lost him again. If he left the station at Footscray, which we suspect he did, then he was in a new disguise."

"So, are we making progress or not?" asked Marino.

"Yes, we are. Here are our conclusions. He likes to use public transport, especially trains and trams. He likes to change disguises, but generally keeps them simple. Sunglasses, facemasks, false beards and facial hair. A hijab as part of a female disguise. But he transitions into a new disguise one element at a time. There's no phone-booth moment unless he's doing something exotic. Like the woman, or Cyrano, which is what we've dubbed his big nose disguise from Voss's DVD. But whether by accident or design, the slow change tends to trick the computer scanning the CCTV. Facial recognition depends on memory to a large degree, certain assumptions and algorithms. And the bias is definitely white and male. So, if he darkens his face, he is virtually invisible. Up until now, because I've programmed for that possibility. But our most important breakthrough has come from our geographers. While his disguises are random, his pattern of travel is becoming predictable. And despite the exceptions given above, one thing is emerging as a constant: he almost always leaves and returns via Footscray."

Ringer pondered the situation for a moment and made a decision. "Nita, let's devote resources to Footscray Station. Undercover and surveillance with uniformed units in support."

"Yes, boss," she said, consulting her chart and circling the elements she would deploy.

"And if you need more bodies, ask me."

"Yes, boss."

"Well done, Ray." Ringer looked at his team. They needed a win.

"Let's go and catch this bastard."

———

Jane invited Ringer across the road for a drink at the Zanzibar.

"I should apologize. I guess you could have done without the bike ride?"

"No, I loved it. Cleared the head and saved me the calories of a Showbag burger run."

"So, how did the weekend go?"

"I'm sorry?"

"Wasn't this one to be with your daughter?"

"Had to cancel. The life of a cop. More important things to do."

Jane gave him a look.

"You don't think so, do you?"

"No. You ignore family life at your peril."

"Spoken like a veteran."

"You bet. I'd swap places with you tomorrow to have a Caroline in my life."

"What's brought this on?"

"Spending time at the hospital with Melissa Woods's children and mourning the ones I never had."

"What about Zoe?"

"Not mine. Adopted. Step."

"Are you seeing someone about this?"

"Used to. But what's the point? Got involved with a man who had a child and didn't want any more. And because I loved him, and valued what I thought was my freedom, I capitulated. I will love her as much as my own, I said, and she will love me back. And we were probably ninety percent there. But however loving and generous and well-meaning we were, it never came close to the bond she had with her father. Or even with her mother—who put out a contract to have her father killed. Can you imagine that? You would think that would be the end. But it wasn't. Blood is thicker than daughter. How I envied that. The ability to be appalling and be forgiven. So don't cock things up with Caroline, Eric. Treat her like the gift she is."

"I don't know where to start."

"One day at a time. With no cancellations. Or you'll end up with a bag of regrets that you'll pour out over a gin and tonic to someone who doesn't want to hear."

Jane downed her drink and left to pay the tab.

She turned and waved before heading off, leaving Ringer with his empty glass. She wanted to stay but didn't trust herself, not in a cozy bar like this.

How do you find the right partner in life? How many goes do you get? Why, in the midst of this terrible case, was she even thinking she and Ringer might have a future? A future with this imperfect, incomplete, irresistible man who needed so much help with his daughter? And why, despite everything she'd said to herself, did she like it when he paid her attention?

Jane wasn't coping. She missed Ben every day. She didn't know how to continue without him. She hated everything about her single life, about how easy it was to feel superior and give others advice without the daily checks and reckonings of an intimate companion?

Jane was happy to warn others about the stress this case was taking. Did she think she was immune? Time, she thought, to stop lecturing others and heed her own advice.

23

Melissa Woods had had a remarkable recovery. No longer in ICU, she had been moved to a private room for observation. Apart from a sensitivity to light, she had few other physical symptoms, but her doctors wanted to make sure her mental well-being was being addressed. She was pleased to see Jane though self-conscious about her circumstances.

"I guess I should thank you for saving my life," she managed, unfamiliar with being in anyone's debt.

"I'm relieved we got there in time," said Jane.

"I have a favor to ask, as if you haven't done enough already. They want me to see a counselor but I don't like the ones they're offering. I'm wondering if you would take me on?"

"I don't really have private patients," said Jane, off-balanced by being asked. "And more importantly, I'm conflicted. I'm working with the police on your husband's death."

"Well, tell them you're not anymore. Whatever they're paying, I'll double it."

Jane frowned an apology. "I'm sorry, it's not about money."

"I need someone who understands what I've been through, and you have suffered in much the same way. Maybe worse—your partner was beside you when it happened. And I think you and I could be friends."

"You don't need to be friends with your counselor, Mel. In fact, it could be a disadvantage."

"You're one of the few people, Jane, who doesn't treat me like someone from outer space. You seem to understand the burden of being a billionaire. That with great wealth comes great responsibility. Which is why we set up the foundation. Of course, people like to say it's all about avoiding tax, but we preferred to see it as benevolence without government interference, that we can multiply the value without the bureaucratic burden."

If she only knew how far away from hers Jane's politics really were . . . Jane had made her position clear and there was no need to repeat it. But she was happy to let Melissa do the talking.

"The sensible thing to do would have been to cash it all in at fifty and enjoy the bounty of our labors. Establish a wing of a hospital or something and spend the rest of our lives having fun. Learn how to keep bees or make cheese or something. Nigel would have been happy making wine. Then none of this would have happened." Melissa Woods came as close to crying as she had managed since her husband's funeral.

"I had a nice talk to George," said Jane, changing the subject. "He told me about his father's death. That must have been very hard."

"For heaven's sake, he was four at the time, he barely knew him."

"Hard on you, I mean."

"It was a different life. I don't think about it anymore. And neither should George. Nigel's the only father he and Charlotte ever had."

"Do you think it was an accident?"

Melissa stiffened. Jane was stepping on forbidden ground.

"Stewart had the great misfortune to have an embezzler as a partner," Melissa said. "He fleeced the business then disappeared, destroying the records in a fire that killed my husband."

"Do you think your husband was murdered?"

"No. I think it was accidental. Stew often worked late and slept over at the office. I don't think his partner knew he was there."

"Is that what the police concluded at the time?"

"Can we talk about something else?"

Jane was content to let it go for now. The police file would confirm the truth.

"What did you do before you were married?"

"What on earth has that got to do with anything? Hardly a feminist friendly question, but I get the implication. If you must know, I was a receptionist and bookkeeper, totally untrained, but a very good one. Happy?"

Jane had touched a raw nerve. Was Melissa sensitive about her lack of tertiary education, or her past with a husband whose business had been a disaster? Or was it simply not in keeping for the former wife of a former rich lister—now a rich lister herself—to be reminded of her origins?

"Mel, as I said, I can't take you on as a client, but I'm more than happy to recommend someone else."

"No, thank you," said the billionairess. "I must ask you to leave. I need to rest."

Summarily dismissed, Jane departed, once again intrigued by Melissa Woods, absorbed by the motivations of a woman who had traveled from nowhere to the very top of Melbourne society. Fortuitous or deliberate, the woman's motives remained impenetrable. But maybe that goes with the territory, maybe vast wealth becomes a barrier normal people can't breach.

Or maybe Melissa needed more help than anyone, still traumatized by the horrifying circumstances of her husband's murder and her forlorn attempt to end her life. Jane resolved to put her prejudices aside and keep out a weather eye.

————

As the team assembled for the daily briefing, Nita Marino handed Jane a large, untidy file. It was the police file on the death of Melissa Woods's first husband, Stewart Vizor.

"I warn you, it's totally out of order. Looks like somebody's dropped it."

"Thanks, Nita, I'm sure I'll find the bits I want."

Ringer entered and called the meeting to order.

"Everything in place at Footscray, Nita?"

"Yes, boss."

"I meant to ask—why can't we trace Kurtza's movements using his Myki card? You can't use public transport these days without tapping on and tapping off."

Everyone turned to Ray Cheung for the answer.

"It is possible to get a card anonymously from a vending machine. As long as you don't register the card, it's not linked to your identity. Of course, you're not protected if you lose it or it's stolen."

"The dead hand of the civil libertarians strikes again," said Ringer, unable to let the moment pass. "Mustn't compromise personal freedoms."

"A right we'll fight for as long as we can," said Jane, unafraid to be the odd one out.

"Anyone got anything positive to offer?" added Ringer, eager to get his leaders back into the field.

"I might have," Jane said. "Though it's just a theory."

"Fire away."

"I think the evidence is building that if Kurtza is our killer—he's not working alone."

Jane suddenly had everyone's attention.

"In repetitive crimes of this nature there is usually some aspect of ritual. The criminal wants to leave his signature, some proof of ownership. It is also usual to declare his motive in some way, to reveal his purpose even if his purpose is only to shock. I have always sensed some greater purpose or message behind these crimes, but the killer's failure to leave any sign or symbol can mean one of two things. Either this is sadism, pure and simple—let's call that the Showbag Theory—or he's committing these crimes on someone else's behalf."

"As a hired killer, you mean?" said Marino, trying to understand.

"Possibly. The absence of any link between the killer's victims rules out personal animus. So maybe that lies with someone else."

"Where do we look for that?" asked Showbag.

"First, by accepting it as a possibility and looking at the evidence from that point of view. To see if there's someone else who links the victims. To see that person as the principal and the killer as the actor."

"I like Showbag's theory better," said Ringer.

"Thank you, boss," said Showbag, happy to take the credit.

"Don't think I'm ruling that out," said Jane.

"So where do we find this other person?" asked Marino.

"If it's Kurtza—then other prisoners he might have had links with. That's where I would start. The planning of these crimes is so meticulous, it probably began when he was still in jail."

"Thank you, Jane. We'll give it some thought. But whether you're right or you're wrong, the best way to stop this bastard is to catch him. Correct?"

"Of course."

"So, let's get out there and do it. Let's go."

Jane and Ringer remained as the others dispersed.

"I hope that wasn't a hand grenade," said Jane.

"No, we should consider all possibilities," conceded Ringer.

"You're putting a lot of faith in Footscray."

"Yes, I am. But one thing we do know is he hasn't left the area. Not yet."

"You're due for a break in your fortunes, Eric."

"Yes. We both are." As usual, his look seemed to imply things beyond the investigation.

"Good luck."

"Yeah. Thanks."

"I'll go water my theories."

24

A fat man on a small motorbike is bound to turn heads. But motorists only laughed and looked no closer as Kurtza, wearing his latest disguise, rode a Honda monkey bike over the Westgate Bridge. Convincing the seller he was a serious buyer who needed to take it for a spin, he had left his mobile phone to show his bona fides. It would be forty-eight hours before the owner, with police assistance, recovered the motorcycle, abandoned in an alleyway in the city. The mobile Kurtza had left as security had been stolen too.

Discarding his fat suit to reveal the dirty clothes he wore underneath, Kurtza used the motorbike's rearview mirror and a cardboard stencil to apply a large red-wine birthmark to cover almost a third of his face. With some additional grime to conceal any imperfections and verify his homelessness, Kurtza headed along William Street. He made no attempt to disguise his eyes with tinted glasses or colored lenses; no one looks a homeless man in the face, it's too confronting. Or worse, he might ask for money. He was as safe from being noticed as if he wasn't there.

Kurtza took up a position across the street from Ravi Patel's chambers, sitting on the pavement with a sign selling ballpoint pens. No one bothered to buy one, preferring to show their munificence by tossing the odd coin in his hat. But he wasn't there to sell stationery or beg for money. He was there to count heads.

It wasn't the first time he'd been there. He had been watching the building on and off for a week, variously disguised as a street sweeper, parking inspector and someone collecting for UNICEF. The busiest times were before and after court and around the lunch break. The barristers were always back in their chambers by 4:10 p.m. to see a stream of clients or prepare for the following day. Patel's associate, Celeste, arrived at 7:00 a.m., never went out for lunch and left promptly at 3:30 p.m. Patel also arrived at 7:00 a.m. via the carpark, before heading to court at 9:20 a.m. He typically worked late at night, was frequently still in his office at 8:00 p.m. before pampering himself and his waistline at one of the city's better eateries. Sunday was his day off.

Of course Ravi Patel had no idea he was being watched—or why. And the police were focused on Footscray. No one expected the next attack to be in the heart of the city's judicial precinct, with police ferrying criminals back and forth and buildings bristling with security guards and sophisticated equipment.

The police might expect Kurtza knew not to reuse his old disguises, but of course he didn't. His change of heart on this day was simply dumb luck. He was getting bored and felt like a change.

Now, as the police computer churned its way through the city's CCTV, Kurtza's matches had dwindled to zero.

———

Ravi Patel wasn't the only one working late. Ringer and his team were assessing the operation around the Footscray

Railway Station and the fact the computer wasn't coming up with matches. They had rightly concluded that Kurtza was changing disguises, but with the monkey bike still another day from being discovered, they did not yet know he was operating in the city.

Jane popped her head though the muster-room door as she was leaving. "Should I be part of this?"

"No thanks, Jane," said Ringer. "We know you don't like pizza with the lot."

"What have you got against margherita?" asked Jane.

"She a low-down cheating moll."

As always, Showbag's deadpan response reduced everyone to laughter.

"Okay, team, let's keep it together," said Ringer. "I do not want to be here all night."

As Jane's car emerged from the carpark, the glass towers of the city mirrored the setting sun. She lowered her window; it was good to be outside. The Homicide Squad offices were, as they should be, focused and intense, but the fresh air was liberating, reminding Jane that life went on beyond the world of Tomas Kurtza.

Her mobile rang.

"Hello, Jane. It's Ela Bey. I'm sorry to phone you like this, but I've decided to show you some letters."

Jane wanted to shout out her delight as focus and intensity came crashing back. Instead, she kept her response subdued.

"Ela, that's great. When can we meet? I could swing by on my way home?"

Building relationships. It's as important in psychiatry as it is in police work. It's about earning trust. As Jane drove to Richmond, she wondered what had happened to change Ela's mind.

She even wondered if she was walking into a trap. She

hadn't informed anyone of where she was going. Had she been a cop, they would have drummed her out of the service. No one in the force operates alone for very sound reasons and it was specious of Jane to think she wasn't bound by such rules. She was part of a homicide investigation, she knew the procedures and the dangers of going solo. But she didn't pick up her phone, she pressed on.

Jane buzzed Ela's intercom, heard the lock disengage and pushed in through the door. Was her enthusiasm to get the letters about to place herself in danger? Had she taken the bait? Who else was waiting inside?

Ela opened the door. She had changed from the clothes she had worn to work into a pale gray shift. She'd been crying.

"Ela, are you okay?"

"Yes, I'm fine. Just been reading my letters again. Memories are better left in the past."

Jane noticed a small pile of handwritten letters on the dining room table and couldn't wait to read them. But Ela's tears were unsettling and reinforced the possibility she wasn't alone, that her crying had not been caused by the letters at all.

"Is there someone else here, Ela?" Jane asked, taking the risk of seeming foolish.

"No. Why do you ask me that?"

Jane flinched as a noise came from the kitchen.

"It's all right. It's only the cat coming in through the flap in the back door. I'll feed her and make some coffee. Those are the letters on the table."

As Ela left, Jane quickly texted Ringer.

At Ela's reading letters. Will report.

At least they would know where she was.

Jane sat down at the table, put on her specs and took up the first letter.

Sunday, 15 April 2018
Dearest Ela,

I have written a new play and Cayden has sent me some notes. He says I get lost in my subject and forget the stagecraft, but it's all a learning process. It's a love story about a man in jail on the last day of his life inspired by The Last Day of a Condemned Man by Victor Hugo. At least I know I'll get out one day, but it's good to review your life against a known end date—even if it's only a fictional one. The play is about letting go of the things he can't control, accepting that regrets are futile, accepting he will never see the woman he loves and that she will never see him, except in a wooden box at his funeral. I have taken what looks like a wasted life and tried to give it purpose. He sees injustice everywhere and is overwhelmed by the need to avenge it, even though he knows it's wrong. His imaginary cellmate is God—or is it the devil? Or are they both reflections of him? Are we all in prison cells of our own creation, insignificant, without power, utterly alone?

But it's only a play. I don't feel alone with your letters to keep me company at night, to know there's someone out there who cares, who writes to me with the same intimacy as I write back to her (within the limits of the bloody censor!!!). My letters start out as erotic fantasies but end up like something my grandmother would have written. If you only knew my vulgar heart . . .

Ela returned with the coffee.

"Can I take these with me?" asked Jane.

"No."

"I could photograph them," said Jane, taking up her mobile phone.

"I am letting you read them. That's enough."

The truth was that Jane wanted to analyze them closely. *Letting go of the things you can't control* and *injustice everywhere . . . and the need to avenge it* had her mind racing already and she was only on the first letter.

"I don't want to waste your time while I sit here and read them, Ela."

"You're not wasting my time. I want to know what you make of them, Jane. If you are reading the words of a callous killer."

Instant analysis and feedback. Ela was no better than the police.

"Do you mind if I take notes?"

"If you have to."

"Is this all you have?"

"I know you think you're different," said Ela, "but you do sound like a cop sometimes. And if you send them back with a warrant, those letters won't be here. I'll burn them before that happens. You're making me wish I hadn't agreed to this."

"You want to know what I make of these, Ela, and I don't want to make mistakes."

"Then take your notes. And take your time."

Jane continued to read the letters, logging key phrases in the notebook she had taken from her bag. By the time she'd finished, she had been there for almost an hour.

"Moment of truth," exclaimed Ela, like someone secure

in the letters' lack of incrimination. She had clearly selected them with care.

"He writes very well," said Jane, genuinely impressed. "What made you decide to show me?"

"So you could see he can't possibly be the person who's doing these terrible things. To show you it must be someone else. Does a callous sadist write letters like that or send his wife flowers? Or do you think that's another form of torture?"

"I'd like to read more of these, Ela."

"No."

"They could help."

"Help put him away?"

"Help us—and you—understand."

"He's not psychotic, Jane. He's as sane as you or me. I think someone has stolen his identity, a former prisoner. I think he is being framed."

Jane looked at Ela, deeply conflicted. On the one hand, the suggestion was close to her theory that Kurtza was not acting alone. But there was nothing in this selection of letters that verified that. This was a man with many demons, though he tried to distance them from himself by attributing them to the characters in his plays. A man who was angry with the world, whose sense of frustration and bleak assessments allowed for no light or purpose, a man whose heroes harbored deep resentments that were ultimately cruel, if only aimed at themselves. Even in love letters Jane could see the suppressed sadism Kurtza tried so hard to hide. But what was she going to tell Ela? Would she betray this woman who had finally found love through her letters? Was it her role to take that away? Jane was working with the police and Ela was sitting on a cache of correspondence. What if those letters could help the police find the killer and stop him before the violence that drove him exploded again?

"Ela. We just want this to stop. Whether it's Tomas or someone pretending to be Tomas, we need to examine every possibility. There's nothing incriminating in these letters but there's nothing that helps us either. The sooner this stops, the better for everyone, most of all Tomas."

"Tell me about the Thomas Embling Centre?"

"It's a hospital, Ela. A psychiatric hospital where people with mental health issues are cared for and treated."

"At Her Majesty's pleasure."

"It's not a prison."

"You think he's mad?"

"I can't tell from reading a few letters and I have never had the chance to assess him. But I suspect Tomas is punishing himself for something, possibly his original offense. That he struggles to move beyond something that happened a long time ago under circumstances we don't understand."

"Which manifests itself in unspeakable tortures?"

"Maybe he is torturing himself."

Ela's tears returned. She clearly loved this man deeply.

"In case Tomas does make contact—" started Jane.

"That's not going to happen."

"He sent you flowers."

But Ela shook her head.

"In case Tomas does make contact, I want you to think about what we might be able to do to help. That's all."

"And do people ever get out of these places?"

"Yes, they do. Her Majesty is known for her compassion."

25

Ravi Patel was working late and feeling hungry. He had almost finished dictating his closing address to the jury on a case that would conclude the following day. Celeste would type it up when she came in at 7:00 a.m. Patel liked the way the address was going and phoned his favorite restaurant to put in his order before the kitchen closed. He would be there in half an hour.

"Ladies and gentlemen, if you take only one overarching thought with you to the jury room, let it be this: Why would my client risk everything for nothing? His wife, his family, his reputation, his standing in the community, his business, his fortune—for nothing? He wasn't on medication. He wasn't taking drugs. He didn't drink any more than the rest of us . . ."

Patel thought better of the last sentence and told Celeste to strike it out before continuing.

"He didn't have a mistress or a secret life or a gambling addiction or social-suicidal impulses. So why would he risk everything—everything that he had in the world—for nothing? For vanity? For ego? For hubris? None of it makes any sense. Nor has the other side advanced any reason . . ."

In the street below, Tomas Kurtza entered the building

carrying a mop and a green plastic bucket filled with cleaning products. A crooked scar ran down his cheek below his left eye, which was covered with an eye patch. He followed some other cleaners in and, feigning to reach for his security pass in his pocket, spilled his cleaning materials on the floor. While some of the cleaners helped him gather his things, someone else swiped the elevator access pad and Kurtza indicated the floor he wanted. It was so simple, he had to laugh his gratitude and, as the lift doors closed, had everyone else laughing too. What a klutz.

When Kurtza walked into the outer office of Patel's chambers and snibbed the lock, Ravi Patel wasn't pleased. The cleaning company knew they were never to clean while he was there.

"I'm still working. Come back in an hour," he called, expecting the intruder to scamper away.

Instead, Kurtza entered Patel's office and locked the door behind him.

"Hello, Mr. Patel."

Patel could not conceal his shock. "Tomas . . . is that you? What in the hell are you doing here?"

Kurtza removed his eye patch and carefully peeled off his latex scar. Cold fear crawled up Patel's skin like rising damp.

"I need some advice."

"Well, I can't do it now. I need to be somewhere else. Maybe if I make a call . . ."

Kurtza's eyes followed Patel's as they moved to his mobile on the desk. Kurtza picked up a small marble bust of former Chief Justice Owen Dixon and smashed it down on the phone.

"I need your undivided attention, Ravi. I may not have much time. With CCTV and artificial intelligence as it is these days, you never know how long you've got. Can I see your life line?"

"My what?"

"It's the line on your palm that runs up from the middle, below your line of fate. Are you right- or left-handed?"

"You have to leave!" Patel was immobilized with dread.

"Right-handed, as I remember. So, show me."

The barrister was struggling to breathe, terror welling at the back of his throat. Desperate to placate his visitor, he extended his right hand. Kurtza took it tenderly and placed it, palm upward, on the desk. Then, taking up the marble bust again, he brought it down on the lawyer's hand with as much force as he could muster.

Patel howled in agony. It was music to Kurtza's ears.

"You don't need that hand anymore, Ravi. The dominant hand is to do with the past and the present. Let's look at the left one to see what the future holds."

Kurtza was now holding Patel's left wrist in his powerful grip. Only the pain from his shattered right hand was keeping his victim conscious.

"You probably know what I've been up to. So, I want you to tell me, as quickly as you can, what possible defenses do I have?"

Patel was crying.

"Come on. There can't be that many. And please don't tell me the obvious."

"Your only hope . . . is you plead insanity."

"I asked you not to tell me that." Kurtza took up a scimitar-shaped letter opener with an elaborately carved handle and brought it down with such force it pinned Patel's left hand to the desk.

The barrister slumped to his knees and whimpered for help. But help wouldn't come.

"Tell me about noninsane automatism, Ravi? There must

be some mileage in that. Or a fugue state: that's a doozy. There's got to be plenty of angles there." Kurtza wheeled Patel's chair in behind him. "Take the weight off your feet—which I might do next—though I need some kind of agenda or we'll be all over the place.

"Head, shoulders, knees and toes, knees and toes.

"Head, shoulders, knees and toes, knees and toes.

"And eyes and ears and lips and nose . . . We'll get to them all in the end."

Kurtza took out a small pair of bolt cutters from his jacket and proceeded to remove the toe caps of the lawyer's patent leather shoes. "I think these would be better as sandals, don't you? No, no need to take them off, Ravi. Your tootsies are as soft as butter."

All Kurtza's crimes had been unspeakable: Nigel Woods's slow death on his Judas cradle; the excruciating dislocation of Franco Bernero's limbs on the ladder; the primitive disembowelment of the fallen priest, Michael McGill, on something as benign as a hose reel.

Ravi Patel's suffering wasn't greater than theirs—nor the trauma the police officers suffered in having to attend the crime scenes—but for one appalling factor: the entire obscenity was recorded on Ravi Patel's Dictaphone, which Jane and the police would have to listen to again and again.

Kurtza's guilt was at last beyond question.

26

A polypropylene tensioning tool had been used to bind Ravi Patel to his chair at the knees. Similar bands of green pallet strapping had been placed around his shoulders and chest. A coil of the strapping, which had a breaking strain of 500 kilograms, had been taped inside the bottom of Kurtza's plastic bucket so it didn't spill out when he staged his "accident" in the foyer. The tape remained in the bucket for the police to see. The tensioning tool and a set of 350 mm bolt cutters had been discarded beside Patel's desk. The police would learn that both items had been stolen from Franco Bernero's factory.

It was difficult for the detectives to determine the order in which the various stages of the torture had been completed, even with the aid of the audio recording. But the strappings had been tensioned to the point where Ravi's knees and shoulders had been dislocated. Without the autopsy, the effect of the tensioning bands around his chest were more difficult to assess but the last one had probably caused his asphyxiation. The mutilation of the eyes, ears, and nose had been carried out by both tools together with the letter opener, which suggested a degree of spontaneity. But in general, the punishment came under the crushing and ripping category of Nicholas Mandel's

History of Medieval Torture. The professor would no doubt acknowledge that, this time, despite the modern variation, the killer had done his homework.

As repulsive as the physical evidence was, it was the audio on the barrister's Dictaphone that most of the officers found too disturbing to take. Cheung was the first to leave, closely followed by Marino. Ringer made it clear that no one was obliged to listen, and in the end, it was only he and Jane who had the stomach to stay. That both had the facility to look beyond the horror was testament to their ability as investigators to put some distance between the crime and their emotions.

The recording came to an end and Jane looked at the notes she had written.

"Do you want to hear it again?" asked Ringer.

"No, not straight away." Jane wasn't as unaffected as she appeared.

"So, what do you think?"

"He's manic, elevated, possibly rattled. He's talking to his victim but looking for justification. I doubt he's done that before."

"How do you know?"

"I don't. But this is a victim he knew. And he seems to have wanted Patel's approval. For him to accept some blame in taking so long in getting Kurtz's case to court. But more than that, this time he's reckless. There are witnesses to his arrival and evidence left at the crime scene he was meticulous about removing before."

"Meaning?"

"I think he's entered his endgame, though one only known to him. As I've said, I've been missing something, the thing that links the first three victims together. And I think the recording confirms it: that there is someone else; that Kurtza has not been acting alone."

"An accomplice?"

"Maybe even a principal."

"What makes you think there's someone else?"

"On the recording, Kurtza mentions 'we' more than once."

"A figure of speech?"

"Possibly . . ."

"Will it make Kurtza easier to catch?"

"I don't know. But it broadens our approach."

"Or makes the job twice as hard." Ringer wasn't enjoying the theory as much as Jane. "As I've said before . . ."

"You just want to catch the bastard. Then I can analyze him as much as I like."

"Something like that. Unless you can tell me where to look."

"A former inmate—"

"We've done that. Former prisoners with links to any of the three victims. Crooks with links to organized crime who could have approached Kurtza to carry out a contract. Like-minded sadists, close friends and associates, anyone inside he could have hatched a conspiracy with. And we came up with nothing. The man was a loner who kept to himself."

Jane had to admit that her theory was largely speculative, that it filled in gaps in her profile of Kurtza that had previously been unexplained, such as his lack of any contact or interest in the Catholic Church. But what Ringer needed was evidence.

"I've got a briefing to go to. I'll leave you to your theories." Ringer headed for the muster room, his mind already on other things.

Jane wasn't offended by his abruptness. Cops want results not explanations. They leave that to the experts and the courts. Jane looked at the Dictaphone, confronted by what it contained. Then, taking her mobile and setting it to record, she started the device to live through the horror again.

———————

Following Patel's murder, Kurtza had once again been traced to Footscray only to "disappear" the moment he left the station. Ringer had decided to commit all their resources to the suburb and called for reinforcements from area command. Marino was beginning to doubt the decision. She preferred her units to remain nimble and mobile. Apart from Nigel Woods, all the murders had occurred in the city and that's where she thought they should stay. But once the decision was made, she marshaled her forces and put Ringer's plan into action.

The operation worked on a number of levels, both uniformed and undercover. Ringer wanted Kurtza to know they were looking, but to be distracted by what was obvious. He reasoned that if Kurtza focused on the increased police numbers, he might think all he had to do was avoid them. It was the undercover police who had the real task of detection, to look for reactions to the patrolling officers, to look for evidence that Kurtza was as cocky as ever about his ability to avoid detection.

Ray Cheung briefed the detectives at the local station.

"His favorite game is to confuse CCTV. Computers can be fooled in a number of ways—sometimes as easily as pinning a photo of someone else's face to your T-shirt. Makeup and face paint works as well. It's about breaking up the image. Facial tattoos, scars, birthmarks. Covid has been a disaster for facial recognition. Put on some sunnies and a face mask and you virtually disappear. The good old Aussie hat with corks,

Red Nose Day noses, a workman with safety glasses or an oxyacetylene mask. And look for umbrellas—they are very good blockers. Or a shirt or any fabric printed with multiple faces, which can send a computer into meltdown.

"We know he has some favorite disguises and generally likes dressing down. Homeless men, workers, cleaners, parking inspectors. He hasn't once put on a suit and tie. But don't rule it out. That might be next. And don't think he's playing a game here. This perp is as bad as anyone we've ever encountered, a sadist whose murders are excessively cruel, a crook who's laughing at us behind his knife. A murderer who's killed at least four times and has nothing to lose. So good luck. And stay safe."

Ringer checked in with Marino at her temporary command post. Plain-clothes officers had visited boarding houses and shelters for the homeless. They had searched derelict buildings and culverts where someone might camp out or hide. They were patrolling the railway station and the Footscray markets and the banks of the Maribyrnong River. And they were following in the wash of the uniformed patrols to detect anyone paying unusual attention. It was laborious, repetitive policework, but it had to be done.

———

Showbag had established a crime scene around the stolen monkey bike in an alley behind the law courts and was now on his way to Williamstown to interview the owner.

"He seemed too big for the bike," explained the collector of classic motorcycles. "Like he was going for some kind of comic effect." The owner insisted the buyer didn't look anything like Kurtza's mugshot. "His nose was really big and his eyes quite small. And his teeth crooked and yellow. No, that's not the guy at all."

Though Showbag knew the man was wrong, he didn't argue. Fatman was just another disguise with a false nose and false teeth to add to Kurtza's ever-expanding gallery.

"Oh, there was something else. I think he was peeing himself when he left."

"Peeing himself?"

"Literally. It was running down his legs."

Showbag didn't explain that either. When they had found the fat suit, it had water bags inside to add to the costume's authenticity. In his quest for a trembling obesity, Kurtza had obviously sprung a leak.

If the recording of the barrister's torment hadn't been so present in Showbag's mind, he might have found it amusing.

———

It was late when Jane got home. Her apartment was beginning to look like an extension of her office at the Homicide Squad: there was a whiteboard on an easel that mimicked the one in the muster room and she had taped various diagrams and photos to the windows. Books and papers lay everywhere. The dining room table was spread with the various elements of the Stewart Vizor file, which Jane had been putting back in order while reading its principal reports.

Everything pointed to a tragic accident after Vizor's partner, Terry Tressyder, had set fire to the premises to destroy the evidence of his embezzlement, not realizing that Vizor was asleep in his office. For a moment, Jane pondered if there could be any link between Melissa Woods's first husband and Tomas Kurtza. Or between Kurtza and the fugitive, Tressyder, believed to be in hiding somewhere in South America. But the notion was implausible. Jane was beginning to believe her own conspiracy theories and desperately needed some sleep.

Instead, she poured a glass of Sarah Crowe's exquisite 2019 Yarra Yering pinot noir and settled down to listen, for the third time, to the sickening audio of Ravi Patel's torture. Despite the glory of the pinot noir, Jane would need a very powerful sleeping tablet to keep her nightmares at bay tonight.

I need a defense, I need a way out. I'm not responsible for everything I do. Nature or nurture or something else: lack of a nurturing nature? Don't squeal, Ravi. There's no one here. The other cleaners on this floor have already come and gone and I canceled yours. I said I was phoning on Celeste's behalf and they took me at my word.

Patel pleaded for his life, but the relentless ratchet of the tensioning tool made his words hard to decipher. Kurtza kept adding bands to his knees and shoulders, each one tighter than the last.

The shoulders are designed to carry loads—not for bending forward like this. It will be interesting to see when they snap. Think of it as an experiment, Ravi, like Habeas Corpus versus the Parole Board. Like your vanity versus my life. Do you realize what that cost me? I could have been a contender. We will never forgive you for that. Whoops, did I hear something crack? Here we go!

Jane fast-forwarded though the lawyer's pitiless cries.

And eyes and ears and lips and nose. But we're getting ahead of ourselves. Let me add another band to your chest. It needs to be tighter to help your breathing—or not. Oh, Ravi, your advice was not the advice I wanted, not the advice I need from you now. I need a get-out-of-jail card, Ravi, a magic wand, to make the pain go away. We trusted you, we believed what you said. We never thought it would take even longer than saying what they wanted to hear. And shame on you, Ravi, you wasted my poor Ela's money.

Oh, stop it, Ravi, you are such a wuss. Knees can be reconstructed, shoulders too, but not life-changing opportunities. You only get one of those. So it's right that you suffer some pain for your indiscretions. And the good thing about agony is it passes. Unlike fifteen years of incarceration for the most important years of your life.

I think this tensioning device is clever, don't you, with its cutter when you reverse the handle. Sorry, did that hurt? Clumsy, clumsy, in trouble with Mumsy, as if she ever gave a shit . . . Was that your girlfriend you were screwing on the carpet last night? I can't see your wife doing that. I was doing a recce to check the lay of the land and got the lay of the year instead. What an arse! I'm so glad you put her on top.

Jane clicked off the recording and topped up her glass. Then, as if she was seeing it for the very first time, she looked around her apartment and let out an audible gasp. It didn't look like a version of her office at all, it looked like the home of a crazy person, someone obsessed with work to the exclusion of everything else. This would never have happened when Ben was alive, her work would never have invaded her home life, at least not in such a tangible form. So why was it happening now she was single? Did she have nothing else but her work?

Grabbing her wheelie bag from the bedroom, she packed everything inside: the books, the papers, the files—everything. She took down the photos and diagrams and cleaned away the marks the tape had left on the glass. The whiteboard was consigned to the laundry and the artwork that usually sat on the easel returned to its rightful place. How could things have got like this without her realizing what she was doing? This wasn't the behavior of someone who worked too hard, this was someone losing perspective, someone in danger of losing herself in the case.

Jane put the wheelie bag by the door. She would take it with her in the morning. She crossed to sit in the big chair by the window and looked out at the city. She felt safe up here, remote from the teeming streets and the cruelty of Kurtza's crimes. This was her sanctuary, the place she had moved to in order to heal, the place where the second bedroom was set up for Zoe, if she ever came back from New York; her difficult stepdaughter, the only family she had.

"So come on, Ben. You're the wise one. What am I going to do now?"

You know what to do. You don't need advice from me.

"But I do. I need you to tell me to leave my work at the office."

You've already told yourself that.

"I don't like being alone anymore. I'm not a solitary person. I don't know what single people do. I'm not designed to live like this."

You're missing me, Jane. You're missing me in your life and in your bed. You're missing the warmth of my naked body and the comfort of holding me close.

Jane had to smile. She was putting words in his mouth. But that's what you do when you talk to someone who's suddenly gone, someone you thought would always be there. Mad people talk to themselves but grieving people converse with ghosts. And drink wine twice the price they would normally drink because now they're drinking for two but need to contain consumption.

"I love you, Ben."

I know you do.

"What will become of me?"

You'll find someone new. Younger, cleverer, someone who likes to sail boats.

"But I don't like sailing. I don't like how they lean over. I like something with a motor and an even keel."

Yachts are better for the environment. And you need to learn a new skill.

"Why?"

To help you forget me.

"I'll never do that."

I know. I'm irreplaceable.

Jane was lonely but she didn't pity herself. She pitied Ben for a life cut short. She pitied Zoe for the loss of her father. She even pitied Zoe's mother, for all her transgressions, whose tenuous bonds of motherhood were now even further distanced by being incarcerated for twenty years. Twenty years! The same sentence Kurtza had received—and what had it done to him?

Daughters and fathers, daughters and mothers—for Jane, everything came back to that. It would have been so much easier if John Halifax had simply aged and retired and become a normal old man with bad hearing and a dodgy prostate. He would have become more fallible that way, less of a peerless advocate with such high expectations of his only daughter. Why had he checked out before his time? Was he sick, in love with another woman, leading a double life? Or was he simply depressed and covering it brilliantly, no one he felt he could talk to, no closest friend, no community beyond his profession? Jane knew enough about depression to know it was the most plausible explanation.

And why had Jane's mother returned to New Zealand to be with her sisters instead of remaining near her daughter? She said it was her yearning for the landscapes of her youth, for the majesty of the Central Otago mountains and their gold, arid pastures and the cozy warmth of their holiday house at Lake Hawea. "I am going there to end my days playing tennis and golf and to laugh and drink with friends around an open fire. You can come and visit any time you like." But Jane only went once a year, for her mother's birthday. Like anything else, you have to work at family. Jane was in no position to criticize Zoe.

Since Ben had died, Jane had discovered how much time relationships demand. That it was possible to have too much time on your hands, to become too reflective, too self-absorbed.

And here she was talking to ghosts.

Maybe the time was right to find someone and risk everything on a relationship once again.

27

The torture killer now had a name. His photo was all over the papers as the police appealed to the public for help. Cayden Voss sat in Ringer's office, insisting on police protection. Gone was the self-assurance of the nascent author. Now all Jane could see was his fear.

"I need twenty-four-hour protection, Inspector. He has obviously become unhinged. His victims are no longer political targets, now he's turning on people he knows."

"Political targets?" queried Ringer.

"Or whatever they are. This vendetta against the Church."

"So why do you think he's changed?" asked Jane.

"You're asking me?" Voss was almost shouting. "You people haven't got a clue, have you? You can't catch him, you've no idea where he is. I'm in danger. I need to be in witness protection."

"I'm not sure you're a witness at this point of time. Why do you think he'll come after you?" asked Ringer.

"Because I let him down as well. I'm sure he went after his lawyer because he took too long to get him parole. And he'll come after me because I failed to set up the film we were going to make, the film that would make him famous."

"Is that enough of a reason?" asked Jane.

"It is when it's all you've got."

"You'll need to explain," Ringer said.

"It was a low-budget thing but even low budgets are hard to raise. He'd written the lead for himself, I was going to direct. Does it matter? Can't you offer me temporary relocation?"

"We have been keeping you under surveillance, Mr. Voss. You haven't been unprotected."

Jane looked at Ringer. This was news to her. He returned the glance as if she didn't need to know, as if it was like their surveillance of Ela Bey—maybe supported by a warrant; maybe not, strictly speaking, legal.

Jane tried to lessen the heat in the room. Voss was entitled to be scared. A lot of people were. "He went to Patel for advice, to see what his options were. That doesn't mean he'll come after you."

"Dr. Halifax, your assurances are no protection. Have you seen what he does to people?"

"Unfortunately."

"So why won't he do it to me?"

"I'll have a word with the Witness Security Unit. And increase our surveillance measures," said Ringer.

"Can you supply me with a gun?"

"No, sir, we can't do that. Do you know how to use one?"

"You point it and pull the trigger, don't you?" said Voss with rising agitation.

"You can get a license and buy a gun. But I strongly suggest you learn how to use it first."

"He's going to kill me next!" Voss was almost in tears.

"Do you know something we don't?" asked Ringer.

"Yes. I know Tomas Kurtza."

———

Jane knocked on the open door of Marino's office. She was returning the file on Stewart Vizor.

"It's now back together, in proper order. If you ask me, someone threw it at the wall in frustration."

"What makes you say that?" asked Marino.

"A man dies in suspicious circumstances, the coroner feels inclined to leave an open verdict but doesn't—and the police do basically zilch. Everyone agrees the fire was arson and there are two obvious suspects. Vizor's partner, Terry Tressyder, who wanted to conceal his embezzlement. Or Vizor himself, who was also trying to destroy the records and could have died by misadventure. Most of the file is about proving the dead man's identity—ultimately by looking at his dental records—but no one raises the possibility he was murdered."

"I thought they concluded the arson was committed by Tressyder who didn't know Vizor was asleep in his office?" said Marino, recalling what she could remember of the file.

"Which is one hell of an assumption. There's no evidence that was the case, apart from a statement from Melissa Woods—then Melissa Vizor—that her husband often worked back late and 'liked to kip on the couch.'"

"Are you saying Melissa's first husband was murdered as well?"

"It's a possibility. And if it's true, then that's suspicious. I will concede one murdered husband is bad luck. I belong to that club myself. But two? I'd like to know the odds on that."

"Melissa Woods killed both her husbands?"

"No. I'm not saying that. What I'm saying is it's possible that both of Melissa's husbands were murdered. No more, no less."

"Have you run this past the boss?"

"He doesn't want theories. He wants Tomas Kurtza."

"Yeah, well, I'm with him on that one."

"Could you get me another file? Pretty please?"

"I'm guessing the boss said something like 'we're not the Cold Case Unit'?"

"You got it."

"Hit me. I've got nothing much on." Marino's irony had a personal as well as a professional edge.

"Can you get me the file on Terry Tressyder? I'd like to know how hard they tried to find him. How much effort they made to track him down, if Interpol was involved, if they actually sought extradition."

"Which will help us catch our killer, yes?"

"Yes. No. Perhaps. Maybe."

"I bet you give Ringer the shits."

Jane contorted a smile; there was a reason she was asking Marino instead of Ringer.

"I might fancy the Cold Case Unit after this," mused Marino. "No more bloody crime scenes."

"Thank you, Nita. I'll buy you a drink."

"Careful. I might put something in it. And don't think I'm joking. Never underestimate a woman with no one to go home to."

———

Showbag sat in a coffee bar near the Footscray Railway Station, watching the passing foot traffic. Someone in a koala suit was raising money for Animal Welfare. It probably wasn't Tomas Kurtza, but how would you know? Showbag considered asking the bear to show his ID or remove his head. What better way to stay hidden while raising some cash on the side?

Showbag finished his coffee and headed across the road to make a donation.

"Can I trouble you for a receipt?"

"Only if you use a credit card," said the bear, offering to hand back the cash.

"Nah. Keep it," said Showbag, content the koala sounded too young to be Kurtza.

Two constables walked past on patrol, guns and tasers prominent on their belts. Showbag stood and watched for a moment, not the cops, but everyone else, mentally logging reactions. Most people paid no attention: a few greeted them with half-hearted nods, pleased their suburb, which had had its fair share of trouble, had a stronger police presence at last. As the constables disappeared around the corner, Showbag followed, maintaining his distance while keeping an eye out for unusual behavior. He knew the likelihood of seeing Kurtza was remote to nonexistent, like those coincidences you only see in the movies. But he also knew it wasn't impossible. They weren't called plods for nothing.

The constables stopped for a homeless woman who was high on something and needed to talk. The brain cells that hadn't been fried were struggling to make sense, but the police showed her respect and patience.

Across the road, a man emerged from an alleyway and pulled back into the shadows. It was as if he'd forgotten something and had turned on his heel to go back. Then he reemerged to peer around the corner, as if assessing what the police were asking the junkie. Maybe he was her dealer? Maybe he wasn't?

As the man disappeared, Showbag followed. The man was the same height, bulk, and age as Tomas Kurtza and his beard didn't match his hair. Showbag had read somewhere that Christian Bale had dark hair and a ginger beard, although he couldn't recall the explanation. Genetics, he seemed to remember.

This was madness. Showbag was clutching at straws. Plenty of people are wary of the police, especially law breakers, but was this the law breaker they wanted?

The man ducked into an empty lot and slipped up and over a fence. Showbag followed with a grunt and a little less grace. Weren't there younger officers to do this? And weren't police officers, on their own and at imminent disadvantage, supposed to call for backup?

Showbag was a cop who did most things by the book. And he knew Standing Operating Procedures 1.01: Deviate at your peril. If you follow the system, the system protects you. It's designed by wise men and women to keep police officers safe, not to mention the public at large. How hard would it have been to make a call or send a text?

By now the man knew he was being followed. He quickened his pace and Showbag quickened his too. He was gaining but tiring. If he took out his phone, he'd lose him. The man knew the area, Showbag didn't.

Turning into Shelley Street, the man suddenly wheeled and turned to confront him.

Showbag held up his badge and took out his gun. "Police. Hold your hands in the air where I can see them."

The man gave a smirk and opened his hands to show they were empty.

"Hold them up!"

The man slowly raised his arms. Showbag came closer. The man's unkempt hair was black with streaks of gray, but it was the edges of the ginger, almost red, beard that gave him away. It seemed to stand proud on his face, as if it wasn't connected, as if it was false. Holding his Smith & Wesson in his right hand, Showbag grabbed the man's beard with his left hand and pulled as hard as he could.

The man pitched forward, sprawling on his hands and knees.

"Fucking bloody hell," cried the man as he inspected the grazes on his hands and a rip to the knee of his trousers. "What in the hell was that for?"

"Face down, roll over, put your hands behind your back," demanded Showbag. He cuffed the man's wrists and took the wallet from his back pocket to check his ID. "What's your name?"

"Robert Polk."

"Address?"

"2/27 Station Street."

"Occupation?"

"Invalid pensioner."

With a sinking heart, Showbag confirmed the information was correct. "Okay, you can stand up, Robert." He removed the cuffs. "So, tell me, why did you run when you saw me?"

"It's pension day. I thought you were going to mug me."

In a world of trouble, Showbag went into reparation mode as, from his mural above them, the Furniture King, Franco Cozzo, arms outstretched, gave them his blessing. Some antiseptic cream from a chemist for Robert's hands, new jeans—better than he had ever owned "in his entire life"— and a slap-up meal at the Viet Hot Pot & BBQ and Showbag had made a new friend.

Robert had washed and dyed his beard the night before. It had fluffed up more than he wanted but it was better red than the blue it was before. Well, according to his mates at the community center it was. He knew why the cops were in the area. He had seen Kurtza's photo in the papers and hoped Showbag would catch him soon. And as he pointed out, the detective was also the same height, bulk, and age as the wanted man and had given him quite a fright.

"It's one thing to be mugged, quite another to have your guts made into garters."

"Okay, Robert, I'd better get moving. Anything else I can do?"

"Yeah. I'd love to see a movie."

Showbag didn't have the time but gave Robert some money—more than enough with his pensioner discount—and sent him on his way.

Showbag's shift had ended hours ago, but he wouldn't be claiming overtime. Some days you take your losses on the chin.

As he headed back to his car, he gave the koala another donation.

"Thank you," said a female voice, a new volunteer inside the costume. "Have a nice day?"

"Doin' my best," said Showbag. "Doin' my best."

28

A notice on the door of Stages In Acting announced that classes had been suspended until further notice and advised students to consult the website. Jane phoned Cayden Voss to tell him she was at the door and he headed down to let her in. With bars on the windows and heavy steel doors that dated back to its warehouse origins, the building was already a fortress.

Voss led Jane upstairs to his apartment. It had been erected in the roof space and was long and narrow with windows at either end. The far end contained his bedroom and bathroom, the rest an open lounge and kitchen with a long dining table and eight Gothic chairs, suggesting a man who liked to cook and entertain.

The apartment housed Voss's valuable collection of memorabilia from the Grand Guignol, the famed theater of the "Great Puppet" that operated in the Paris Pigalle district from the late 1890s until the early 1960s. The posters were collector's items and Voss couldn't resist taking Jane on a tour. A form of naturalistic sensation popular in Elizabethan times—even Shakespeare paid tribute to the style in Titus Andronicus—Grand Guignol was at its height between the two World Wars before falling out of favor.

"How are you?" asked Jane.

"Terrified."

"You didn't think of going away for a while?"

"Like where? At least I feel safe in here."

Jane didn't share what she was thinking: that if Kurtza did get in, Voss could find himself trapped in a building from which there was no easy escape. A fortress can quickly become a vault. But he was stressed enough as it was.

Voss suggested tea and put on the kettle.

"Did you know Kurtza's wife?" asked Jane.

"Which one? There were so many."

"Ela Bey."

"Oh, the one who claimed to have married him? We met briefly at the court case. I was appearing as a character witness and she was paying the bills."

"Did you sense any antagonism then? Between Kurtza and his barrister?"

"He hadn't let him down at that point."

"But how did he let him down? Didn't he get him paroled?"

"Yes, but too late for the film we were going to make. He missed the funding event and it was all downhill from there."

"And that's why you think he was murdered?"

Anguish contorted Voss's face. "It's complicated. I hope that's why he killed him, because he blamed everything on Patel. But if he knew the truth, he would've killed me. I'm the reason the film wasn't made. And I'm terrified, Jane, that he either knows this or is about to find out."

A piercing scream came from the kitchen as the kettle boiled. Jane settled her nerves as Voss withdrew to make the tea.

They sat at the big table and Voss explained.

"My mother had bought an old church in the country

which she was going to convert into a holiday house, but like most things in our dysfunctional family, plans rarely come to fruition. So, I made it our hero set and spent a fortune fitting it out. The idea was to hold a lavish function there for potential investors so they could see what we were going to do. Everyone of any significance was invited: bankers, investors, all the film bodies. But nobody came. Apart from my students, who enjoyed the party of the year for free. That was the reason the film wasn't made—no one was remotely interested. I was meant to contribute to the court case fees but had spent all of my money on the set. That's it over there."

Jane crossed to look at the scale model on a side table. It was like the models architects make to show clients and future buyers their intentions. Intricate, professional, with a removable roof and obviously expensive. The church had been redressed as Satan's church, with the Grand Guignol as inspiration. There was a human sacrifice on the altar, a guillotine decorated with the heads of recent victims, maidens in imminent threat of violation, and priests being stretched on the wheel.

"What kind of film were you making?"

"Modern horror with a Gothic twist, tongue in cheek, of course."

"A splatter movie?"

"A date movie, Jane. Keep up with the times."

"Written by Tomas?"

"And starring Tomas. It was going to announce him to the industry."

"Can I read the script?"

"No. I haven't got one anymore."

"But weren't you the director?"

"And producer. But I burned everything in that potbelly

over there, along with the budgets and schedules and marketing campaign. I couldn't stand being confronted by my failure anymore. If that model hadn't cost five thousand dollars, I would have burned it as well, but it seems to go with my collection."

"There must be something on your computer . . ."

"I wiped the files. Same reason."

Which was suspicious. Jane had been around cops long enough to know that you can never really wipe anything from a computer and made a mental note to suggest Ringer get a warrant. She even wondered, given his penchant for working outside regulations, if Ringer had hacked Voss's computer already. Jane was looking for a possible collaborator in Kurtza's killings, an accomplice, someone covered by Kurtza's use of the royal "we" on his barrister's Dictaphone. Voss's fear was palpable, but was it the terror of a man in genuine fear of his life—or something more?

As Jane excused herself to use the bathroom, Voss got up to remove the teacups. With a jarring clatter, a handgun hit the ground and skidded past Jane on the polished floorboards. Shock jostled with panic as she tried to make sense of the moment. Was this a deliberate act, a warning—or worse, a failed attempt on her life?

Jane stared at the weapon, unable to move, wanting to believe it was a prop from Voss's collection. But it wasn't.

Slowly, she turned to confront her host, now standing directly behind her.

"Sorry. Slipped from my belt. Still getting used to the bloody thing."

Jane reached down and picked up the Glock 17AG4. "Is it loaded?"

"Yes."

"Is the safety lock on?"

"It doesn't have a safety. They told me a safety would slow me down."

"Did they teach you how to use it?"

"I fired twenty rounds at their range. That was enough for me. It frightened me to death."

"The trouble with inexperience and firearms, Cayden, is that accidents happen. Or worse—the weapon can be used against you."

Jane removed the loaded magazine, checked the breach was empty and handed the magazine and the weapon back to Voss. "Just keep it like that till I leave, okay? Firearms make me nervous."

Voss took the weapon and the magazine. Tears were welling in his eyes, but the acting teacher wasn't acting. Jane could see this was real. A man in genuine fear of his life, someone who knew Tomas Kurtza as well as anyone and seemed convinced he would be his next victim.

―――――

It was a perfect day in Melbourne. Port Phillip Bay wallowed in the sun, the air tempered by a cooling breeze. A small tender picked Jane up at the St. Kilda Pier and ferried her out to a 40-meter yacht. The luxury vessel with five staterooms and accommodation for a crew of six seemed an unlikely place for a meeting but that's where George Woods had stipulated and his reasons soon became clear.

"Why did my mother and Maurice Engels tell me not to meet you?"

"I've no idea," said Jane. "Did they offer a reason?"

"They said the police can't be trusted. That you say you're

looking for one thing while all the while you're looking for something else."

"Then that's all right. I'm not a cop."

"But you work for them."

"To help them catch the man who murdered your father."

"Stepfather."

"Didn't Nigel adopt you? I thought you'd taken his name."

"I took my mother's name when she remarried. At six, I didn't have a lot of say in the matter."

George seemed relaxed and at ease on the boat. He wore dark blue shorts and a white short-sleeved shirt printed with tiny anchors. His feet were bare and he wriggled his toes to celebrate their liberation from the business suits and shoes he normally wore to work. He had the air of a privileged scion who was skipping out on expectations and loving every moment. The crew and caterers were his age or younger and you could sense his secrets were safe with them.

As Jane took a canapé, George explained he wasn't drinking. "I have to go back to the office this afternoon. But you can have anything you like."

Jane asked for sparkling water, eager to provide him with no advantage.

"So, fire away. I'm intrigued."

"Do you have a theory? As to why your stepfather was murdered?"

"No."

"Or who might have done it?"

"Wasn't it this Kurtza fellow?"

"Yes. But he may not have been working alone. And once you consider that possibility, other things emerge. Like someone else with the motive, but not the capacity. Like a principal who was using Tomas Kurtza to do his or her bidding."

"Her?"

"I was being politically correct. I have no one in mind. Do you?"

"I thought it was some religious fanatic with a beef against the Church."

"And it might be. Can you think of anyone who might answer that description?"

"No. Apart from me. I hate the institution."

"How much do you know about your father's death? Stewart Vizor, I mean."

"Hardly anything."

"Or his business partner, who supposedly committed the arson?"

"I couldn't even tell you his name. That part of our lives was canceled, Jane. My mother found it untidy. I know she loves me and my sister but as far as she is concerned her first marriage was a mistake that never happened. And our father was Nigel Woods."

"How important is wealth and power to your mother?"

"It's the air she breathes."

"And now she has even more."

"Are you suggesting my mother had Nigel killed?"

"No. I'm not suggesting anything. Just running the possibilities."

"I'd like to see you put that to my mother," said George with a grin.

Jane was surprised how far she was pushing her theories, even more by the fact that George hadn't pitched her over the side of the boat.

"My mother loved Nigel, as we all did. If anything, he was the calming influence. He wasn't a Papal Knight for nothing. He was hard in business but outside that, an utterly decent man. And I miss him. So will Mum."

"And the possibility of Kurtza having an accomplice brings no one to mind?"

"I'm sorry. No."

"How well do you know the business?"

"As the executive 'office boy,' I know almost everything."

"So, if threats were made, you'd know about them?"

"Yes."

"So why has the company—and Maurice Engels in particular—been so unhelpful?"

"Because it's in their nature, Jane. The rich start with an assumption that everyone's against them. It was worse in the beginning when it looked like Nigel was the only victim but somehow the other murders have made things easier to bear."

"Maurice Engels seems worried we're going to find something else."

"Like tax avoidance and foreign entities and spurious political donations? You probably will. But if you try and pursue those off the back of a murder investigation, I think you'll find our friends are bigger bullies than yours."

It was said with such ease. George Woods mightn't have liked a lot of things about the Catholic Church or his family and the way they wielded influence, but he saw the power that came with money as part of the natural order.

"We're used to being suspected of everything from anti-competitive behavior to running drugs. How else could I afford a boat like this? Why else would I need one except to outrun Customs? I don't have many friends, Jane, and most of them are here on this boat. But we don't sell illicit drugs, we buy them like everyone else on the open market. It's called capitalism and I applaud it."

Was Jane looking at the new face of power? The children of the mega-rich on ten-million-dollar yachts, wagging work with their friends while the rest of the world struggled to make a buck?

"So, what's your prediction? About Nigel Woods and Associates?"

"That Mum will double the business in less than ten years. And that Maurice Engels will become stepdaddy number two. In which case I will take my share, bail out, and sail off into the sunset."

"I thought Maurice Engels was married?"

"To a dormouse, Jane, with no libido. It won't survive the summer."

As the tender returned Jane to the pier, her mind was in overdrive. With the hubris of an Elon Musk, who was probably his poster boy, George Woods, while ostensibly telling Jane nothing, had established the following:

1. The Woods did have secrets to hide but;
2. Felt utterly protected by high-placed friends;
3. Melissa Woods was no society maven, running some benign charitable foundation—she knew as much about the business as her deceased husband;
4. She was probably having an affair with Maurice Engels.
5. George Woods, despite his easy way, was as sharp as a stiletto and was not going to answer anything directly— especially about people he thought may or may not be in league with Tomas Kurtza.
6. That the Woods were ruthless and capable of anything.
7. That the last point needed repeating: The Woods were ruthless and capable of anything, which were the same words Cayden Voss had used to describe Tomas Kurtza.

The House of the Stolen seemed to represent everything:

the masterwork of an aging sculptor, destined for public display but snatched instead by a private collector to enhance his own endowment. A sculpture that became an instrument of torture, diabolical yet somehow inspired. A sculpture which could have been gifted to a major gallery—with stringent conditions it not be displayed for fifty or a hundred years—but which instead was callously destroyed by the victim's widow.

Though she was no closer to putting a name to Kurtza's accomplice, Jane was convinced more than ever that he had one.

29

Ringer was late for dinner but he had a good excuse. "I had to take Caro to swimming lessons. It was great. You have to get into the pool as well and help with the drills. And I was the only dad."

"I'm sure the mothers all said nice things about your body."

"Only with their eyes." He handed Jane a bottle of champagne and pecked her on her cheek, his chlorine tang and tousled hair betraying his shower had been perfunctory.

"So how was your day with the hideously rich?"

"Caviar, scallops, and lime-infused mineral water. You won't be getting that tonight."

"I didn't come for the water," said Ringer, popping the cork of the Moët & Chandon and pouring two generous glasses.

"The next generation of Woods is more charming and probably twice as deadly. They give the impression they can do what they like—and they probably can. Shall we go out on the terrace?"

At least Jane had made her own canapés: smoked eel and white anchovies on Danish black bread, which went perfectly with Ringer's champagne.

"And how was your day at the rockface?"

"I've put a lot of eggs in one basket with this Footscray operation. I've got Neuter looking a query every time I make a decision."

"I didn't know Showbag's nicknames traveled that far up the chain?"

"I live in fear of calling her that to her face."

"You know what he calls you?"

"Ding dong. It's pretty harmless. Unless he means my . . . ding dong."

Jane smiled to herself. Was he only getting it now?

"Why does he call me Campbells?"

"As in the soup?"

Jane didn't understand.

"A hearty meal."

"I'll take him to the Human Rights Commission," said Jane with a grin.

"He means it as a compliment."

"It isn't."

They sipped their champagne and looked out at the city where the lights would stay on all night as if the Loy Yang Power Station didn't burn coal anymore and the Glasgow Accord had their backs.

"I wonder what Kurtza's doing right now?"

Jane assumed Ringer was thinking the same thing.

"Do you ever give yourself a break?"

"Not very often. At least you went swimming with Caro?"

"Only to keep you off my case."

"I am hoping that's a joke," said Jane.

"Up to a point. You can stay on my case all you like."

With his larrikin charm and easy smile, it was hard to know when he was joking.

Jane regretted bringing up the killer's name. This was a

chance to escape things at work, a chance to pretend they led ordinary lives, a chance to decompress and talk about normal things, whatever normal things were. But there were three of them there: Ringer, Jane, and Kurtza—and Jane didn't know how to make it just two.

"Did you tell anyone at work I was coming to dinner?" Ringer asked.

"No. Did you?"

"Not that it matters. They think we're doing it anyway. Waste of a bloody good rumor if you want my opinion."

Was he thinking what she was thinking, could he read her mind, were his thoughts as unhidden as hers?

Jane watched Ringer loll in the half-light, his long limbs extended, his shirt two buttons open when one button would have done.

He watched the bubbles rise in his glass and savored the taste. "Mmm, salt like the sea. I don't usually drink champagne. You're bringing out my classy side." He beamed his dimpled smile and kicked off his shoes and wriggled his toes like George Woods had done.

Jane wished she could shed her skin so easily.

"So, what are your plans when this is over?" Ringer asked.

"Go to New York and see Zoe. What about you?"

"Christmas with the kids at Torquay. The ex's family have a beach house down there. She and her boyfriend take the first two weeks, I get the rest. Seems to work. I'm going to teach Caro to surf."

"Are you trying to impress me?"

"You bet."

"What happened to your marriage?" asked Jane, slipping into dangerous waters as easily as she sipped her champagne.

"My fault entirely."

"Another woman?"

"Worse. Unbridled ambition. A year in Sweden studying Command and Communications. Four months in New Zealand on Restorative Justice. Then the promotion to the Feds."

"Leaving your ex to bring up the kids. Did she have a career?"

"Yes. She taught Early Childhood Development."

"Which made bringing up the kids sound right up her alley."

"Got it in one."

"Well at least you're trying now."

"And what are you looking for, Jane?"

"I wish I knew. I won't be alone forever."

"Maybe, when this is over . . ."

"Eric, you're not the problem. I am. If we were together, I'd be tremendous for Caro—like a favorite sister."

"What's wrong with that?"

"I'd be doing what you should be doing. What you're starting to do by taking her surfing. And I'm happy to advise from the wings . . ."

"But?"

"I've got my own life to get together. Repair things with Zoe. She's been with me for most of her life."

Ringer scrutinized her with his smile.

"What are you after, Eric? Emergency Sex?"

"What . . ."

"It's a very good book by three friends who worked for the UN in Cambodia and Somalia in the 1990s and sought relief from the hell they were in."

"Sounds perfectly human to me."

"Which is probably what we did twenty-three years ago."

"When we didn't overthink things out of existence."

"Probably."

"So, what does that make us now?"

"Wiser. More cautious."

"And ever-so-slightly dull?"

"Okay. Here's the deal. You want sex and I want sex. And we seem to be in a war zone. So my best offer is this: a one-off ES, never to be repeated or mentioned again, followed by dinner, laughter, absolutely no advice on children—and a total absence of expectations from this day on."

"Deal."

"So take it for what it is, Eric, and don't be greedy. And don't call me Campbells or you're going home." She led him through to the bedroom where they undressed each other and fell into bed as easily as they had two decades before. Back then she had told him to keep his eyes open or he was only making love with himself. This time there were no instructions. No rush. No inhibition. No meaningless conversation.

Jane hadn't made love with anyone since Ben. She didn't think she would be able. She thought she would be confused by a body that wasn't his, that she'd be all at sea without the subtext of seventeen years. She thought she would cry for what she had lost, that Ben's memory would be overwhelming, that she'd call it off before it began and hand in her resignation the following day.

But the magical powers of ES protected them both as they swam to the moon and back. And Jane didn't care what Eric was thinking: for the first time in two long and painful years she was claiming part of herself back again.

The Footscray operation was on the verge of being abandoned. In the days since Patel's murder, the computer had not come up with a single match from CCTV footage. The troops on the ground, both plain-clothed and uniformed, had found no trace of Kurtza and detectives posing as railway employees were convinced he was no longer using the station.

"I think an obvious police presence was a good idea at the time, but it hasn't flushed him out," said Marino. "So why don't we pull the uniforms and leave everyone else in place?"

"I agree," said Showbag. "If he's gone to ground, it could encourage him to come out."

"I think he's left the area," said Cheung with the certainty of a man who only put his faith in computers.

"Jane, you said before that he's entered his endgame. Could you tell us what you mean by that?" asked Ringer.

It was a theory Jane had only shared with him but he was right to get her to explain it to everyone else.

"The first three murders had a lot of things in common. They were meticulously planned and executed. And there were no witnesses. With the fourth—the murder of Ravi Patel—he was reckless. He let witnesses see him before and after the event. He left fingerprints and other evidence behind, which he had never done before. That can be interpreted a number of ways. He no longer cares, he thinks the game is up, or the fourth murder was an afterthought—an add-on beyond his original purpose."

"Which was what?" asked Marino.

"His glorification of the medieval," said Jane without conviction.

"You also believe it's possible he's not working alone?" added Ringer.

"As you know, we have been unable to find any links between

Kurtza and the first three victims. Or indeed any links between the victims and each other. But there will be connections, there always are. So a possible explanation is that the links lie elsewhere, with someone else, and that Kurtza was acting as an accomplice or hired killer in the execution of someone else's agenda."

"And what evidence do we have of that?" said Cheung.

"To date, absolutely none."

"Or he's just a sadist who doesn't need an agenda beyond his own twisted gratification," said Showbag.

"Which is also possible," conceded Jane.

"So what do we do?" asked Marino in exasperation.

"Withdraw the uniformed troops and leave everything else in place for forty-eight hours. Then we'll regroup and review."

Ringer's decision was clear and unequivocal but it didn't lift the mood in the room. They knew who the murderer was and had tracked him to the area from which he was operating. They had established a gallery of his known disguises and the computer had, up until recently, successfully tracked him—albeit after the event. They were watching known associates closely, especially Cayden Voss and Ela Bey. They had failed to penetrate the walls of the Woods citadel, but Franco Bernero's and Michael McGill's worlds were open secrets—and still they had nothing.

"Okay, everyone—let's make these next forty-eight hours really count," said Marino, urging her troops to ignore tiredness and defeat for one final push.

Showbag couldn't get his wife on the phone so left a message. "Sorry, luv, won't be home for a couple of days. We've got a bit on at work. A closing door kind of situation and we're going to give it a real hot crack. On Saturday, I'll take yer out to dinner and hopefully celebrate a well-earned victory. Or not. Wish me luck, sweetie. We're overdue for a win. Love yer to pieces."

It would be the last time she would hear his voice.

30

Kurtza noticed the police foot patrols had stopped and that there was no longer a uniformed presence at the railway station. He was impressed the police had tracked him that far. He had made his last transformation on the train from Flinders Street after killing Ravi Patel. His combination of earlier disguises was risky, but better than remaining in his cleaners' clothes, which might have given them a real-time trace. He still felt safe in Footscray, a suburb he knew well and where he had remained since breaking his parole. Still, he was a wanted man and his mug shot was everywhere. He treated everyone as a potential informer.

He considered Digger his consummate creation, an aging one-legged man in a wheelchair with powerful spectacles that made his eyes look like distorted saucers. The creation certainly attracted attention, but no one thought it could possibly be Tomas Kurtza. His bulbous and purpling drinker's nose and the deep lines that ran down his face took two hours at the makeup table, but it was no more than many actors do every night before a performance. And the rewards were many. Free bread and bakery items that "would only be thrown out anyway, luv," people stopping traffic so he could cross the road and random contributions of charity when he would suddenly cry out in pain. The pain was real, the consequence of having one leg folded into a compartment under the seat of the wheelchair, which cut off his circulation and could only be relieved by pushing himself up on the armrests to get the blood flowing again.

In two short months, Digger had become a familiar presence, living in the caretaker's flat on the roof of an old factory down by the river that was marked for demolition. He explained he was there by an arrangement with the owner to keep the squatters and druggies away, though nobody checked or asked any questions or wondered how a one-legged man negotiated all those stairs. It was amazing what people took at face value. Even the police officer who called by the factory accepted his story. Digger even volunteered to keep out a "weather eye for the bastard" and took a card from a young detective, promising to phone her if he saw anything suspicious.

"What do you think the maniac's up to?" he'd asked.

"We wish we knew," she'd replied. "Sometimes some things don't make any sense."

"Oh, it will make some sense to him," said Digger, with the wisdom of the old and the guilty.

———

Showbag was in his element, working alone and by his own rules. He had parked his car down by the markets and was drinking from a bottle in a brown paper bag when the old man rolled up to join him. He was Showbag's fourth visitor that afternoon and the beginnings of his second bottle of wine. Not that he drank much himself: the bottle was Showbag's prop.

Showbag introduced himself as "Bob," a refugee from a busted marriage, though his companion, like those before him, was more interested in the wine than his personal story and gratefully accepted a swig.

"Sleeping in yer car tonight?" asked the old man, who introduced himself as Digger.

"Haven't thought that far ahead," said Bob. "Still in the adjustment phase—though it's an option. Unless you can recommend somewhere cheap?"

"Newell's Paddock, down by the wetlands. Sleep under the stars for free."

They chewed the fat for an hour or so and covered a range of topics. How Digger had lost his leg in an industrial accident. How Bob blamed his misfortune on the booze. The advantages of life with and without a woman. If dogs were better than cats. If the North Melbourne Shinboners could ever win another premiership flag in the next twenty years. But they never mentioned the torture murders, or the recent police presence in Footscray, or who Kurtza might be or where he was hiding or what he was trying to achieve.

But all the while Showbag was watching. How Digger seemed to sweat around the edges of his face, how his nose was big but his nostrils comparatively small, how he rose up in his chair from time to time to release the pressure in his back, lifting the thigh of his missing leg. Showbag was no physiotherapist, but even with his primitive understanding of the human muscular system, it made no sense at all.

When the wine ran out, Digger took his leave and rolled off down the street. Showbag watched him go and wondered if Kurtza's disguise could be that good. Digger seemed like a man well north of sixty-five—but for one unconcealable feature: his voice was not the voice of an older man.

Showbag gave him a block's lead then followed on foot, keeping his distance but never letting his quarry out of his sight.

Through a maze of back streets and alleys, Digger arrived at last at a derelict factory ringed by a high chain-link fence. The gate was secured with chains and a broken padlock. Digger slipped in through the gate and wrapped the chains behind him. Showbag paused and messaged Marino.

> I'm in Wylie Street, number 62.
> Put some backup in the area just
> in case. Might need it, might not.
> Still checking. I'll let you know.

Showbag pushed in through the gate, leaving the chains as he found them, and followed the wheelchair tracks to the rear of the building. The empty wheelchair stood at the bottom of external steel stairs that extended four stories to the roof. Digger was nowhere to be seen.

The big roller door to the ground floor of the building was rusted and broken but its access door was open. Maybe Digger had gone in there?

Showbag edged his way to the opening and peered into the gloom. He knew that the moment he stepped through, he would present himself as a target against the light, so his next movement was swift and deliberate. He flinched as a flock of pigeons suddenly took flight in a confusion of wings and panic. It was difficult to know who'd received the bigger shock, but Showbag's main emotion was one of relief, as it confirmed that no one had entered this way before him.

As he turned to leave, his eyes slowly adjusting to the light, he became aware of something against the far wall, a heap that looked like sand but wasn't, a dye maybe, or powder, something industrial or chemical whose most obvious feature was its color. Even in the half-light it was a dull but discernible blue, the blue of cobalt, the blue of oxide, the unmistakable blue of the feet of a certain clutch of captured *Rattus rattus*. Rats that had been caged and starved so they would burrow into a man's gut. Rats that were territorial, according to Jane, though for all Showbag knew she'd been making that up. But rats with blue feet was incontrovertible.

Showbag headed into the gloom for a closer look, filled his fist with the blue substance and held it up into a shaft of light. If anything confirmed Digger was Kurtza, it was this. Showbag pulled out his phone and whispered his message.

"Me again. Send backup now. I think I've found him."

Kurtza had slipped out through the police cordon in Richmond and Showbag was determined he was not going to do it twice. Taking his Smith & Wesson from his ankle holster, he climbed the stairs as soundlessly as he could. The door to the caretaker's flat was open but there was no sign of anyone there. With his gun at the ready, Showbag sidled inside. The premises had not been officially occupied for years but someone was living there now. There were blankets and a soiled mattress on the floor and a kettle and unwashed crockery by a kitchen sink with a leaky tap. The only organized part of the room was the racks of clothes. Hi-vis vests and overalls and jackets with company names and logos. There was a small section of women's clothing, a nurse's uniform and a burka and coats and jumpers and T-shirts and jeans, all set out on dry-cleaners' wire hangers and looking as if they were mostly sourced from charity bins. Above the racks, hats and scarves were pegged on a makeshift line while below were rows of shoes, arranged with the toes pointing outward. There was rainwear and ponchos and a collection of totes and back-packs and in the corner a table with a profusion of makeup, latex, and wigs and three unmatching mirrors surrounded by a fringe of naked lightbulbs.

Showbag cautiously opened the two doors that led from the main room. The first was a dank and barely functioning bathroom with a bucket to flush the toilet. The second room was stacked with broken furniture and rubbish, the repository of what had been cleared to make the main room marginally livable. There was no apparent sign of the absent resident but if Showbag had been more observant and less adrenalized, he might have noticed that not all of the shoes under the racks were empty and that the sneakers five pairs from the end were occupied by someone standing behind the line of clothes.

Showbag headed outside to the small landing which commanded spectacular views of the area and the city beyond. The day was still and perfect and Showbag felt he could see forever. The wheelchair remained at the base of the stairs which provided the only access to the roof and Showbag worried that Kurtza had waited for him to climb all the way up before making his escape yet again.

But the killer was closer than the detective thought and as Showbag took out his phone to give Marino a sit-rep and instruct the backup to surround the building, Kurtza rushed from behind and shouldered him over the railing.

In those slow-motion moments people experience when time inexplicably slows, Showbag noticed he was still holding his gun and mobile phone and wondered how much it would hurt when he hit the ground.

31

The moment was palpable, a sudden intensity that was at the same time louder yet quieter than before. It was how Jane remembered earthquakes in New Zealand as a child, a feeling so manifest you actually stop breathing as you wait and listen for the aftershock you hope won't come. But the building that housed the Homicide Squad wasn't shaking, well, not in any physical sense. Maybe the change Jane felt was electrical or barometric? She got up from her desk and looked out through the glass wall of her office. Officers were running but no one was talking. It was like an urgent, disciplined fire drill by people who had trained for an event like this all their lives.

Jane headed along the corridor to Ringer's office and stopped in the open doorway. Ringer was on the phone, Marino and Cheung at his side. It was clear something momentous was happening.

"Did we get him?" asked Jane, though the faces of the three detectives suggested anything but that.

"No. He got us. Showbag. They're airlifting him to hospital now."

Jane could not find the words to respond to Ringer, who returned to his phone call.

"No, Marino will run it. We're on our way down to you now." Ringer hung up the phone and shared the latest with the others. "Kurtza just carjacked a Mercedes. But PolAir's got a fix and there's more units on the way."

As the detectives headed for the lift, Jane hesitated. This was operational and it was not for her to follow unless invited.

"Come on," said Ringer. "I'll fill you in on the way."

The Mercedes coupe drifted around a corner into Ascot Vale Road at 130 k's per hour, side-swiping an approaching vehicle, forcing it over the curb and through a plate-glass window. As pedestrians scattered, remarkably, no one was injured.

Kurtza hadn't driven any car for sixteen years and the C Class CLA-180 he had commandeered from its terrified owner was nothing like the clapped-out VL Commodore he owned before he went to prison. The power of the Merc was unbelievable, its acceleration out of this world. Kurtza was riding a missile.

Which was both good and bad· for Marino. As Jane and Ringer stood behind her and Cheung in the control room, the senior sergeant watched the screens and, like a subaltern at Kandahar, gave instructions without emotion. The chase was a danger to the public and Marino ordered the pursuit cars to "back off and follow." Kurtza's capture would have to be strategic but with PolAir tracking him from above and multiple units on the ground, Marino felt she had the upper hand.

"He seems to be heading north—to the M79. Units 307 and 510, put roadblocks and spikes at the first two exits and confirm," ordered Marino.

Unlike Marino, Kurtza was barely in control. As the lights ahead turned red, he accelerated and cornered wildly to join the flow of the crossing traffic, slewing onto the wrong side of the road and avoiding an oncoming truck before veering back to the left-hand lanes. His speed increased.

"Suspect now heading east on Buckley," reported Marino as she followed PolAir's eye in the sky.

"Running red lights like that, this may be over before we think," said Ringer.

Jane had to agree. There was something suicidal about Kurtza's driving, but like the others, her anxiety wasn't for him but the public at large. "Can't you turn all the lights to red?" she suggested. "Bring everything to a grinding halt?"

It was a sensible suggestion but regrettably beyond their capacity.

Marino scanned the map. "I'm looking ahead. If he sticks to this course, we'll have an opportunity in three to four minutes. 237 and 919, hold and pursue."

But Kurtza wasn't headed east for long. As two more pursuit cars joined the chase, he broadsided into a turn and headed back toward the city. The helicopter wheeled above him, tracking his erratic course.

"Give me a southern perimeter."

As Cheung plotted roadblocks to the south, Marino's eyes didn't deviate from the screens.

"307 and 510—stay where you are. He could change direction again."

"I hope he's not going where I think he's going," said Ringer as his eyes scanned the map for possible destinations.

"The Footscray Railway Station," said Jane, reading his mind. "The only place he feels safe."

"301 and 443, relocate to Footscray Railway Station," said Marino into the microphone on her headset. "Will arrange support."

Anticipating her instructions, Cheung speed-dialed Footscray Command.

"And I want the railway station's CCTV up here on my screens."

That took Cheung a little longer, but he did that for her too.

"301, you're parallel and one block ahead. Turn left, turn left now and hold the intersection."

On the ground, Kurtza had damaged something in the front suspension and the smell of burning rubber from body-work chafing on tires told him that his race was almost done. Up ahead, the pursuit car slammed to a stop, blocking his path, its four body-armored officers spilling from the vehicle with weapons drawn. With nowhere to go, Kurtza floored the accelerator and aimed his car at the police. The officers fired, taking out the Mercedes's windshield but not the driver. The Merc cannoned off the police car and barrel-rolled along the road.

An eerie silence descended, broken by the sound of leaking fuel. Cautiously, the officers approached the Mercedes, their weapons held at the ready. When the first shot was fired, they thought it was one of them, the unmistakable sound of a Smith & Wesson service-issue revolver. But it wasn't the police who fired first—it was Kurtza, using Showbag's gun. An officer went down then another, before the returning fire of their squadmates ignited the wreck, which exploded in a ball of flame, an inferno no one could possibly survive.

PolAir radioed what had happened and trained its camera on the scene so those in the control room could see. As Marino marshaled ambulances and police reinforcements, the two uninjured officers retreated to their wounded colleagues, who were mercifully still alive.

Kurtza stood on the other side of the blazing wreck, shaken and disoriented, a dark pall of smoke obscuring him from the eyes of the chopper above. He had crawled through the shattered windscreen seconds before the car exploded.

As startled onlookers cautiously approached, Kurtza held up Showbag's badge. "Police. I need to make a phone call."

A number of people offered their mobiles. "No. I need to use a landline."

"Come with me," volunteered a middle-aged woman, eager to assist.

As she led him to her house across the road, Kurtza was still struggling to formulate a plan. The trusting woman led Kurtza to her phone, which he pretended to dial and initiate a conversation.

"This is Paulson. We had a collision, two officers down."

Kurtza asked the woman her address and repeated it into the phone.

The woman looked at his injuries and wondered if she should dress them.

"Do you have a car?" he asked.

"Yes, in the garage out the back."

"Can you take me to the hospital?"

"Yes, of course. I'll get the keys."

As the woman disappeared momentarily, Kurtza considered his options. When she returned, he hung up the phone and held out his hand for the keys.

"It's too dangerous—he's still out there. It's safer if I drive myself. Vic Police will cover expenses. You have my word."

The woman handed Kurtza the keys and led him out through the backyard, pressing the remote to open the garage door to the lane.

"The quickest way to the highway is to take the lane all the way to the end."

By the time the police discovered there was no one in the burning wreck, it was too late. Kurtza—this time without any disguise whatsoever—had slipped through their net yet again.

Jane sat in Intensive Care and wondered if she would be the one to inform Showbag what had happened. It was remarkable he was still alive. He had been in an induced coma since he was pushed from the factory roof, a fall of thirty meters onto the remains of a demolished shed, the rusty sheets of corrugated iron saving his life but not his spine nor his ability to walk again. But telling him about his injuries wasn't what Jane really dreaded—or letting him know that Kurtza was still at large. Far more tragic and heart-rending was the death of Showbag's wife, Leilani, who had suffered a fatal heart attack on being informed of what had happened to her husband.

Leilani had fought heart disease for a decade. Showbag had considered early retirement and an easier life at their fishing shack in Mallacoota but was trapped by the need to keep their private health insurance intact to cover his wife's medical expenses. Some people create an online shopping monolith and jostle for the dubious honor of the world's richest person. Others eke out a living as first responders and put their lives on the line. Where is the fairness in that?

While Ringer and his team widened their search for Kurtza and interviewed the woman who had willingly handed over her car to a man whose face had been in the media for weeks, Jane kept vigil beside Showbag's bed and wondered where her thinking had taken the investigation. If Kurtza had an accomplice, he or she hadn't helped him escape or offered refuge. If Kurtza had an accomplice, there was zero evidence they had been involved in any of the murders. Maybe Kurtza was, as Showbag had suggested, no more than a heartless sadist, a man who had pitilessly tortured Nigel Woods, Franco Bernero, Michael McGill and Ravi Patel for no reason beyond his own psychotic pleasure. And could the Catholic connection between Woods, Bernero, and McGill be nothing more than coincidence? Catholics were the largest Christian grouping in Australia, accounting for a quarter of its population. As coincidences go, it wasn't that much of a stretch.

So why couldn't Jane shake this feeling there was someone else involved, someone between Kurtza and his victims that would make his crimes make sense? Melissa Woods and her clannish family had resisted the investigation at every turn. Her first husband's death was highly suspicious, as was his former partner's disappearance. Cayden Voss's fear for his life was understandable, but the destruction of the documents relating to the film he had planned to make with Kurtza was odd to say the least. The only person Kurtza had sought to contact since his release was Ela Bey. But for police intervention, she may have been implicated or worse—become another victim. She had hidden or destroyed her cache of letters and refused to show them to the police, which at least made sense to Jane given her hybristophilia. Yet Ela remained unconditionally committed to the man she loved—whatever atrocities he'd committed. She had mortgaged her house to pay for his appeal. She couldn't be ignored.

Jane looked at Showbag, his head pinned in a halo vest to protect his cervical spine. She checked his monitors, troubled by what he would face when he awoke. What transgressions had he committed in this or any other life to deserve what fate had dealt? None, of course: life is not a reckoning but a vale of hopes and tears. "Celebrate the dawn, wonder at the night and try and achieve three things every day: something in the morning, something in the afternoon—and something for yourself before bed." It was her father's advice, the mantra of an ambitious man who had tried to make his life make sense up until the moment he'd departed, at a moment of his own choosing. He left no note or explanation, no confession of his sins. Little wonder Jane had devoted her life to looking for answers.

That night Jane did something for herself before bed—she deleted Ben's mobile number from the favorites list on her phone. It wasn't because she didn't think of him every day, or miss his smile or his gentle humor—usually at her expense.

It was simply time—time to stop pretending he was still around and about to call to say he was running late or had booked their next holiday or ask if she could give Zoe a lift somewhere.

As she pressed delete with a silent "sorry," Jane couldn't help wondering if Melissa Woods had already deleted Nigel's name from her phone.

32

Jane left the hospital and went to the crime scene. Forensics had done their work and Marino and her team were tagging items of interest to be taken back to Homicide for use in evidence. The mood was somber. Showbag was still in danger and two other officers were in hospital with serious gunshot injuries. Everyone had heard about the death of Showbag's wife and held Kurtza responsible for that as well.

The rooftop squat was as close as any of them had come to their elusive killer. His spartan ways and the extensive wardrobe of disguises that had allowed him to evade the law for so long were chilling reminders of his discipline and attention to detail. His makeup table and clothes lay abandoned. Kurtza was now on the run as himself, without disguise. Jane's assessment that he had entered his endgame, that his work was done, seemed prescient.

Jane took in the details of his monkish existence. There was nothing to give him comfort or distraction. No radio, no television, no writing materials. No books, no newspapers, no evidence of alcohol. She noted that he appeared to have survived on canned food and instant coffee. There was a box of mobile phones, no doubt stolen, all with their SIM cards removed. The police checked those first but there was nothing of a sexual dimension, no pornography or items of self-abuse as were frequently utilized by sadists. He had continued to live as he had in prison with only the most basic requirements, seemingly sustained by his inventive disguises, his singular crimes, and his cruelty and absence of pity.

"He's pathetic, isn't he?" said Marino.

"Or single-minded," said Jane. "A man on a mission."

"You still think there's someone else?"

"I can't see how he developed his targets from a prison cell. Apart from his lawyer, I can't see a connection with any of his victims."

"Does there have to be a connection?"

"Where the tortures are so personalized—yes, I think there has to be."

"Is there anything here that helps you?"

"No. Not immediately," confessed Jane. "Though I see nothing that indicates he thought about the future. Wasn't he supposed to be a gifted actor? There's not a text or a play-script in sight."

"Which tells you what?"

"I don't know. Maybe his murders were his performances."

The search for Kurtza was now nationwide. The car the middle-aged woman had so obligingly provided had been abandoned in a service station on the Hume Highway where Kurtza stole another vehicle while its owner was paying for fuel. It looked likely that he was now headed north to New South Wales and checkpoints had been established on the border. Then the second car had been discovered as well, abandoned on the side of the road. How he had continued on from there was unknown. Maybe he had hitched a ride with someone—but if so, in which direction?

Jane slipped out from Ringer's briefing. Finding Kurtza was policework and there was little she could do to help. When she returned to her office there was something from archives on her desk: the Terry Tressyder file. As Jane opened the file she wondered what Ringer might say about her interest in Melissa Woods's past—"Going the long way round again, are we, Jane?"—and maybe he was right.

Like the Vizor file, this one was also filled with inconsistencies. Press articles suggested Tressyder had disappeared after the fire in which Vizor had died, while Melissa Woods was insistent that her husband's partner had left Melbourne days before. The eagerness of the police investigators to declare Vizor's demise "death by misadventure"—adamantly supported by Melissa Vizor—was nothing short of astounding, an opinion also held by the coroner, who sent the matter back to the police for further investigation.

The coroner, Betty Noachic, was someone Jane knew, though she had retired years ago to devote herself to her garden. Betty had one of those wonderful gardens that grow so well in Melbourne. After spending too many years investigating suspicious deaths in the Garden State, she had embraced the rhythm and harmony of the seasons and made her home a showplace.

"My God you look like your father," said Betty. "Such a handsome man."

"People say I'm more like Mum."

"Well, you're both female. But you've got your father's bearing and smile and eyes. Come on, I'll make us some tea."

She made a pot of French Earl Grey in accordance with

George Orwell's rules. "Take the teapot to the kettle and not the other way round" didn't make any sense these days when kettles didn't bubble away on coal stoves, but she did it anyway and they sat outside beneath a bower of lemons and limes and nibbled on homemade shortbread.

"I can tell this isn't social," said Betty, "though I am terribly pleased you've come. I probably miss your father as much as you do."

But Jane wasn't about to pursue any of that. "Do you remember the death of Stewart Vizor and the disappearance of his partner, Terry Tressyder?"

"How could I forget?"

"According to the file, you were critical of the investigation from the very beginning."

"You bet I was. The detectives were charmed by Vizor's wife and took everything she said at face value."

"Melissa Vizor."

"Now Melissa Woods. Have you met her?"

"Oh, yes."

"Now there's a force of nature. She insisted Tressyder hadn't been around for days and that he wasn't even in the country. But records showed he didn't leave until the day after the body was found. To California and New York, then down to South America somewhere, never to be heard of again. Wouldn't that make you suspicious?"

"Melissa admitted the company was drowning in debt and about to collapse, and that someone—either Vizor or Tressyder—may have wanted the records destroyed. She maintained her husband, who was a smoker, frequently napped on the couch in his office and had probably fallen asleep."

"A theory happily embraced by the police."

"So, what's your interest, Jane?"

"I'm not sure yet. I am working on the Kurtza case—the torture murders."

"Thank God I don't do that stuff anymore."

"I think one violent death of a husband is unusual; two distinctly worrying."

"You think Melissa Woods murdered her husbands?"

"No. Well, certainly not the last one. We know Thomas Kurtza did that."

"But . . ."

"I don't think Kurtza is working alone, yet I'm struggling to come up with connections."

"And you think it could be Terry Tressyder?"

"Melissa Woods was a wealthy woman, even before Nigel's death. If Tressyder had something on her—well, she'd be a perfect target for blackmail."

Betty shrieked with laughter, not because Jane's theory seemed fanciful but because it was so deliciously plausible she wanted it to be true.

"Didn't anyone think Tressyder's disappearance was fortuitous?"

"Well, I did."

"How hard did they try to find him? Was Interpol ever involved? Did they trace which country he ended up in?"

"Pass," said Betty.

"Did anyone think the circumstances surrounding Vizor's death weren't at least passingly suspicious and deserving of further inquiry?"

"Only me."

"So, you sent it back . . ."

"And still nothing happened. I came very close to an open finding."

Jane's impressions of the Tressyder file were being confirmed.

And Vizor's file had not been reassuring either. Maybe policing wasn't as exacting back then in the pre-digital age.

"Stay for dinner, Jane. I've got some Mount Cook salmon and fresh veggies from my garden. We'll open a decent Riesling and talk about your father. Such a handsome man."

Jane and Betty workshopped Jane's theories over dinner and Jane wondered if Betty and her father had ever got together. She wouldn't have been surprised.

"The thing about Melissa Woods," said Betty in her cups, "is that she has to do it her way. She wanted me to go on the board of her foundation but I wasn't going to be anyone's rubber stamp. We're both very close to the premier and I think she bullies him, too."

———

When Jane called by the Homicide Squad on her way home, Ringer was alone in his office. He had just come from the hospital where Showbag had come out of his coma. It had befallen Ringer and Leilani's brother to inform the detective that his wife had died. Ringer was still shaken by the experience. Showbag was yet to learn about the seriousness of his injuries but he didn't seem to care.

"He apologized for not waiting for backup. If he hadn't gone up there alone we probably would have got Kurtza. Typical Showy, taking responsibility for everything. He told me to tell you that you were right about the rats. He should have had the place surrounded as soon as he saw that heap of blue powder on the factory floor."

Ringer produced a bottle of scotch and poured a couple of slugs.

"I know you hate the long way round but could we take

another look at the Tressyder file, make some effort to find him? I've just been with the coroner who handled the case and she thinks—"

"I'm not against anything, Jane. Not at this point. Your theory that Kurtza didn't invent this vendetta in the isolation of a prison cell makes sense. There's got to be someone pulling his strings."

"I didn't expect to hear you say that, Eric. I thought I was whistling in the dark."

Ringer gave Jane a cab charge card, took one for himself and walked her to the taxi rank across the street. As he opened the door of her cab, Jane gave him a hug. They held each other tightly. They were in this together, they'd get through it together. Any way they could.

"See you in the morning, Jane. Sweet dreams."

"Yeah, well, that's not going to happen."

33

The business Stewart Vizor and Terry Tressyder had built was a classic case of failed expectations, strategic mistakes, and unrealistic pricing. It was an era when the mortgage broker was king and the industry was fueled by advertising. Marketing was Tressyder's area but he outspent their earnings at an alarming rate and the whole business was modeled on a growth they could never achieve.

As the accountant, Vizor spent most of his time juggling the books, not that he had much to work with. All he could do was put up fees or invent new ones, neither of which made his customers happy. But he would convince them he was losing more than they were and that they would save thousands in the end, so they'd grumble and write a check.

The money supply was the key to everything and Tressyder's trip to the States had been planned for weeks. He was having trouble pinning the Americans down and flights had been booked and canceled a number of times. According to Melissa Woods, he had been waiting in Sydney at his parents' house for their middleman in America to confirm the deal was on. He finally flew out of Sydney the day after the fire, which the investigating officers did not consider suspicious.

Shouldn't they have expected him to stay? To attend his partner's funeral and console his partner's wife?

With Marino and everyone else focused on finding Kurtza, Ringer had allocated Ray Cheung to reopen the case.

"I've got the FBI checking things out at the other end. They're sending me his arrival information and all movements following that. And I've asked them to send me a copy of his passport."

"I'm sorry," said Jane. "Why would you need to do that?"

"It wouldn't be the first time somebody left a country on one passport and arrived somewhere else on another."

Jane was impressed. "You're more suspicious than me."

"It's called being a detective," said Cheung, pleased to be relieved from his typecasting as the unit's computer expert. "Most criminals who don't want to be traced travel on a number of passports, some fake, some legitimate, though it's harder to do it these days. The technology's so much better. Most people think it's just a matter of matching a face with a photo. But if the underlying data is different, provided the photos match, you can effectively have two identities."

"You mean you can get on an airplane as John Doe and leave it as Richard Roe?"

"People with dual citizenship and dual passports do it all the time."

"And that's permitted?"

"Yes. And there's no system that matches the passport you present when you leave with the one you present on arrival in another country. Each country controls its own borders."

"Until someone like you wants the systems matched?"

"Precisely."

It wasn't surprising that the chief commissioner had asked to see Ringer for an update on the investigation, but it was quite unusual that she had asked for Jane to come as well.

"Perhaps she thinks I'll need a psychiatrist after she finishes dressing me down," mused Ringer as they waited in reception. "Or perhaps she just wants to meet you?"

"We'll know soon enough." Jane grinned, surprised by Ringer's apprehension. "I'm looking forward to meeting her too."

Chief Commissioner Cheryl Hursthouse had been a controversial appointment. She was a woman of sizable girth and opinions. Her close connections with the state government and testy relationship with the union had made her unpopular with the rank and file. Two of the force's deputy commissioners had been seen as more suitable candidates, more qualified and more experienced, and her recruitment of Eric Ringer from the Federal Police to head the Homicide Squad had had its critics as well.

"You had this man in the palm of your hand," Hursthouse began.

"Well, not exactly," said Ringer. "There was an accident. And two officers were wounded."

"Wasn't there a helicopter overhead?"

"Yes, but the suspect's car caught on fire and the smoke obscured their view."

"So the two uninjured officers, assuming the perpetrator was in the burning wreck, retreated to assist their fallen comrades."

"Yes."

"Did you give them that order, Inspector?"

"No, I didn't."

"Or countermand their actions, until the whereabouts of the suspect had been established?"

"No, I didn't. There were other units on the way."

"Yet you were watching proceedings, were you not, from the control room in this building?"

"Yes."

"While a junior officer ran operations."

"She's a senior sergeant."

"Still junior to an inspector, Inspector?"

"Should I be here for this?" interrupted Jane. "As you people like to say, it's operational."

"We're paying you, are we not, Dr. Halifax? I will come to you in a moment." With Jane put in her place, the commissioner continued. "You behave like you're running a task force, Inspector?"

"Maybe."

"But you haven't asked to be upgraded to that?"

"I considered it. We nearly had him earlier on."

"Ah, the debacle in Richmond. I should have pulled the plug on you then."

Jane had heard enough. There is only one way to handle a bully.

"Commissioner, you may well be paying for my consultancy, but I don't have to listen to this. The inspector probably does, though if he wants my advice he should either resign or file a bullying claim or both, and I will happily be his witness."

The commissioner was momentarily taken aback, so Jane continued.

"I've been part of this operation from the beginning. I've been to four unspeakable crime scenes, seen images of human suffering I will not unsee for the rest of my life and glimpsed what the suspect is capable of to the point where I have seriously questioned the meaning of life. But I've held things together while three members of your police force—not mine, your police force—have been seriously injured. One may never walk again and has lost his wife as a consequence of this investigation. Do you really think this tirade is helpful? I am, as you say, a mere consultant, but if you need some help kicking people when they're down, I'll go home and get my boots."

"Are you finished?" asked the commissioner.

"I guess that's up to you," said Jane.

"I would have preferred to have heard that from the inspector, but fair enough. I like a woman with balls. Which brings me to you. What's your problem with Melissa Woods? Don't you think she's suffered enough already?"

"I'm sorry—"

"You went to see the coroner who handled her first husband's death."

"Yes."

"While your colleague here is looking into the taxation records and political donations of Nigel Woods and Associates. Can either of you explain what any of this has to do with Tomas Kurtza and the people he's murdered? And in case you think this is just me being a bully—I received this very complaint from the premier this morning."

"As you would know, Commissioner," said Ringer without any trace of sarcasm, "in a homicide investigation you look at everything."

"Do you really think Melissa Woods is involved in her husband's murder? And the death of her first husband as well?"

"Commissioner, I'm not ruling anything in or out," Ringer said. "But Melissa Woods and her lawyer have been pushing back on this investigation from the very beginning. I've no idea what it is, but they're hiding something. And if you're asking me to limit my investigation, then you can have my resignation."

Cheryl Hursthouse could dish it out but she could take it too. She was blunt to the point of rudeness and didn't mind when others were the same. "Okay. Then take this as a warning. Do what you think you have to do. But if it turns out that there's no basis to these inquiries but prejudice or wild assumptions or personal hubris, then heads will roll. Your heads. That's all."

With a tight smile of satisfaction, the commissioner gestured them toward the door. Her final "Good luck" was a warning. They had better be right.

———

"I came close to giving her my resignation," confessed Ringer over a scratch meal at the Magic Mountain. "But I'm seeing this through, if only for Showbag. Then I'm back to the Federal Police."

"I didn't see that coming," said Jane.

"They want me to head the Melbourne Office. I'm better at administration—I've been away from investigation too long. I think I've lost my edge."

"You and me both."

"But the difference is you don't think you're wrong."

"And you do?" His doubt wasn't helping their cause.

"I worry my dislike of the billionaire class is getting in the way. 'Personal hubris,' as the commissioner put it. What if she's right?"

"Well, none of that is fueling me, Eric."

"I've been giving things a lot of thought. I think I want a normal life. Regular hours, more time with the kids. Find someone who doesn't put labels and limits on sex—"

"Ouch."

"Pushing paper is nine to five—catching crooks is total commitment."

"And leaves you with no life—like me?"

"I wasn't having a go at you."

"I know. I suppose it's why I went into teaching."

"So why did you come back?"

"I guess I'm obsessed."

"With what?"

"The transgressive mind."

Ringer didn't understand.

"I don't divide people like you do, Eric, into criminals and law-abiders. I think we're all on the spectrum. We're not all murderers, some of us just park illegally. Or drink and drive. Or lie to our partners. Or tell them we love them when we don't. But we all transgress. Sometimes more, sometimes less. I think it's what makes us human."

Ringer laughed. "You think too much."

"And I don't hate Tomas Kurtza—"

"Well, you should."

"—I wonder what makes him tick. Why all his victims are men—apart from his first crime, the one that sent him to prison? I wonder how much pain he is in, why he needs to be so cruel? Who let him down or hurt him so much? If he hates himself more than he hates his victims?"

"And if there are no rational answers to these questions?"

"Then I'll keep looking until I find them."

———

After the meal, Ringer headed back to Homicide and Jane to her apartment. The whiteboard had found its way back onto the easel, the latest version of the muster-room chart replicated with all its color-coded dot points. So many dots and no way to join them.

Jane changed for bed and checked her voice mail. There was an apology from Betty Noachic for "speaking to the premier out of school" and a message from Zoe in New York, asking for a loan when she really meant a donation. But Jane was happy to support her stepdaughter's music career in the toughest town in the world. In that sense, Zoe was just like Jane, taking the harder path in life as if the degree of difficulty justified the journey.

Jane wondered if Showbag was comfortable in his halo device and if the FBI would find Terry Tressyder; if Cayden Voss still feared for his life and if Melissa Woods still felt invincible; where Tomas Kurtza was sleeping right now and if Ela Bey was rereading his letters.

And she thought about Eric Ringer reordering his life and reviewing his priorities. Was he rejoining the Feds so he wouldn't have to work with her again? Was he clearing the decks for her? Was he putting personal happiness ahead of career? Did he see the two things as a contest? Jane certainly didn't. Or was none of this to do with her? Was he simply getting on with his life?

The fifties is a tricky decade, especially if you find yourself alone. The closer you get to the Big Six-Oh, the more you feel the options narrow. Jane remembered thirty as coming too soon but forty was okay. Fifty was a shock, but the prospect of sixty was beyond comprehension, and only three short years away. Maybe she should have taken that job with the International Criminal Court in the Hague when it was offered to her last year; a new life and a new career on the other side of the world.

With so much on her mind, Jane wouldn't have nightmares about torture tonight. But she knew they'd return soon enough.

34

Kurtza hadn't hitchhiked after abandoning the second stolen car. At least, not immediately. The dog squad had followed his trail across farmland to a dam, where he had probably bathed to clean away the blood from the accident. But the dogs couldn't find any trail leading away from the dam and police divers searching the water found no body. Not that Kurtza's scent would have been lost by entering the water but a trail, once broken, is harder to rediscover—especially if Kurtza had walked west by wading along the creek that fed the dam.

Photographs of Showbag and the two injured officers had motivated the public, who were phoning the hotlines at last. The faces of policemen injured in the line of duty had an impact that reports of the tortures and murders had never achieved as the police and the press rightly protected the privacy of the victim's families and safeguarded the detail of the investigations. But most of the sightings were historic or vague and nothing pointed to Kurtza's present whereabouts.

Jane called by Cheung's office to see if he'd heard back from the FBI. He hadn't, but his computers had come up with something else. It related to Ela Bey.

Unable to detect any place at her apartment where she

might have hidden Kurtza's letters, Cheung had programmed his computer to log "repetitive patterns" of Ela's movements at work. After eliminating predictable trips to the cafeteria and bathroom, Ela seemed to return several times a week to a particular box in a storage room. Jane agreed it was worth checking out, so Cheung made a call and arranged an appointment with Kim Leveson, the library's chief executive officer. What better place for Ela to hide her letters than in a library housing five million items?

When Jane and Cheung arrived at the library, they did not expect to see Ela Bey waiting in her boss's office. Kim Leveson explained that she was uncomfortable the police had accessed the library's security cameras despite the fact their warrant gave them express permission to do so. "Maybe it was a failing on my part, but I think I should have warned my staff they were being watched."

Jane was sympathetic. It felt invasive and it was. The chief executive had supported Ela after her initial arrest and had kept a close eye on her welfare. "I think Ela should be here, Ms. Leveson, and I applaud the concern and support you've shown her. We hold no animus toward Ms. Bey. We're only doing our job."

"By accessing personal correspondence that's none of your business?" scoffed Ela. "I've already shown you some of the letters. They're not going to help you find him."

"Can we do this please?" said Cheung.

The two women led Jane and the detective down into the bowels of the library to a storage room where Early European Australian History was kept—or "Records of Invasion," as Jaroslav Petranovic might have called it.

The cameras had not been able to identify the actual box Ela had accessed so often, but alongside a file-box marked *The Letters of Charles Hotham, First Governor of Victoria* was another called *The Further Letters of Charles Hotham* with a distinctly recent label. No one was surprised it contained none of the governor's correspondence. Instead, there were more than 350 letters to Ela from Tomas Kurtza.

Cheung wrote Ela a receipt, which she signed, and carried the box to the lift.

"Will I get them back?"

"I've no idea," said Jane. "We'll have to read them first."

"Will you do that?"

"Probably."

"If I don't get them back, I'll have nothing of him. Nothing to show for seven years."

"I'll do what I can," said Jane, aware of the enormity of what Ela was losing.

As Jane and Cheung left the library, it didn't seem much like a victory. More like police overreach and an unnecessary invasion of privacy.

"Well, we don't have Kurtza but we've got the bastard's love letters," said Cheung hoping his joke might lighten Jane's mood.

It didn't.

Jane and Cheung were introspective as they drove back to police headquarters. Garrulous "Gary" was always going to be the one to break the silence.

"Do you really think these letters are going to help?"

"They might reveal more than his prison file did," said Jane without conviction.

"I've never come across a perp like Kurtza. Not using mobile phones so he can't be tracked. Only using their cameras to photograph the sites of his intended crimes. One phone for each, multiple visits, documented like a secret agent. At least there was one he never got around to completing."

Which was news to Jane. "I'm sorry?"

"Five phones—four crime scenes," said Cheung. "The Woodses' place, Bernero's factory, McGill's garden, and his lawyer's office."

"There was a fifth intended crime scene?"

"A church, probably run by some wayward priest, except it didn't look Catholic to me. A strange-looking place. We talked about it at the briefing. I think you were visiting a coroner."

As soon as they got back to Homicide, Jane had to see for herself. The five mobiles had been tagged and sealed as evidence but Cheung had uploaded the images to the computer. He scrolled through the various crime scenes until he came to the series of photographs labeled "Mobile 5."

A simple wooden church stood on a hill overlooking tinder-dry farmland. Its grounds bore the remains of some kind of event, a church fete or marketplace. The access road was a dusty track, the steeple unusually tall, as if it had been extended to be seen from afar. Most of the photographs featured the inside detail. The design was overwrought, much like the steeple, an exaggeration of the form. Country churches are typically sparse and utilitarian: this one was filled with embellishment.

"We think it's the site of an intended crime," explained Cheung, "one Kurtza planned but didn't get around to committing."

Jane took over the keyboard to scroll through the photos again.

"Something the matter?" asked Cheung. He could see how unsettled she was.

"I think I've seen it. At least in model form. At Cayden Voss's studio."

It seemed Voss was right to fear for his life after all.

———

Voss sat alone in an interview room, somewhat puzzled as to why he was there. As Ringer entered with Cheung, he was about to find out.

Jane adjusted the monitor in her office. Though invited by Marino to watch the interview with her, Jane wanted to watch on her own.

"Mr. Voss." Ringer was formal but not unfriendly.

"What's happened? Have you got him?" asked Voss.

"Not yet, but we will. In the meantime, we'd like you to look at some photos."

Cheung placed the photos of the church on the table.

"How did you get these?" said Voss.

"Do you recognize the place?" asked Ringer.

"Yes, of course. I inherited it from my mother. She was going to turn it into a holiday house."

"We believe these photos were taken by Tomas Kurtza. Did you take him there?"

Voss hesitated, considering his answer. "Yes. Yes, I did."

"When?"

"After he was released from jail. We were going to use it for our film that never happened. I wanted him to see I had been serious about the project, to see where my money had gone."

"Did you take him there again later?"

"No."

"How many times did you see him after his release?"

"Once."

"So this was the only time?"

"After this, he broke his parole and went to ground."

"You never mentioned this before?"

"You never asked."

"What's this?" Ringer pointed at a photo that showed the area in front of the church.

"Oh, it's supposed to be a kind of fairground. I used it as a fundraiser when I tried to finance the film."

"Were you aware he was taking these photographs?"

"No."

Ringer studied Voss, needing to be convinced.

"I remember leaving at one point to close the gate, to keep the neighbor's cows out of the property. Perhaps he took them then."

"How disappointed was Kurtza to discover that the film wasn't going to happen?"

"He was devastated. Just like me."

"I'd like to see the script of the film. And any documentation."

"As I explained to Dr. Halifax, everything was destroyed. The whole thing became too depressing."

"What about your computer?"

"Wiped. For the same reason."

"Well, luckily, Mr. Voss, there's not much we can't recover. So, we will take a look. The detective here will arrange to have your computer collected. And we'll need your mobile as well."

Voss didn't hide his irritation. "You should be offering me protection, not putting me on the stand."

"Did you know Nigel Woods?" The question seemed to come from nowhere.

Voss balked. "No."

"Or his wife?"

"Of course not."

"Did you approach their foundation for money?"

"We went to everyone."

Ringer waited.

"I wrote and asked for a meeting but they wouldn't see me. They told me to send in an application."

"And did you?"

"Yes."

"And?"

"It was dismissed out of hand. By form letter."

"What about Franco Bernero?"

"Who?"

"The second victim. Did you know him?"

"No."

"Are you sure?"

"I'd heard of him, of course. Wasn't he a Labor politician?"

Jane's attention didn't stray from Voss. His eyes, the way he sat, the way he adjusted his position.

"Or Michael McGill?"

"This is ridiculous."

"Did you know Michael McGill, Mr. Voss?"

"No."

"What about Ravi Patel?"

"We met twice, during the court case. I was a character witness for Tomas."

"How many times did you meet or speak with Tomas Kurtza after he was released from jail?"

"Once."

"The day he took these photos?"

"Yes."

"On this date?" Ringer pointed to the time and date on the bottom of the photo.

"If that's what it says."

"How many times did you see him in prison?"

"I didn't keep count. Multiple times. He was a member of my drama group and I directed most of his plays."

"Then out he came and that was that—apart from this one occasion?" Ringer gestured at the photos on the table.

"I told you. Once he broke his parole, he was a wanted man."

"Let's take a short break. The detective can get you refreshments."

Ringer left the interview room and met Jane and Marino in his office. "What do you think?" he asked.

"He's lying about Franco Bernero," said Jane.

"How do you know?"

"Body language. The pursed lips, constantly altering the way he sits, feigned confusion at routine questions. He's agreed he knew Nigel Woods or at least applied to his foundation. And there's something about Michael McGill as well. He is just not telling the truth."

"Can we run a check, Nita? Look for connections. See what we can find," asked Ringer.

"Yes, boss," Marino said, leaving to get her team to run some checks.

Ringer turned to Jane to ask a question, although he already knew the answer.

"Want a go?"

"You bet."

———————

Voss was surprised when Jane entered the room instead of Ringer, more so when she dismissed Cheung, though that seemed to put Voss at ease.

"Don't get too relaxed," warned Jane as she indicated the camera on the ceiling. "Big Brother is watching. You and me both."

Voss seemed confused.

"I should apologize. I misjudged you. I didn't believe you when you said you were afraid of Kurtza. I thought you were acting. I thought you were proud of what you'd created."

"I didn't create him, Jane. Discovered him maybe. Discovered a monster?"

"If things had turned out differently, if the Nigel and Melissa Woods Foundation had funded your film—"

"They weren't the only ones we approached."

"If the film had been financed—by anyone—do you think any of this would have happened?"

Voss took a long time to consider Jane's question.

"No."

"So why did you give up? Surely there are other ways to raise money . . ."

"Are you blaming me for Kurtza?"

"No. I'm just wondering at what point everything changed. At what point you decided it was hopeless."

"You can only bash your head against a wall for so long."

"So, you give up and Kurtza goes on a killing spree?"

"I am not responsible for that."

"If it was the other way round, if you gave up because you realized your star was a sadist and a killer—that I would understand."

Voss's eyes glanced up at the ceiling camera. He knew he was addressing the police as well as Jane. "I did everything I could possibly do to make that film."

"And it would have changed everything?"

"Yes, it would."

"Made you famous, made Kurtza famous, changed your lives forever?"

Voss didn't answer.

"Not everyone wants to be Cate Blanchett or Geoffrey Rush." Jane was quoting Voss's lecture, the first words she had heard him say, though she continued with words of her own. "But most of us know we won't be and settle for something else, something achievable, a normal existence. And then there are others who seek something else altogether. Notoriety. Like Ivan Milat or Jeffrey Dahmer."

Voss's unblinking eyes looked at Jane, unmoved by her theory.

"Is it possible that that's Tomas Kurtza?" said Jane.

"Why are you asking me?"

"Because you are the only person I know who had any kind of personal interaction with him. You knew him better than the prison governor."

"I don't know if that's true, but yes, I knew him and I saw his talent."

"Did it surprise you that he was capable of what he has done?"

"I am not sure I understand."

"That he was capable of such cruelty?"

"How would I know that?"

"Because you knew him. Because you knew his writings."

"I had no idea."

"And when you did find out—when you realized the torture and the killings had been committed by Tomas Kurtza—what did you think?"

"I thought how little we know our fellow man."

Jane studied Voss closely. Such glibness, she thought, from a man supposedly in fear of his life. How little we know of our fellow man? Did Voss only see what he wanted to see, an actor of unlimited talent? Had Kurtza concealed so absolutely the cruelty and sadism that drove him that Voss never sensed who he truly was? Or was Voss's narcissism so extreme that he dwelled in a bubble of his own self-importance, unrelated to anyone else?

Ringer knocked then entered and gestured Jane outside.

Cheung came in to be with Voss as Jane joined Ringer and Marino in the corridor.

"We sent a car out to the church," explained Ringer. "Someone's there, almost certainly Kurtza. We're surrounding the place and going in. He's not going to get away this time."

"Have you been watching me and Voss?"

"Some of it—until this came up."

"Let's take him with us."

"Why?"

"If we get into a situation, he might be able to help."

"How, exactly?"

"A familiar voice? If you want to take Kurtza alive . . ."

"To be brutally honest, Jane, taking him alive is not exactly top of my list right now."

"It could be a waste of time," said Jane. "But what have we got to lose?"

"I want to catch Kurtza and you want to prove a conspiracy?"

"Something like that. But I want to catch Kurtza too. If he's dead, we may never know why he did it."

"Does it matter? It could save the state a lot of money."

Jane gave Ringer a look. Did he really mean that? Wasn't he as curious as anyone else?

"The trouble with you, Jane, is you're looking for things that don't concern me. I just want to keep the public safe."

"They're not mutually exclusive, Eric. Even you know that."

But she could see that exasperation and a sense of failure was all he was feeling right now.

Ringer looked at Marino.

"Your call, boss," Marino said. "There's room for him on the chopper."

"Okay," he said at last. "Bring him along if you must."

35

The setting sun was an angry orange as the Leonardo AW139 lumbered up into the sky from the helipad on top of the police center, thirty-nine floors above Spencer Street, the blade-vortex pressure of its five composite rotors screaming at a hundred decibels. Inside, the aviation headsets provided its passengers with enough quiet to converse, but the chatter remained operational as Marino marshaled her resources. Ringer was eager to avoid a night operation and they had an hour and a half's daylight at best. He also knew that sieges like this should never be rushed and that Kurtza would be playing for time.

But this time he had a perimeter in place. The Armed Crimes Unit had already left in another chopper. Ringer would have upward of fifty police on the ground plus snipers with night-vision goggles. Area police held the perimeter and the Rural Fire Service and local ambulances were on site. If Kurtza got away, the commissioner wouldn't need to ask for his resignation, it would be sitting on her desk in the morning.

Ringer and Marino were seated behind the two-person crew, Cheung behind them in the second row with his portable screens and equipment. Jane sat in the back with Voss, watching his mixture of alarm and elation at being in a helicopter for the first time in his life. They seemed strange emotions for a time like this, almost juvenile.

Jane worried she had jumped to conclusions again. Voss's lies under interrogation proved nothing more than the fact he was a liar, something she already knew. At their very first meeting she had seen him as the narcissist he clearly was, so what was different now? In her determination to find a co-conspirator, she had at various times suspected Melissa Woods, Ela Bey, and Terry Tressyder—all because her experience told her that there had to be a connection between the victims. But what if Showbag was right? What if the victims were utterly arbitrary, no more than the random prey of a sadist's pleasure?

At the church, Kurtza completed his preparations. Like Ned Kelly at Glenrowan, he watched as the troopers assembled, content he was in control of how his last stand would play— if last stand it would turn out to be. He made a final tour of the church, checking its doors and windows. He felt his pulse, surprised to find his heart rate was normal. He was experiencing a sense of calm he hadn't felt for a very long time.

Back in Melbourne, Ela Bey watched the breaking news on television while, at her compound in Portsea, Melissa Woods did the same with Maurice Engels. A siege was taking place to the north of the city. The press believed, though couldn't confirm, that it involved the wanted fugitive, Tomas Kurtza. Every network had a team on the ground. Like OJ in the white

Ford Bronco twenty-five years earlier, everyone had stopped what they were doing to watch.

———————

The Leonardo landed in a dusty paddock and Ringer and his team headed straight for the portable command post. Voss was taken to the first aid tent where he would wait until required. He asked the police officer assigned to him what his status was. "Assisting us with our inquiries, aren't you?" The woman was being diplomatic. Ringer's orders were to not let him out of her sight. "Shoot him if you have to," he'd said, though she didn't take him literally.

Jane watched as a robot bumped its way along the uneven track that led to the church before stopping short of the building. It was like the robots that bomb squads use to defuse or destroy explosives.

The robot started to speak. "Tomas. This is Inspector Eric Ringer of the Homicide Squad. We know you're in there and we've sealed the area. I am giving you this opportunity to put down your arms and give yourself up. We want a peaceful resolution to this, Tomas. Better for you and better for us. There's a headset on the robot and we'll send it in closer so we can speak."

The robot moved forward only to be met by a hail of bullets. A more powerful weapon than Showbag's Smith & Wesson would have disabled the robot. Was it fair to assume that Kurtza had expended most of his ammunition already? No one in the command post, least of all Ringer, was jumping to conclusions.

The robot continued and stopped at the steps to the church. Kurtza didn't emerge.

"Tomas, we'll give you five minutes to think this over. If you don't want to come out for the headset, the robot can hear you from there."

Five minutes passed, then ten, and Ringer gave him a final deadline. It would be dark in fifteen minutes. Time wasn't on their side.

Jane had experience in siege situations and knew a friendly voice could break an impasse. She went to the first aid tent to speak to Voss. "We want you to try and make contact," she explained. "Let him hear reason from someone he knows."

"I wouldn't know what to say," said Voss, clearly not wanting to be involved.

"Ask him how he's doing. If there's anything he wants. Food or water . . ."

"I'm scared, Jane."

"Scared of what?"

"Of what he might say? He wants to kill me. He wants to take me down too."

"Let's give it a try. He can't hurt you from there."

Jane found Voss's reluctance confusing, but was it fear or something else?

She led Voss to the command post where Cheung gave him a headset and sat him down at a monitor that showed the robot in front of the church. Arc lights lit everything up like a theme park, making the church look surreal.

"Hello, Tomas. This is Cayden. I didn't come here willingly. I'm under arrest."

As Ringer moved to cut him off, Jane raised her hand. What he said wasn't important. Establishing contact was all that mattered.

"Ask him if he can hear you," said Jane off-mike.

"Tomas. Are you there?"

"Ask him if there's anything he wants."

"Is there anything you need, Tomas? A lawyer? A priest?"

Jane frowned. She knew Kurtza wasn't Catholic and Voss probably did as well.

She pressed a button to silence the microphone so she could talk to Voss off-air.

"Are you Catholic, Cayden?" she asked.

"What—"

"Just curious," said Jane, "because I'm sure you know Tomas isn't."

Ringer was becoming impatient. This wasn't the time for Jane to conduct an interrogation. "Keep talking."

Jane released the button and nodded to Voss to continue.

"This is not turning out like we'd hoped, Tomas. It would have made such a good film. All lit up at night like we'd planned. Ironic, isn't it? All the networks are here—and Fox. Half the world is watching."

Jane killed the mike once again.

"What are you doing, Cayden?"

He didn't answer.

"Explain that the cameras aren't seeing any of this," said Jane. "We don't want him going out in a blaze of glory."

"I don't know what to say," Voss whined.

Ringer asked Cheung to turn off the headset. This wasn't getting them anywhere.

"Thank you, Mr. Voss. That will do for now."

The policewoman took Voss back to the first aid tent.

"We're going in."

"You won't take him alive," warned Jane. "And if anyone else is involved, you'll never be able to prove it."

"Do we even know he's still there?" asked Ringer, fearful Kurtza would elude them again.

"He's there all right," said Marino. "The snipers are seeing movements and shadows inside. And we've checked the area for culverts and drains. There is absolutely no way out."

Ringer took up the headset. "Tomas. This is Inspector Ringer again. I am prepared to come in and talk. But you need to put down your weapon and show me you're clean."

It was a bold offer and somewhat reckless; not what Jane had in mind. But Kurtza's response was unambiguous as he emptied the rest of Showbag's clip into the robot.

"Four shots, boss, that's probably all he's got," said Marino. "So, unless he's got more ammunition or another weapon, he's probably unarmed."

Ringer looked at Jane, who reached out to take the headset.

"Hello, Tomas. I'm Dr. Halifax. I'm a friend of Ela Bey's. Would you like to talk to her?"

There was no response.

"She's worried about you, Tomas. A lot of people are. We just want to talk. Take the heat out of the situation. It doesn't have to be like this. We're here to listen, to understand your position. We've got to the point where the police are running out of options. And only you have the power to stop it. I hope you don't mind, but Ela showed me some of your letters. You write very well. I found them very moving. She loves you, Tomas, and I know you love her. She would want you to give yourself up. And so do I."

Jane did nothing to hide her emotions. Her humanity was the last chance Tomas had.

Ringer looked at Marino. who was listening to sit-reps from the snipers through her headphones.

"It's all gone very quiet, boss," she reported. "There's no sign of any movement anymore."

"Okay, let's do this." Ringer kept it simple. "Go."

Adrenaline was high as the Armed Crimes Unit readied their weapons and checked their body armor. They would go in on foot behind an armored vehicle. Their commander radioed Marino. "Moving now."

The fence was cut, concertinaing back to its strainers. The assault vehicle rolled through, unit members running behind.

Suddenly, a single rocket rose up into the sky from somewhere behind the steeple. And then another. And a third, this one exploding in a cascade of falling stars.

"Hold your positions," said Marino, looking at Ringer for guidance.

A line of small explosions ran across the front lawn, like mini blasts at a quarry, followed by a loud thump as the water tank beside the church exploded on its stand. A fine mist descended like summer rain as the fairground came to life. Carnival music blared from an ancient speaker while a children's Ferris wheel, bereft of custom, began to turn. A fairy floss drum spun unattended, drenching the air with its sweet sickly smell. A row of clown heads turned in unison, their open mouths hungry for suckers to come and play. Across in the graveyard, a zombie rose up, its mannequin face a decomposed leer. Another dummy fell from the steeple, jerking to a stop at the end of a noose. The stained-glass window shattered, revealing an elongated body stretched by the wrists and ankles, entrails spilling from a gash in its stomach.

Ringer was not going to be distracted and ordered his troops to continue.

But before Marino could give the order, the entire church erupted in an explosion of accelerant-boosted flame.

Ringer looked at Jane. Were they about to be outwitted again?

On top of the church, a crucifix rose up bearing a body stripped to the waist. But unlike the dummies and mannequins, this one was real, this one was alive. It was Tomas Kurtza. He had a crown of barbed wire on his head and a deep wound in his side that was bleeding freely. The church was now an inferno, and as the flames licked at his feet and bubbled and blistered his skin, Kurtza's face contorted into a scream. But it wasn't a scream of agony.

What Jane saw on his face was ecstasy.

———————

The Rural Fire Brigade had moved in as quickly as they could, but the intensity of the fire was such that the roof, along with Kurtza on his cross, had collapsed into the heart of the blaze before they could train any water on the flames. Though the fire was extinguished swiftly, it was fifteen minutes before the police could safely enter the crime scene.

Ringer and Marino were the first to go in but, with the RFS still putting out spot fires, came out quickly to escape the smoke.

"It's over," said Ringer grimly, as they handed their breathing equipment to Jane and Cheung. "Don't do this unless you want to, Jane."

But Jane needed to see for herself. She and Cheung made their way through the smoldering ruins to where Kurtza's body lay on his great wooden cross and the cables and weights that had lifted it up. With enough flesh on his face to confirm his identity and enough missing to chill the blood, his charred remains meant little to the police. After four horrendous crime scenes, bearing witness to the criminal's demise was a grisly but necessary ritual. But Jane's emotions were elsewhere.

She looked down at the contorted form of a man who had struggled to escape the loops that had fixed him to his cross. Even Kurtza didn't know how he would react once the flames started to consume his body. One hand had been freed—maybe to protect his face—a fleshless arm, half human, half caricature, extended as if pleading for under- standing. But Jane didn't need the symbolism: she already felt like she had failed him.

Was she Kurtza's only advocate, the only one who cared what he had to say, the only one who cared if he died and took his secrets with him? But who takes the side of a sadistic murderer who had made his victims suffer slow and agoniz- ing deaths, or the side of a rapist who had tortured his victim for days? Who else believes there's always a reason, however alien to right-thinking minds? Who else believes in redemp- tion, even for the blackest soul? Who else but priests and forensic psychiatrists?

The dead and wounded had priority, so the command chopper was commandeered to take Kurtza's body back to the morgue for autopsy and identification. Two cars were allocated to take Ringer's group back to the city, and as Ringer and Jane got into the first car with Marino, Jane watched Voss as he got into the second car with Cheung.

"He wanted to see the body," explained Marino with disgust. "But I told him that wasn't going to happen. What did he want? A selfie?"

Voss looked across at Jane like someone who had experienced the most remarkable day of his life—and maybe he had.

She could not get his look of self-satisfaction out of her mind.

36

Sing the wondrous love of Jesus
Sing His mercy and His grace
In the mansions bright and blessed
He'll prepare for us a place
When we all get to heaven
What a day of rejoicing that will be
When we all see Jesus
We'll sing and shout the victory.

Jane didn't know the words in Samoan and only vaguely knew them in English, but the ease with which the people sang in unrehearsed harmony was mesmerizing. A surrender to God, a surrender to His music; a oneness with Leilani, for whom they had come to bid farewell. "Sunrise" they called the date of her birth and "Sunset" the date of her passing, both dates placed beneath her beaming face on the programs and matching T-shirts that many in the congregation wore.

She was barely forty-nine.

Unlike the funeral of Nigel Woods, this one would take several hours, as everyone played their unhurried part. The pallbearers who carried her into the church were large, ferocious-looking men, but they wept without apology, pausing whenever anyone moved forward to touch the casket or say a prayer. Women placed floral tributes and photographs at Leilani's feet and covered her vessel with tapa cloths and delicate gauzes embroidered with large crucifixes in red and blue. The Catholic Church could learn a lot from this, what comfort a genuine belief in heaven can bring. No incense, no Latin, no pomp.

Jane sat behind the immediate family in the third row with Ringer, Marino, and Cheung.

Showbag sat in his wheelchair at the front, breathing with the aid of a respirator. Though Leilani and Showbag were childless, it didn't matter. He was surrounded by his nephews and nieces, who all called him "Papa Gra." In this culture, the children of your brothers and sisters are your children too and the parents of your spouse, your second mother and father. Showbag was not alone.

After the feast, Jane and the others found a tree and sat with Showbag in the shade. They hadn't spoken since Kurtza's death the week before.

"You sure you got him?" asked Showbag, needing reassurance. "Ordeal by fire. The prick's a witch. How did he escape from that burning car?"

"The RFS was on standby and put out the fire. We were able to identify the body," said Marino. "At least he saved us a trial."

"Ordeal by paperwork. I won't be missing that."

"You're not leaving us, Showy?" said Cheung, assuming he was joking.

"Mate, I do the rehab and, as soon as they let me go, I am wheeling straight out that door. On a pension for the rest of my life. Look out for me at the Paralympics in the Special Fishing section."

"Is that a sport?"

"It will be, Gary. It will be."

Jane and Ringer wheeled Showbag to a waiting ambulance. The day had been long and emotional and Showbag was spent.

"That was a lovely funeral," said Jane. "It was a privilege to be there."

"The Samoans don't think people die but that God calls them when He's ready. They believe she's in a better place. So, I'm hanging on to that and hoping she's happy—and keeping a seat for me."

"The police force will miss you, Graeme," said Ringer. "And so will I. They don't make them like you anymore."

"Yeah, boss, I know. And I'll miss you too. And Campbells. You're quite a team. Invite me to the wedding."

The ambos lifted him into the back of the ambulance and closed the door.

Jane and Ringer watched as the vehicle drove away, giving a farewell wave.

"Well, we've got his blessing if we need it," said Ringer as straight-faced as he could manage.

"I'm giving men away, Eric. Had enough of the lot of you."

"Giving them away for what?"

"Special Fishing."

———

Jane and Ringer traveled in silence as a car took them to Spring Street to meet with the premier and the chief commissioner. While Ringer jotted down notes for the press conference that would follow, Jane's thoughts were elsewhere. She was pleased for her colleague and could understand his relief that a callous murderer had finally been stopped. But for Jane, Tomas Kurtza's death had denied her the answers she had so desperately wanted.

How had Kurtza evolved, psychologically, from a man who could rape and torture a woman into someone whose victims were exclusively male? Why had he subjected his victims to such cruel and pitiless tortures? Was he a sadist in the purest sense or a masochist whose victims were martyrs to his own self-hatred and despair? And how had this so-called "model prisoner" maintained an intimate correspondence with an honest woman like Ela Bey while at the same time harboring unspeakable intentions to be committed upon the moment of his release? Jane's psychological profile was incomplete, her evidence scattered and contradictory. The mind frequently defied normal logic but it was seldom as chaotic as this.

Ringer finished his notes and glanced at Jane.

"Have you met the premier before?" he asked.

"No. I'm yet to have the pleasure." Her tone implied the experience might be anything but that.

"I'm told he just likes to be liked."

"Well, he's in the wrong profession for that."

Ringer gave Jane a grin.

"Inspector," said the premier, gripping Ringer's hand like a long-lost friend. "I'm sure we've met. At the Black Saturday Recovery function? The film festival opening? The Working for Victoria Initiative?"

They hadn't.

"Nice to meet you, Premier," said Ringer. "Do you know Jane Halifax?"

The premier was not going to repeat his mistake.

"Dr. Halifax. I've heard so much about you. The commissioner's your biggest fan."

Cheryl Hursthouse moved things closer to safe landing conditions.

"It's been an investigation that has had its up and downs, Premier. I think we're all grateful it's been brought to a conclusion."

"Jane. Can I call you Jane? Jane! Do you know I knew your father?"

––––––––––

Jane woke up screaming. Well, not exactly screaming, but certainly startled and disoriented. The meeting with the premier wasn't the reason. It was an accumulation of stressors from a singularly distressing case. Jane got iced water from the fridge and went out onto the balcony where the sea air eddied on the east of the building, bringing a kinder relief than the air-con. What was she doing in a city of five million people when her heart was still in Shag Point, that little row of coastal shacks north of Dunedin where she'd holidayed as a child before her father decided to bring the family to Australia to further his brilliant career?

Why was she even thinking about that?

––––––––––

Jane was her usual reflective self as she joined the team in the muster room. Wrapping up an investigation is an exacting task, though not as meticulous as preparing for a trial. But evidence needed to be collated and filed and reports prepared for the coroner.

Ringer was happy to share what the premier had said when he'd taken him aside after the press conference: "Maybe now you can back off Melissa Woods?" It had riled him then and it riled him still.

"Send our auditors' report to the tax commissioner," he instructed Marino. "It's our civic duty. Any member of the public can report irregularities. I don't see why we're any different."

"It will come back to bite you in the arse, boss," Marino warned.

But Ringer was almost out the door. Only Jane knew he was heading back to the Feds. The others would be told soon enough.

Jane's mobile rang and she moved out into the corridor to take the call. It was Cayden Voss.

"Good morning, Jane," he chirruped. "How are you today? Do you think the time is right for that interview with the inspector?"

"No, Cayden. Not right now."

"I'm under pressure to get my article finished and produce this podcast. They want it while the news is still fresh."

Fresh? Kurtza hadn't been dead a week.

"I'll have a chat with him when the time is right. There's still a lot to do."

"Well, at least there'll be no trial," said Voss. "I bet everyone's relieved about that."

Maybe. But not as relieved as Voss seemed to be.

Jane had to check herself that this narcissist wasn't getting under her skin, that in seeking to exploit his association with a monstrous killer, Jane wasn't blocking him out of spite.

"When do you think he'll see me?"

"I'll ask him, Cayden, but if you push too hard, he may say no altogether."

"Then I'll leave it in your capable hands, Dr. Halifax. You have my number."

Jane continued on to her office. Her own files would need to be indexed and archived as well. The library box containing *The Further Letters of Charles Hotham* sat on top of a filing cabinet. Jane had read enough of Kurtza's letters to Ela to confirm they were what she claimed: intimate correspondence. Surprisingly tender prison-cell longings from a man who had perpetrated four acts of unspeakable cruelty and a violent rape. Jane marveled at how he'd been able to sequester his life so completely.

For the sake of completeness, she would take the box home and read the rest before returning them to Ela as promised.

It was no idle task. Many of the letters were several pages long. Jane left a trail from one room of her apartment to another. Her work had once again invaded her home, but she made a promise to Ben that this would absolutely be the last time. She read them as she cooked, she read them as she washed up and, by midnight, she was sitting up in bed with some more.

Much of it was repetitive.

Thanks for your letter and the money you put in my account. Buying little luxuries like shampoo and chocolate makes life almost bearable in here . . .

Bad loss by the Kangas on Sunday, but as we've been saying for years, we're in a rebuilding phase. Nothing a new coach, full-forward and crumber won't fix . . .

The book you sent me on the Inquisition was great. Especially how the belief in sorcery and witchcraft was promoted by the Church so they could then turn around and condemn it . . .

I like your new stationery. What's the perfume? Or is it you? I lay the pages out every night on my bed before I go to sleep and ████████████████

████████████████████████████████

████████████████████████████████

████████████

I don't know how much of this gets through the censor. That last bit probably won't . . .

They certainly butcher your letters to me but I can read between the lines. They can delete our words as much as they like but they can't delete what's in our hearts . . .

My new play is about a blind judge who has to touch the faces of everyone who comes into his court. He believes it doesn't matter what they say. He can feel their guilt or innocence. But then he starts having ████████ *under his robes and has to question his own guilty mind, and whether he can be trusted to deliver justice anymore . . .*

The film is progressing well. C knows someone who let him down in the past but is eager to put things right. He says he can put him in touch with a developer who could fund the entire project . . .

My darling, please forgive me if I save my paper for

my plays. I write them only for you—so they are my love letters too. I aim to finish my next one by our anniversary. A special present to the one I adore with all my heart . . .

I think the play was successful, though it doesn't take much to get approval from the audience in here. It tells the story of a man who can't escape his past, however much he tries. Some mistakes are too enormous, some sins irredeemable. But as usual I take an ironic approach. What's the point if you can't laugh at life? If you thought about how sad it was, you couldn't go on . . .

Your devotion sustains me, but I worry your sacrifice is too great. A love like ours gives me purpose, but you're free in the outside world to have normal relationships like everyone else. I know I hurt you when I write like this, that it "insults your commitment," as you've said before. I truly love you and the last thing I want is to cause you pain. But if you found someone else, I would be happy for you and you would have my blessing . . .

The abuse C suffered as a child has been enormously helpful as I build my character, which is beginning to take on a life of its own. It's the power art has: his pain and my satiation. Do you like that word? It's Middle English. I got it from a book you sent . . .

Jane looked across the room at the person looking back at her from the mirror. Illuminated by her reading light, she sat in bed, surrounded by the love letters of a killer she had been reading for most of the day and night. It was 2:00 a.m. She stared at herself as if looking at someone she didn't recognize. She was tired, facts were blurring together. Her desire to make sense of a sadist she had never met and place him in a conspiracy she couldn't prove was testing her rationality.

She went to the bathroom and splashed cold water on her face and buried her head in a towel. She couldn't decide if she was hot from the heat of the night or chilled by where her thoughts had taken her.

"C" was Cayden Voss, of course; Ela's letters, a real-time diary of how the film was progressing. Jane went through to the dining room table where she had sorted the letters into groups of interest: possible clues to Kurtza's psychology; sadism versus masochism; torture and the Middle Ages; failures of the Catholic Church. But she hadn't kept track of the film, which had seemed inconsequential.

The abuse C suffered as a child has been enormously helpful as I build my character, which is beginning to take on a life of its own. It's the power art has: his pain and my satiation. Do you like that word? It's Middle English. I got it from a book you sent . . .

Jane found her mobile and dialed. It went to voice mail. She dialed again.

"Jane?" said Ringer, roused from his sleep. "Is something the matter?"

"It's Cayden Voss. He's Kurtza's co-conspirator."

"Jane, are you drunk? It's the middle of the fucking night."

"It's a folie à deux—where two people share the same delusions." But Ringer was half-asleep and Jane was only making sense to herself.

"If you want me to come over, I can be there in . . . twenty minutes."

"No. I don't want you to come over, Eric. It's the middle of the fucking night."

"I told you that—"

"It can wait till the morning."

"Jane. You woke me up. You're not making sense. And I'm coming over. Put on the bloody kettle."

And with that he hung up and refused to answer though Jane repeatedly called.

So she put on her robe and filled the kettle.

———

In his clothes from the day before, Ringer looked like someone who'd been roused by a fire alarm in the middle of the night—which wasn't that far from the truth.

"You look awful," said Jane.

"Well, unlike some, I need my eight hours. A weakness of the constitution, I know."

"How do you like your tea?"

"Scalding and unforgiving." But his crankiness was just for show. "So, what's your blinding insight? And please don't tell me you haven't got one."

"There's no doubt Kurtza was our murderer and that he delighted in the pain he caused. Whether or not it was because he hated himself even more than his victims is something we'll never know, but I suspect it was probably the case. He had decided his life was pointless, that the die had been cast fifteen years ago when he committed his original crime and that redemption was impossible. So, he carried his regrets and his self-hatreds with him through fifteen years of jail and looked for some symbolic end to it all, some grand exit, some final statement. But his victims weren't personal—apart maybe from Ravi Patel, although that was almost an afterthought, some last-minute attempt to find a way out in the hope a plea of insanity would save him."

"The man's dead, Jane. And I'm sure your analysis is fascinating, for your doctoral students if no one else—"

"Eric, you're missing the point. Kurtza had the capacity to commit these crimes, but the motivation was elsewhere. Which is why we couldn't make any connection between Kurtza and his first three victims—because there wasn't one. He didn't know them. They had been selected by someone else. He's not the principal in this, he's the weapon.

"The real criminal is Cayden Voss."

Ringer sipped his strong black tea and burned his lips. "And how are you going to prove that, Jane?"

Jane pointed to the piles of letters on the table. "That's all the proof we need."

37

The skies at last were overcast, a welcome respite from the summer heat that had punished the city for weeks. It was late in the afternoon when Cayden Voss signed in to the police center for his interview with Ringer. He had been pleasantly surprised Jane had organized things so quickly given what she had said the week before.

Jane met Voss at the lift and walked him along the corridor to Ringer's office, which looked out toward the docks and the West Gate Bridge. Ringer welcomed them and showed them to casual chairs around a coffee table.

"Tea, coffee, water, Mr. Voss?"

"Water's fine."

Ringer got three bottles from the bar fridge and handed them around.

"So, you're making a podcast, I hear?"

"Writing an article first."

"Is there any interest in that?"

"Tomas was a remarkable person, Inspector. To elude you for as long as he did."

"Is that what the article's about?"

"No. It's about his acting. And the man he might have

been. I think I knew him better than anyone. Such talent, such terrible flaws."

"Flaws?" remarked Jane, surprised by the word.

"Well, we know what he did . . ."

"Did you see that potential in him?" asked Ringer.

"No. I didn't."

"Do you mind if I record this, Inspector?"

"Not at all. It's usually us doing that."

Voss placed his phone on the coffee table and pressed record.

"So, what did you want to ask me?" said Ringer, maintaining a conversational tone.

"In terms of your career as an investigator, how would you describe this case? The most challenging? The most unusual?"

"I've never been asked that question before. So, I suppose that makes it unusual."

"What has it meant to you personally or professionally? I'm looking for something I can quote."

"I'll tell you when it's over."

Voss gave a half-hearted laugh as if there was a joke he couldn't see.

"You see, Mr. Voss, the good doctor here doesn't think Kurtza was acting alone."

Voss looked at Jane for elucidation, but Ringer continued.

"You knew Franco Bernero, didn't you?"

"Who?"

"Franco Bernero. Kurtza's second victim."

"No. How could I?"

"When you bought the factory to turn it into a theater-restaurant, didn't you go to Bernero to get the zoning changed?"

"Indirectly. The real estate agent put us on to him as

someone who could fix things with council. My former partner did most of the haggling . . ."

"But you paid the fee?"

"And nothing happened. He couldn't deliver."

"How did you feel about that?"

"I put it down to experience, Inspector. It was a very long
time ago."

"Did it contribute to the breakdown of your relationship?"
asked Jane.

"That's a rather personal question. Probably. None of this
will be in the article."

"Cayden, did you know Michael McGill?"

"No, Dr. Halifax, I did not know Michael McGill. Not
even remotely." Voss was on sounder ground now and clearly
relieved by the change in direction.

"But you knew his type?" Jane continued. "As a child,
didn't you suffer abuse at the hands of a priest?"

"Who told you that?"

"I have a friend who prepared a submission for the Royal
Commission. About a priest called Father Hartigan, who
taught at your school."

"Now mercifully dead and in hell."

"If only your suffering had ended with that."

"You don't know what you're talking about." Voss dismissed
Jane with an icy smile and returned to Ringer. "I'm supposed
to be the one asking the questions."

"Then fire away."

"Did you ever work out what these crimes were about?"

"I thought your article was about his acting?"

"I'm trying to equate his acting with what he did."

"You think he was performing a role?"

"No. Do you?"

"You'd have a better idea than me, Mr. Voss. As someone who 'knew him better than anyone.'"

"These disguises he used," Voss continued, "how effective were they in helping him avoid detection?"

"Extremely."

"Can you elaborate?"

"Not really."

"Why not?"

"It's operational. Facial recognition. It's a sensitive matter, politically. We're allowed to run the odd test or trial, but most of its use is highly regulated."

Jane noticed that Voss wasn't blinking. Blinking too much or not blinking at all, neither was normal.

"Cayden, can I ask a question?"

"No, Dr. Halifax. This is my time, not yours. I don't even know why you're here. Inspector, could you ask the good doctor to leave?"

Ringer didn't answer. He didn't need to.

"This is ridiculous. I'm here to interview you, Inspector, but if you've nothing to say, then I'll waste no more of your time." Voss got to his feet, shaking his head as if in the presence of lesser beings.

"Sit down, Mr. Voss. You should hear what Dr. Halifax has to say. Might be useful for your article."

Voss returned to his chair and defiantly crossed his legs.

"I believe there was a film," Jane began, "and that you genuinely wanted to make it. But as is usual with these things, it's the finance that's the problem. You probably came closest with the developer that Franco Bernero introduced you to—no doubt for a sizable fee. And when that fell through, you went to the Woods Foundation, who dismissed you out of hand.

"Then gradually the idea took root that you could make

the project anyway—if not as a film then as a kind of performance. Or maybe that was the intention from the beginning."

"Oh God, a theory from a shrink. That's all I need. I'm writing about reality, Jane. How talented an actor Tomas was, how gifted, how once-in-a-fucking-lifetime special. The man was a genius."

"Well, he was a very clever and inventive sadist. But he had zero connection with the Catholic Church. Those hatreds came from elsewhere."

"Thank you, Inspector, I am grateful you agreed to see me, but this is a total waste of my time." Voss got up and reached for his phone—but Ringer was closer and got to it first.

"Ah, the iPhone 12. I'm still with the 8. It works okay for me. I'll keep this running, if that's all right? Your record is as good as mine."

Marino and Cheung entered and stood by the door. They'd been watching on the screen in Marino's office.

"This is outrageous. Am I under arrest?"

"Do you want to be under arrest, Mr. Voss? Or shall we listen to Dr. Halifax? Please sit down."

Voss lowered himself into his chair.

"You knew Kurtza was never going back to jail," said Jane. "You told me that yourself."

"So what?"

"You knew that he considered himself irredeemable. That he could never get past his original crime."

"Wrong," said Voss dismissively.

"You knew all about his sadistic thoughts and compulsions."

"No, doctor, I didn't."

"You knew of his fascination with medieval torture."

"I thought you said he had zero connection with the Catholic Church?"

"Because he got that, Cayden, from you."

Voss looked at Ringer, bewildered, and then at the other detectives. "Are you people serious? Are you going to swallow this crap?"

The police said nothing, leaving the floor to Jane.

"You discovered Kurtza and you discovered how like-minded you were. Your hatreds and his sadism, your mutual desire for fame. Your pain and humiliation at the hands of Franco Bernero and the Woods Foundation—and Father McGill for good measure, standing in as Hartigan's proxy. I'm sure Ravi Patel was Kurtza's idea, added for personal reasons. But it was outside your pact and it scared you to death and you were terrified you'd be next."

"Very good, Doctor. Very creative. An imagined conspiracy. How clever. And when did this fantasy happen?"

"In prison, during your sessions with your protégé."

"And how would you know that?"

"From contemporaneous evidence."

"So, Her Majesty's Prisons are bugged, are they? That will come as a shock to the civil libertarians."

"There are other ways to prove what was said."

Voss smiled his condescension. "This is nothing but conjecture, doctor. Wildly inventive, I will give you that. But without a jot to back it up."

Jane stood and crossed to a folder on Ringer's desk. Inside were a selection of Kurtza's letters to Ela, marked with colored Post-Its. She began to read.

"I've added another layer to my film script. It elevates a B-grade film to something more metaphorical. Grand Guignol through a Catholic lens—not that I know much about that. But C does. In fact, I think he's obsessed.

"The film is progressing well. C knows someone who let

him down in the past but is eager to put things right. He knows a developer who could fund the entire film . . .

"It's easier to forgive others than forgive yourself. I know I've done my time in here, but some things are irredeemable. I'm not religious, quite the opposite, but there are things in my DNA, compulsions I cannot deny. Cayden—he actually names you here," interposed Jane before resuming the letter, "—Cayden has always encouraged me to believe that appetites must be sated."

Voss sighed his boredom and glanced at his watch.

"C is starting to wonder if there's not another way to make a statement. Films are so hard to put together. Maybe it's a play or some other performance.

"The abuse C suffered as a child has been enormously helpful as I build my character, which is beginning to take on a life of its own. It's the power art has: his pain and my satiation. Do you like that word? It's Middle English. I got it from the book you sent . . ."

"Satiation?" said Voss with disdain. "Now there's a word you don't hear every day."

"Satiation: to satisfy a need or desire, usually to excess."

"Well, thank you, Doctor. I'm sure that's all very informative."

"And then there's the script we retrieved from your computer." Jane held up another document from the desk. "A story about a man determined to show the world the intensity of his suffering, who wants others to feel the pain he endures, to experience his agony and desolation. It's an attempt to justify sadism, which is not very sound, medically speaking. But then, it's a horror film, it doesn't pretend to be scientific. Shall I go on?"

"No, that will do for now," said Ringer. "Mr. Voss needs to be cautioned and charged."

Voss got up and headed for the door. Marino blocked his path.

"You have no right to keep me here. I want to speak with a lawyer. What do you mean 'cautioned and charged'? Charged with what?"

"Conspiracy to commit murder. Accessory before and after the fact."

"You have got to be fucking joking!"

"And you will be given an opportunity to speak with a lawyer."

Ringer turned off the recorder on Voss's phone. "I'll keep this for now. You'll get a receipt. Take him next door for a formal interview."

Voss lunged for the door. Marino took his wrist and twisted his arm up behind his back. Voss kicked out with his feet and glared at Jane, howling like a kid, "She's making this up!"

Ringer headed outside as Marino and Cheung took Voss by the arms and followed.

Voss stopped at the door and sneered back at Jane, "You'll never prove this, you know?"

"Not for me to decide. The courts will do that."

"Isn't it enough he's dead?"

"No, Cayden. It's not even close to being enough."

The detectives steered Voss out through the door, leaving Jane on her own.

She returned the script to Ringer's desk and gathered up Kurtza's letters. Together, they would be crucial evidence in Voss's trial. Her promise to Ela Bey to return her precious correspondence would not be fulfilled any time soon.

Jane looked out at the city as the rain clouds massed. But it was Kurtza, not Voss, who played on her mind, his torment and his demons, the callousness with which he had been manipulated by a man who had stoked his belief that his transgressions were beyond redemption and that the only good purpose to which his life could be put was to see others suffer as much as he had. Voss had looked into Kurtza's dark heart, seen his own reflection, and loaded him like a gun.

Jane's instincts had been right and, with the letters as verification, had proved her theory. But she felt no sense of victory or validation. Only an overwhelming sadness and the hope, as she left the police center to walk home through the darkening city, that the rain would hide her tears.

38

All hell had been unleashed, as Marino had predicted. A superfluity of senior counsel only a world number one tennis player could afford had applied to the High Court on behalf of Nigel Woods and Associates for an urgent injunction against the tax commissioner. It required him to return the documents Ringer had forwarded and refrain from any "investigation, assessment or review" based on their contents. Maintaining the documents had been obtained improperly as the result of an unrelated investigation and had "potentially contaminated current assessments," the application accused Victoria Police—and Inspector Eric Ringer in particular—of "prejudice and possible malice" in the execution of their duties.

Surprisingly, Ringer's biggest supporter was the chief commissioner, Cheryl Hursthouse. Ringer had already informed her he was heading back to the Feds, but she asked him to keep that between them for now. Despite the premier's appeals to let the courts decide the matter, the commissioner had gone on the offensive. At a press conference she announced Victoria Police would vigorously defend the proceedings and praised Inspector Ringer as a fearless investigator whose resignation she had refused to accept. In private she had gone even further, vowing to support any action Ringer wanted to take, including defamation. Even the police union was impressed.

With Voss's trial now the priority, the ordeal by paperwork had taken a new direction. Jane's expert testimony would be crucial and Kurtza's letters to Ela would provide a record of events. Meticulously cataloging documents was not a task Jane enjoyed so when Cheung walked into her office she was grateful for the interruption.

"Are we still interested in this?" he asked, holding up an international courier satchel. "It's from the FBI."

"I've already got my conspiracy theory," said Jane wryly. "But come on, let's take a look."

The contents were impressive. There was an index, timeline, and even a map. The photocopies were of such high quality the documents looked like originals. The dossier was so comprehensive, Jane's first instinct was to put it aside and read it later, but something had caught her attention: a photograph of Terry Tressyder.

"Well, that's disappointing. Here's a mistake right here. This isn't Terry Tressyder—it's Stewart Vizor."

"Melissa Woods's first husband?"

"Now living under an assumed name—Brian Lightridge," said Jane as she read the caption.

"How could they make such a basic mistake?" said Cheung. He took the document, needing to see for himself. "The FBI are the best in the world."

"Unless it wasn't Stewart Vizor who died in the fire," said Jane. "What if it was Terry Tressyder all along?"

Cheung had to laugh. "You're so suspicious of everything, Jane. How do you sleep at night?"

"I don't."

"So even dental records don't do it for you?"

But Jane wasn't laughing. She was thinking of Melissa Woods.

"What if it wasn't tax she was trying to hide? Or political donations? What billionaire do you know who ever cares about that kind of stuff?"

"I don't know any billionaires."

"With that much money, it's par for the course. A cost of doing business. What the hotel industry calls 'spillage.' Now we know what we're looking for, Gary. And it isn't any of that."

———

The team assembled in the muster room with takeaway coffees, poor substitutes for what Showbag used to make. As they prepared the brief for Voss's trial, they were holding themselves to exacting standards. The evidence had to be incontrovertible. But Ringer hadn't called the meeting to discuss Cayden Voss. They were here to talk about Stewart Vizor.

Jane began. "I have reason to believe that Stewart Vizor killed Terry Tressyder. That he somehow replaced Tressyder's dental records with his own and left the country on Tressyder's passport, doctoring the photo. Much of what I'm about to say is conjecture."

"But we love your conspiracy theories, Jane. Go break a leg." It appeared Marino had taken over from Showbag with the witty one-liners.

Jane waited for the laughter to subside. She moved to the whiteboard and the four headings she had prepared.

"One: Stewart Vizor. Stewart Vizor is alive and well and

living in America under an assumed name, Brian Lightridge. He has used a number of aliases and lived at a number of addresses in the United States and Brazil. He does not have a US Social Security number. His source of income is unknown, although he appears to live very well.

"Two. The dental records. The fire was so ferocious, the victim's body could only be identified with the aid of dental records, which we now know were false. Whoever died in that fire was not Stewart Vizor. What we don't know is how the dental records were substituted and who arranged for that to happen.

"Three. Terry Tressyder. If Vizor didn't die in that fire, who did? Was it Terry Tressyder? Or someone else? Is Tressyder, like Vizor, also alive and well? Were they involved in this together?

"Four. Melissa Woods—formerly Melissa Vizor. We do not yet know if Melissa Woods is aware her first husband is still alive. We do not yet know if he has been receiving money from Australia—either willingly or by extortion. The accounts of Nigel Woods and Associates and the Nigel and Melissa Woods Foundation may or may not provide the answers. I'm a forensic psychiatrist not a forensic accountant, but it's good to know we have them on the team.

"At this point in time we only know three things," Jane concluded. "That Stewart Vizor is still alive. That whoever perished in that fire, it wasn't him. And that the dental records are false."

"Thank you, Jane," said Ringer. "The FBI have issued a warrant for Vizor's arrest and we will apply for extradition as soon as we can. I'm establishing a new team to handle this, answerable to me and Jane. I don't want the rest of you distracted. Cayden Voss is still the main game, though if you come across anything relevant, let us know."

———————

The mansion in Toorak had been listed for sale. The instrument of Nigel Woods's torture, *The House of the Stolen*, had been obliterated, but not the place or memory of his suffering. Melissa Woods had planned a new life in Portsea with her faithful notary at her side.

When Jane and Ringer presented themselves at the gate and pressed the intercom, their reception was predictable.

"Inspector Ringer. What are you doing here?" said the omnipresent lawyer. Engels's wife may well have asked her husband the same question.

"Executing a warrant," said Ringer, holding up his authorization.

"You can't come in here. You're conflicted, the subject of High Court proceedings."

"This says I can. It's signed by a judge. You can read it if you like."

High on the fence, a security camera swiveled to take in the patrol cars full of uniformed officers that Ringer had brought in support. One of the officers was unloading a battering ram. Ringer was here to execute his warrant, with or without Engels's blessing.

"This is outrageous. Expect to be back in court in the morning."

Ringer said nothing. He didn't need to.

The gate's lock clicked in defeat.

Jane walked up the long driveway with Ringer. The night-scented jasmine didn't seem so sweet anymore. The fountain wasn't working and some of the spotlights in the garden needed to be replaced. But how harsh should one be on a grieving widow?

Maurice Engels met them at the door and read the warrant.

"So, what are you looking for this time?" he asked with as much menace as he could muster.

"Not sure at this point," said Ringer. "Let's start with some questions. Can you take us to Mrs. Woods?"

Engels led them through to the lounge with the over-sized couch where their first meeting had taken place. Reg Mombassa still hung on the wall, frowning his perpetual concern.

"Hello, Mel," said Jane, trying to keep things pleasant.

"Do what you have to, Jane, and get out. Should she even be here?"

"Dr. Halifax is part of this investigation," said Ringer. "As an authorized consultant."

Engels placed a cautioning hand on Melissa's. "Let's see what they want."

"I'd like you to look at some photographs," said Ringer, opening a file. "This first one. Is that your former husband, Stewart Vizor?"

"Yes. It was taken before our wedding."

"And this one?"

"From an old prospectus. My God. He looks so young."

"What about this?"

"Yes, it looks like him, though I haven't seen this photo before. When was it taken?"

"In 1999. In June."

"But that's impossible. He died in '98."

"And this one—2003. In Rio de Janeiro. Does it look like your husband?"

"That can't be him. It's fake. Desktop publishing or whatever it's called."

"This one was taken five years ago, in California. On April the fifth. And this one, last year, in Aspen . . ." Ringer laid the photos out in sequence on the table.

"Do something, Maurice," said Melissa like a drowning woman. "They're setting me up."

"And what do you think we're setting you up for, Mrs. Woods?" asked Ringer, his voice quiet and steady.

"Don't tell them anything," interjected Engels, too late to be useful. "You don't have to say a thing." The lawyer looked at the photos then looked back at his client. Her face was as pale as death. "Where did these photos come from, Inspector?" Engels asked, hoping their provenance would be problematic.

"The FBI."

Again, the lawyer looked to Melissa for answers.

"You knew your former husband was still alive, didn't you, Mrs. Woods?"

She didn't answer.

"You've been sending him money for years." The forensic accountants had been swift in their work.

Melissa's eyes rolled back in her head. Jane knew she'd fainted thanks to vasovagal syncope, but given her recent medical history, she told the others to call for an ambulance and sent them from the room.

Jane laid Melissa out on the floor and held her feet in the air. The blood that had pooled in her legs returned to her brain and she began to come around.

"What happened?"

"You fainted. Just stay where you are for a moment." Jane was holding her hand and checking her pulse.

"You should have been an ally, Jane. A fellow suffering widow."

"Don't talk. Just breathe."

"I worried if you weren't on my side, you'd be against me."

"It's not a question of taking sides."

"If only George had kept his mouth shut instead of sharing his father's tragedy. I wonder how he'll take it when he's told. And Charlotte. Poor Charlotte."

"Shh."

"You despise me, don't you? And my lowly origins."

"I've never said that."

"A receptionist, without an education."

"Mel, I never thought that for a moment."

"I should have kept my mouth shut too. I knew you wouldn't leave it there. That you'd keep on digging until you found what you were after."

Jane almost felt obliged to counsel Melissa against saying another word. But the guilty need expiation.

"Lowly Mel with her two young children and a husband with a fraudulent partner. Lowly Mel with her lowly job as a receptionist for a dentist."

Dentist. That was news to Jane.

"Lowly Mel without an idea in her head except how to make it better for everyone. I never did it for me, Jane. As a mother, you must know that? None of it was for me . . ."

Ringer came in with the ambulance crew. Jane stayed on the floor at Melissa's side, holding her hand as her blood pressure returned to normal. She watched as Melissa answered the ambos' questions, asking why she should bring her pajamas as if she had no conception of the circumstances under which she'd be spending the night.

As the ambulance took Melissa to hospital where she'd

be guarded by the police until formal charges could be laid, Ringer walked Jane back to the car. If Nigel Woods hadn't been so pitilessly tortured and murdered, would they ever have uncovered what his wife had done? But for the enormity of Voss's hatreds and Kurtza's uncontrollable need to cause pain, would Melissa Woods's comfortable, envied billionaire's life have continued until she died?

"Did you know she worked for a dentist?" said Jane as they got into the car.

"You never told me that."

"I didn't know. Though we were bound to find out, I suppose."

"She told you?" said Ringer, surprised.

"Yes. She told me. Someone had to have access to the dental records to make the substitution. I think it's been preying on her mind for years."

"I don't," said Ringer as he started the car, "think it's been preying on her mind for years."

"Why not?"

"Because I don't think as much as you do, Campbells. Let me buy you a drink."

The car edged out through the police cordon as detectives filed in to search the house again. But not as a crime scene. This time they were searching the home of a murderer.

39

Autumn was coming, the relentless heat of summer replaced with the cooler days of the football season as Melburnians kept warm at weekly convocations of upward of 70,000 believers. The North Melbourne Kangaroos attracted considerably fewer followers these days. They were in a "rebuilding phase." But Ela was there for round one.

Jane was a lapsed Hawthorn supporter but liked being back at The G and sharing Ela's enjoyment.

"Seven years ago, I'd never been to an AFL game. Since then, I've only missed two. Tomas loved me coming and was hugely amused by my early accounts. I'm better now, it's a habit I guess, keeping a diary of every game."

That's devotion, thought Jane, as she tried to enjoy her plastic beaker of beer and a body-temperature pie. But it's the traditions that make Aussie Rules what it is and she wasn't there to spoil Ela's enjoyment.

"You know you won't get your letters back until after the court case is over?"

"I know, and I'm going to hate being a witness." She turned and howled at an umpire for a ball that was clearly out of bounds "Get a mobility scooter, you mug! Keep up with the game!"

"Your barrister will coach you on what to expect," Jane said. "And let me give you a tip. Don't sledge the judge."

"You know, I never saw it," said Ela, turning to Jane. "What the film was all about. I just took it for what it seemed to be— something he'd do when he got out."

"I think we all felt that. There was no reason to imagine anything else. But when the film couldn't be financed and Voss had built the set anyway another idea emerged: that Tomas could still have his final performance."

"So how did you know Cayden Voss was involved?"

"I couldn't make sense of Tomas's profile. At first I thought his DNA was a mistake—which it wasn't. Things didn't add up. I couldn't resolve these crimes with his original offense. And I couldn't match him with the first three victims. Someone else had to be pulling his strings. The hatreds against Nigel Woods and Franco Bernero were Voss's—as was his vendetta against the Catholic Church. And, sadly, he knew what Tomas was capable of, and he turned it to his own purpose."

"Poor Tomas."

"And poor Tomas's victims."

"Yes," agreed Ela. "They suffered terribly."

"I think Tomas was glad when it was over. I was there when he died and I saw relief on his face. I wish I'd met him."

"Me too. On the outside, I mean. Why didn't he come to see me?" Ela's sense of loss was profound.

"He had to keep you apart from his other reality. He truly loved you, Ela. I'm sure of that. You can see it in his letters. And the flowers he took such a risk to deliver."

"Could you have helped him?"

"If I had broken the bond with Voss? Maybe. But first, you have to see it."

"A folie à deux. I've been doing some reading."

"It's a label, Ela. It only tells you so much."

"Beaten by the oldest man on the field," screamed Ela, unleashing another sledge as a North Melbourne veteran side-stepped a defender and set off toward the goals. The Kanga supporters groaned in unison as the kick missed the big sticks and sailed through for a behind. It was going to be another long season. And a long, hard winter for Ela.

"Stay in touch, won't you?" said Jane. "I'm here to help if you need me."

"You going already? There's three quarters to go and we're only three goals behind."

Jane touched Ela lightly on the arm. "Go the Mighty Kangas."

"Shinboners forever," parroted Ela as Jane slipped away through the blue and white.

The Homicide team had their farewell dinner for Ringer and Showbag in a private room at the Magic Mountain. Cheryl Hursthouse had sent Jane and each member of the team a personal letter of thanks. Despite her rough edges, the commissioner was proving to be a surprise.

After the meal, Marino rose to make a toast.

"Boss, Showy, we'll miss you. Boss, because we won't have anyone to make up baseless rumors about anymore. And Showy, for your grace and sensitivity, and your daily reminders of why we don't do things like we used to."

"I'm not going to stand," said Showbag. "Even if I could. I wouldn't treat any of you with that much respect. I have carried you on this case, every inch of the way, on my own broad shoulders, my own broad arse and my own extremely broad opinions, mostly from the nineties. But, hell, they don't make decades like that anymore. It's all body cams and tasers now. In the old days they issued you with gaffer tape to cover the number on your badge and a telephone book to help the customers see reason. Progress? I don't think so. So, I'm out of here. And good riddance to the bloody lot of you. I won't give you a second thought."

The others laughed and cheered and cried. He was going to be missed.

"Well, thanks for letting me follow that," said Ringer. "I should have gone first."

"Which is what Gary's been saying all year," said Showbag, unable to resist the opening. "Well at least you're going now."

Ringer enjoyed the joke as much as anyone, but his style was different to his sergeant's.

"In this job, we get to see the worst of humankind sometimes, and this has been one of those cases. They say that attending one bad car accident can affect you for the rest of your life. Well, we've witnessed four of those. But we've seen the best of humankind as well—in the commitment and staunchness and personal sacrifice of the men and women around this table. There's a cost in doing what we do. No one gets to go home free. So read that letter from the chief commissioner. And read it again if you need reassurance. She means it and so do I. So, thank you—from the bottom of my heart. Be kind to yourself, seek help if you need it, and keep each other's backs. It's been a privilege."

***

"You wrote those letters for the commissioner, didn't you?" said Jane as they shared a cab back to her apartment.

"What makes you think that?" asked Ringer.

"The words you used, the syntax . . ."

"Oh, so now you're a writing expert as well as someone who reads body language."

"I'm the complete package. But thank you. I value what you said very much."

"And thank you. For extending my education. A folie à deux. I doubt if I'll see one of those again."

"Didn't I give you two? A folie à deux à deux? You've forgotten Melissa Woods and Stewart Vizor. What do you think will happen to her?"

"I suspect her money will come to her rescue as it usually does."

"You showed great restraint by not mentioning that at dinner."

"You should have said something yourself."

"It had all been said. I'm not one for making speeches."

"What about the one about the transgressive mind?"

"I didn't think you were listening, Eric. I'm impressed."

"I seem to remember it covers everything."

Jane had to laugh. "You can say that again."

She smiled to herself as she ran through a list in her head. From Kurtza's unbridled sadism to Voss's heartless manipulation, from Melissa Woods's involvement in murder to Maurice Engels, coveting all he surveyed. From Michael McGill's corrupted concept of love to the vanity of Ravi Patel. From Showbag's shame and attraction as he watched Ela Bey in the shower to Father Keeley, clinging to his faith like a lifebuoy lest a rogue wave swept it away. And what about Ringer and herself? At least he was taking steps to build a relationship with his daughter. Jane resolved to do better with Zoe and with her own mother too. And at last, after all this time, to finally forgive her father for leaving.

The cab drew up outside Jane's apartment.

"So, it's come to this?" said Ringer.

"Until it comes to trial and we drag ourselves through it again. But you'll be with the Feds by then and off on other adventures."

"Admin is not an adventure, Jane."

"Then adventures with your family."

"That I will take."

"Be kind to yourself. Seek help if you need it."

"I thought you didn't like making speeches?"

Jane leaned across and kissed him, long and sweetly, on the lips.

"What was that for?"

"To stop you talking. And wish you well. It's been a blast."

Jane got out of the cab and headed across the street.

"Goodbye, Jane Halifax."

Ringer watched her go, hoping she might turn back for a final wave.

But Jane had made a resolution. From now on, she was only looking ahead.

40

Jane found the cathedral inspiring. She hoped it was architectural rather than spiritual, that her nonbelief was intact. She had been similarly moved by other great churches: Westminster Abbey, Notre-Dame de Reims, and the Hagia Sophia. Man can elicit awe as much as God.

"Hello, Jane. What are you doing here?"

"I've come to light some candles."

"That's nice. Did you make the sign of the cross correctly?"

Jane grinned at Father Keely with affection. "Isn't it enough I've ventured into enemy territory?"

"We take all comers without judgment, Jane. How many candles would you like?"

"Three."

"Weren't there four victims?"

"I'm not here for them. And the fourth was Hindu. I won't presume to know what they do. Give me three."

"You can say a prayer if you like."

Jane lit the first candle. "For Leilani, who I never met. Though I know she dwells in heaven."

Keely made the sign of the cross and made a silent prayer of his own.

"That's the good thing about religion," said Jane. "If you're a believer, you can go where you like."

She lit the second candle. "For Tomas Kurtza, who I also never met and is maybe in another place. For his pain and agony and lonely despair. Forgive him his sins, if you can."

Keely added his blessing.

Jane lit the last candle. "For Ben. Who everyone loved. Who deserved a longer life. Who I miss every day and will always adore. Who was good and kind and selfless. And irreplaceable. And weak. And who I forgive for continuing to see his first wife when he was supposed to be only with me . . . Where are you, Ben? Where did you go?" Jane turned her face away from Keely and hurried outside.

The priest remained to light a candle of his own, for the lost soul of Michael McGill, and joined Jane in the garden.

"Forgive us our transgressions for all of us are weak," said Jane.

"Are you having an epiphany at last?"

"No, Father, I remember it from Sunday school."

"Psalm 32. Blessed is he whose transgressions are forgiven."

"Except we Proddies don't have a priest between us and God like you."

"I sense a little bit of religion there, Jane?"

"No, Father. Humanist to the bitter end."

Keely smiled and studied her closely.

"Someone wrote me a letter. Well, he got someone else to sign it. But it helps to know you're valued and not alone."

"I could have told you that."

"You stick with your flock and I'll stick with mine."

"And who are they, Jane?"

"The tired, the poor, and the huddled masses."

"You're baiting me, aren't you?"

"There's more than one way to skin a wildcat, Father."

They sat for a while in the peaceful garden with its falling waters, enjoying each other's company.

"How are you traveling, Jane?"

"I'm traveling okay. Thanks for asking. I'll be fine. Until the next one."

Cayden Voss was found guilty of conspiracy to murder Nigel Woods, Franco Bernero, and Michael McGill and sentenced to life in prison without parole.

———

Stewart Vizor was extradited to Australia from Brazil and found guilty of the murder of Terry Tressyder. He was sentenced to twenty-five years with the possibility of parole after nineteen years.

———

Melissa Woods was found guilty of being an accessory to the murder of Terry Tressyder and sentenced to seven years which was later reduced on appeal to three years and eleven months. The Crown is currently appealing that decision.

Read on for a sneak peek into book 2 of the

HALIFAX SERIES

Jane felt ill. She declined another glass of wine and asked instead for a weak black tea. As Peter went through to the kitchen to put on the jug, she found two Panadol in her handbag and washed them down with what was left of her sparkling water. Though the water was flat, it had enough fizz to release another wave of nausea and Jane wondered if she should simply excuse herself and leave straight away. Instead, she moved out to the terrace to see if some fresh air would help.

Her car stood across the street under a streetlight, advocating her escape. The evening had gone on long enough and she had lost count of the wine they'd consumed. The wiser choice was to call for a cab and collect her car in the morning, but Jane didn't want to leave it in the street overnight with its precious cargo in the boot.

She was grateful Peter had agreed to give her access to his personal files despite the ethical implications, and they had placed the three heavy storage boxes in the car before they sat down to dinner. He had needed some persuading. As a prosecutor, it was improper to share his files with the other side, but the case was twenty years old and he knew Jane wouldn't misuse them. Her interest was personal not official, an opportunity to end a mystery that had dogged her for years. The Millard case: a client she had failed to keep from going to jail, a young man who had committed suicide within months of his guilty verdict; a rare and haunting failure that still kept Jane awake on those random nights when his ghost came to sit in silence at the foot of her bed like her father did after she'd been punished as a child.

Jane drew deeply on the cool night air and convinced herself it was helping. A passing giddiness and nothing more, a reaction to one of the exotic ingredients her host had added to his excellent if over-spiced meal.

Peter arrived on the terrace with her tea and a glass of Laphroaig for himself. "This is what you really need," he suggested. "Peat, smoke, salt-sea air, and iodine. It's literally medicinal."

Jane declined the scotch and scrutinized her companion. Had Peter been spiking her drinks? They were old friends and the thought he was resorting to a date-rape drug only confirmed she was having delusions.

The tea hadn't helped. Jane was feeling unsteady again. Maybe she should call that cab and take the risk the files would be safe? Or ask Peter to swap his car with hers so it could have the added security of his garage? But as always with Jane, pride and stubbornness prevailed.

As Peter waved her car away from the curb, she turned up the air-con and opened the windows, Google maps guiding her home. Distance 21 kilometers, time twenty-three minutes. The journey would be over soon enough.

Not that the SUV behind her was helping, its headlights switched to high beam. Was he doing it to annoy her or was her fever affecting her patience? Jane lowered her rearview mirror and concentrated on the road ahead, but the pest was still behind her when she turned off Bridge Road and headed round Yarra Boulevard toward Toorak. So, he was heading in the same direction. No reason for a rational person to become paranoid over that.

Now shivering from the cold, Jane flicked off the air-con and closed the windows and slowed to let him pass. Her shadower slowed as well so Jane sped up and so did he. Matching every variation in speed, the only change being that he was now blatantly tailgating a matter of meters behind. Jane's rational mind struggled for context. A young male, having fun at her expense? Someone she'd offended—had she cut him off at the lights? Or was it her expensive sports car that brought out the worst in the other driver? Road rage is so commonplace these days it's like trolling, anonymity giving license to do what you like.

It happened as she planted her foot to burn him off on a sweeping right-hander. Under normal circumstances she would back her BMW Series 8 against his lumbering Telluride any old day of the week and under normal circumstances she would have been right. But this wasn't any old day—or any old night of the week. Jane was sickening with something or had had an allergic reaction or her food was tainted or her alcohol spiked, or maybe it was blind panic. As the Kia nudged her right-rear fender, the BMW spun out of control, rolling over and over at a hundred kilometers an hour in an explosion of glass and metal and air bags and blood that ended with the car caught in a tangle of vegetation not ten meters from the river in which she would certainly have drowned.

The mocking sound of the Telluride retreated into the night as Jane lay there, unable to move, the taste of blood metallic in her mouth. Her car's headlights appealed helplessly to the moon as the mournful wail of the car alarm called out in the hope some passing Samaritan might hear the cry and come to Jane's assistance before her lifeblood ebbed away. The Samaritan would come and her life would be saved, but only in a manner of speaking. For when Jane awoke twenty days later she would remember nothing of dinner at Peter Debreceny's—or her name, address, and date of birth; or her father's name or her mother's face; or childhood holidays by the sea or her grandmother's reassuring embrace by an open fire in winter. Even the image of herself in the mirror brought back nothing of her past. All she saw was a stranger with questioning eyes who reminded her of Robert Millard's little sister.

Would Jane Halifax ever recover to be Jane Halifax again?